Praise for *The Roll of the Drums*

"*Roll of the Drums* is a well-written novel centered around an Amish family and their tight-knit community during the Civil War."

Interviews & Reviews

"This historical romance is a thoughtfully crafted love story. . . . It reads like an intricate tapestry of love set against a counterpoint of evil."

The Historical Novels Review

"A heartfelt Amish novel. . . . Complicated, charming, and sweet, *The Roll of the Drums* is a great read."

Urban Lit Magazine

Praise for *The Sound of Distant Thunder*

"Twenty-year-old Jonas Weaver can't resist fighting the evil of slavery by joining the War Between the States. Off to the army he goes, despite strong objections by his family, his Amish church, and his sweetheart, Katie Stuckey. When Jonas's letters stop coming, Katie has to face something from her past she has tried to ignore. Jan Drexler's *The Sound of Distant Thunder* combines historical research with compelling characters to create a memorable story of love in the time of war."

Suzanne Woods Fisher, bestselling author of *Anna's Crossing*

"In *The Sound of Distant Thunder*, the sweetness of young love, the conflict and sorrow of the War Between the States, the wisdom of couples long married, and the cost of making a stand for what one believes are blended into a story that kept me turning pages. The way Jan Drexler's Amish characters spring to life off the page will leave readers wanting to know more about the people in this Amish community. For sure and certain."

Ann H. Gabhart, bestselling author
of *These Healing Hills*

"Faith, family, and freedom are tested by the crucible of war in this haunting love story of a gentle people whose lives—and hearts—are disrupted by the sound of distant thunder. Historically rich and rare, this is a unique glimpse into a nation divided that both captures the mind and nourishes the soul."

Julie Lessman, award-winning author of The Daughters
of Boston, Winds of Change, and Isle of Hope series

"In a beautifully woven story, Jan Drexler once again gives her readers a true look at the struggles of faith, hope, and love facing families, churches, communities, and a nation during a time of turbulence."

Ruth Logan Herne, award-winning author

SOFTLY
BLOWS
the BUGLE

Books by Jan Drexler

Journey to Pleasant Prairie

Hannah's Choice

Mattie's Pledge

Naomi's Hope

The Amish of Weaver's Creek

The Sound of Distant Thunder

The Roll of the Drums

Softly Blows the Bugle

SOFTLY BLOWS *the* BUGLE

JAN DREXLER

Revell

a division of Baker Publishing Group
Grand Rapids, Michigan

© 2020 by Jan Drexler

Published by Revell
a division of Baker Publishing Group
PO Box 6287, Grand Rapids, MI 49516-6287
www.revellbooks.com

Printed in the United States of America

Library of Congress Cataloging-in-Publication Data
Names: Drexler, Jan, author.
Title: Softly blows the bugle / Jan Drexler.
Description: Grand Rapids, Michigan : Revell, a division of Baker Publishing
    Group, [2020] | Series: The Amish of Weaver's Creek ; 3
Identifiers: LCCN 2020005245 | ISBN 9780800729332 (paperback) | ISBN
    9780800739232 (hardcover)
Subjects: LCSH: Amish—Fiction. | GSAFD: Christian fiction. | Love stories.
Classification: LCC PS3604.R496 S67 2020 | DDC 813/.6—dc23
LC record available at https://lccn.loc.gov/2020005245

Scripture used in this book, whether quoted or paraphrased by the characters, is taken from the King James Version of the Bible.

This is a work of historical reconstruction; the appearances of certain historical figures are therefore inevitable. All other characters, however, are products of the author's imagination, and any resemblance to actual persons, living or dead, is coincidental.

The author is represented by WordServe Literary Group.

20 21 22 23 24 25 26   7 6 5 4 3 2 1

To the Morning Coffee Circle at Greencroft Manor IV in Goshen, Indiana: thank you for welcoming me into your group a few times a year and sharing your stories. I always enjoy your insiders' look at growing up Amish.

Soli Deo Gloria

Wherefore seeing we also are compassed about with so great a cloud of witnesses, let us lay aside every weight, and the sin which doth so easily beset us, and let us run with patience the race that is set before us, looking unto Jesus the author and finisher of our faith; who for the joy that was set before him endured the cross, despising the shame, and is set down at the right hand of the throne of God.

Hebrews 12:1–2

1

Life and knitting. Each one goes along smoothly, needles and events gliding against each other to form a seamless whole, until the day you look back and see the one missed stitch that has affected the entire fabric.

Elizabeth Kaufman dropped the ruined sock into her lap and closed her eyes, leaning her head against the back of the rocking chair on the shaded front porch. A bird sang somewhere above the roof, its fluid call carrying through the quiet afternoon air like an autumn leaf falling. It rose, then paused. Rose again, then swooped down only to end on a high trilling note.

A shriek from inside the house brought an abrupt end to the birdsong. Katie Stuckey's feet pounding on the stairway and more shrieks brought Elizabeth to her feet, her knitting falling to the porch floor.

"He's coming!" Katie slammed the wooden screen door

open and grabbed Elizabeth's arms, spinning her in a circle. "I saw him from the window! On the road!"

Katie jumped off the porch and headed down the lane toward the road, leaving Elizabeth breathless and alone on the porch.

"Who?" Elizabeth called after her, then laughed to herself. Who else could it be? The long-awaited day had finally arrived. After three long years of serving in the army, Jonas—her brother and Katie's intended—was home.

It was a happy day, for sure. Elizabeth picked up her yarn and needles and went into the house. She added more ham and water to the pot of beans cooking for their dinner. Then she mixed up a big batch of cornbread, knowing *Mamm* would have many mouths to feed today. As soon as Jonas's letter had come telling them he was returning home, Mamm had started planning the celebration. They hadn't been sure which day to expect him, but they knew it would be sometime this week. The whole family hung in expectation, but as anxious as Elizabeth was to see her brother, she would let him have some time alone with Katie first. She would arrive at the home farm in time for supper.

When the cornbread was finished baking, she wrapped the dishes in towels and placed them in the back of the pony cart. As she hitched up Pie, a sudden longing to see Jonas swept over her. She hadn't been close to him since she married Reuben, but her life was different now. Jonas was her little brother, and he was home. Had the war changed him?

She hurried Pie along as quickly as she dared with the pot of soup sloshing in the back. As Elizabeth crossed the stone bridge into the yard of her parents' farm, Jonas stepped out of the door to meet her. She jumped from the cart, not bothering to tie the pony, and ran to her brother. He lifted her in strong arms.

"Welcome home, Jonas," she said into his ear.

He set her down and looked into her eyes. "How are you?"

"As good as can be, now that you're back." She pulled back slightly. "You are home, aren't you? You don't have to return to the war?"

Jonas grinned, looking more like the boy she remembered. "Mamm asked me the same thing. *Ja*, for sure I'm home. I've been mustered out. The army doesn't want me anymore."

Katie appeared behind him. "Come in, Elizabeth. Jonas brought a friend home with him."

Jonas propelled her toward the door. "I left Aaron in Mamm's hands, the poor fellow."

A lean man sat at the kitchen table, a spoon halfway to his mouth. Jonas had been right. Mamm had dished up a bowl full of chicken and noodles for the stranger, and he had already finished most of it. He put his spoon down when he saw Elizabeth and rose to his feet.

Elizabeth forced herself not to stare as the man grabbed a pair of crutches and hobbled toward her, one trouser leg pinned up at the knee.

"Aaron Zook," he said, thrusting a hand toward her. "Jonas told me about his family. I'm guessing you must be Elizabeth."

Stunned, Elizabeth shook hands with him. Her thoughts swirled. Aaron spoke in Englisch. He wasn't Amish.

"Ja . . . Yes," she stammered. "I'm Elizabeth."

His lower face was covered with a long red beard and

mustache, but underneath she could see hollow cheeks and pale skin with a gray cast. His welcoming smile stopped at his mouth, not reaching his shadowed eyes. The expression in those dark blue eyes reminded her of the man she had been trying so hard to forget.

"Aaron and I met in the hospital where I was stationed in New York," Jonas said, grasping his friend's shoulder.

"Were you a medic too?" Mamm asked.

Aaron's smile disappeared as he turned away from Elizabeth. "No, ma'am. I was a wounded prisoner. A Confederate soldier."

Elizabeth's head swam. A Confederate soldier, just like her husband, Reuben, had been. She took a step back as Aaron went on.

"Jonas saved my life in more ways than one, and I owe him a great debt. With my family and property gone, I had no reason to return to Tennessee. Jonas suggested I come here to Ohio with him before I move on."

"You're welcome to stay as long as you like," *Datt* said.

Elizabeth took another step back. What was Datt thinking, inviting this man to stay?

"I'd like that," Aaron said. "I'll work for my keep. Don't worry about that." He patted his right leg. "I don't let this slow me down much."

"We'll talk about that later," Datt said. "Our older son Samuel will be here with his family soon, and his oldest boy has gone to tell Jonas's other sisters that he's come home. Today is a day to celebrate."

Elizabeth slipped out to the porch, then leaned against the wall, her heart pounding. Somehow, she would have to join with the rest of the family in welcoming Aaron to the community. Swallowing hard, she closed her eyes, dread seeping into the place that had held such joy only moments ago.

She shook her head, trying to clear it away.

He isn't Reuben. He might not be anything like Reuben.

She wiped the dampness off her upper lip and rubbed her palms on her clean apron. If Aaron Zook stayed in Weaver's Creek, nothing could be right again.

~~~~~~

The house was crowded, noisy, and hot. Aaron's head pounded with the strain of being pleasant, the flat tones of Yankee talk mingled with the harsh Pennsylvania Dutch words Jonas's family and friends used among themselves, not realizing he could understand only some of what they said.

Finally, supper was over, and Aaron slipped out of the house. He needed quiet. Peace and quiet.

The porch off the kitchen was crowded, too, but folks moved aside for him as he hobbled through. The sun had gone down, leaving an orange glow in the western sky. Aaron went toward the outhouse, then swung past it and ended up at a board fence. A dark meadow faded into the dusk, a horse standing nearby was a black shadow against the night sky. Aaron leaned his crutches against the fence rail and grasped the post, glad for the breeze that cooled his hot skin.

Frogs croaked. Aaron closed his eyes. An early owl hooted from somewhere to his left. The voices he had left behind were faint, then someone laughed, the sound rising above the others for a brief moment.

Footsteps in the grass behind him. Aaron turned to see Jonas. Ever since they had met in the hospital after one of the many battles in the Siege of Petersburg in October, Jonas had been the one to keep Aaron's path straight. But it wouldn't be long before they would go their separate ways. How did he ever come to be friends with a Yankee?

"Are you feeling all right?" Jonas rested his arms on the fence rail next to him.

"You aren't a medic anymore."

Jonas gave a soft chuckle. "It has become a habit." He rolled his shoulders. "It feels good to be home, but . . ."

Aaron let the silence grow between them. He sighed. "It isn't what you remembered?"

"It's still home, but not much has changed. It is as if the war didn't happen at all."

"But the war changed you." Aaron let his mind go back to the angry, fiery young man he had been, hot to kill any Yankee he could find after a scouting party shot Grandpop and left him to die with his blood seeping into the Tennessee land he had loved. "Both of us. War will do that."

Jonas looked out over the meadow. "You're right. We've both seen things that Katie and my family can't fathom. And I don't want to tell them. I don't want Katie to know how terribly cruel men can be."

"Do you still think war is wrong?" Aaron looked at his friend. "Your side won. The Confederacy is dead."

"And the slaves are free." Jonas bowed his head. "But the cost . . . The cost is so great. I was willing to give my life so others could be free, but when I think of how many others paid the ultimate price, it grieves me." He passed a hand over his face. "Yes, I believe war is wrong. I pray that our country will never be in another one."

After a few minutes of silence, Jonas changed the subject. "What do you think of my family?"

Aaron let a smile tug at the corners of his mouth. "You described each one perfectly. Except your sister Elizabeth. I wouldn't have been able to choose her out of a crowded hog wallow if I didn't hear your mama say her name."

"Elizabeth is different than I remember, but she didn't spend much time with the family when her husband was alive."

Aaron leaned on the fence post, easing the weight pressing on his good leg. "She's a widow?"

"Mamm said Reuben was killed at Vicksburg."

"I thought you said that the Amish don't fight."

"Reuben wasn't Amish."

Aaron shifted again to ease his aching leg. Elizabeth was a puzzle, but he wouldn't be around long enough to sort it out. Jonas, on the other hand, was home. He had often talked about his plans on their journey west, and his doubts.

"Did you talk to your pa about getting married?"

Jonas turned and leaned back against the fence, facing the house. "I mentioned it, but Datt didn't know how the ministers would handle the situation."

"I don't see what the problem is. She's your girl, ain't she? Just up and marry her."

"I have to join the church first. I can't get married until I do."

Aaron turned and leaned his back against the fence post. Someone had lit the lamps in the house and warm golden light spilled into the yard through the windows.

15

"I don't think I'll ever figure you out. What does joining some church have to do with marrying Katie? They can't tell you what to do. It isn't like you're still in the army."

"It's the way we live. I've always been part of the church, but to be baptized and become a member means that I am committed to being part of the community. And we don't allow members to marry before they're baptized."

"You've got your life all planned out, then, just like you said. You'll join the church, build your house, marry Katie, and have a passel of youngsters."

"One step at a time. The first thing I need to do is find out if I'll be allowed to be baptized after being in the army." Jonas turned toward him. "What do you intend to do? Will you stay around here for a while? Or will you head west like you keep talking about?"

Aaron shifted again, trying to ease the strain of bearing all his weight on one leg. He missed the silence of the Tennessee woods and the cabin Grandpop had built when he finally settled down after leaving Pennsylvania as a young man, but that peaceful home was gone forever. Burned to the ground by Yankee scum. They had eradicated his past as thoroughly as they had destroyed his future. But they hadn't succeeded in taking his life. His thoughts shied away from the ravenous black pit of death.

Aaron grasped at the dream he had held fast during the long nights in the prison hospital. "I heard the West is open territory. No one to get in your way."

"I heard the men talk about that too. It sounds pretty lonely." Jonas's eyes reflected the lamplight from the house. "It would be mighty hard for a man to build a home out there."

"Some men do better alone." Aaron glanced at Jonas. "You want to be part of this community, with your folks and your girl. That's what you want. But I've always been on my own, taking care of myself most of my life. I'm itching to hear nothing but the sound of the wind in the trees again."

Silence fell between them. The owl in the woods hooted. Frog song echoed from the creek. Somewhere on the other side of the pasture, a bull complained in the darkness.

"A healthy man with two sound legs might be able to survive on his own," Jonas said, his voice quiet. "I worry that you won't. It hasn't been that long since you nearly died from blood poisoning."

A familiar flare of anger at his situation rose in Aaron's chest. "I won't let a missing leg stop me."

Jonas chuckled, his face hidden in the darkness. "I don't imagine you will."

~

"Lydia, did you hear about Young Peter Lehman and Margaret Stuckey?"

Elizabeth froze as Salome Beiler's voice drifted into the front room from the kitchen. She was Bishop Amos's wife, but where Amos had grown in his tact and wisdom since becoming bishop a couple years ago, Salome was as thoughtless in her comments as she had ever been.

"I know they've been keeping company." Mamm's words were quiet. She never liked to listen to Salome's gossip.

"I heard a wedding will take place this summer."

Mamm didn't answer and Elizabeth continued tidying up the front room.

"Isn't it about time your Elizabeth married again?" Salome's voice took on the wheedling tone that set Elizabeth's teeth on edge. "She's been a widow far too long."

"I'm not concerned," Mamm said. "The Good Lord knows what Elizabeth needs, and he will provide."

"Now that she has repented of her unfortunate marriage to that outsider and has joined the church, my Levi might consider marrying her." Salome sniffed. "The Good Book instructs widows to marry, and your daughter has many good childbearing years ahead of her."

Elizabeth sank into the chair she had just straightened. The front room was empty now that nearly all the community had returned to their homes. The night was growing late. Elizabeth longed for her own bed and a good night's rest, but Salome had insisted on staying while Mamm cleaned the kitchen. Elizabeth wouldn't leave when there was still work to be done, but with Salome in the kitchen, Elizabeth was stuck unless she wanted to face the gossip head-on. Surely the woman knew that she was in the next room, able to hear every word of her conversation. But that had never stopped the busybody before, and it wouldn't now.

"Abraham and I will let Elizabeth make her own decisions concerning her future." Mamm's voice had an edge to it that told Elizabeth she was trying to hold her temper.

Salome grunted. "You should have reined that girl in years ago, before she ran off and married that reprobate. If she was my daughter—"

"She isn't your daughter, Salome," Mamm broke in.

Another grunt. Elizabeth leaned over far enough to see Salome cut another slice of cornbread for herself, then smooth the dish towel over the pan on the table. Mamm was facing the window and didn't see part of tomorrow's breakfast disappearing.

"I think Amos is ready to leave." Salome's chair scraped across the wood floor as she rose from the table. She stood, tying her bonnet. "I'm happy for your sake that Jonas is finally home," she said, moving toward the back door. "The past three years haven't been easy for you with your son off in the outside world, doing who knows what."

Mamm pressed her lips together as she moved a chair out of Salome's way. "*Denki*, Salome. We are very thankful to have him home with us again."

Elizabeth joined Mamm in the kitchen as Salome left. Mamm took a handkerchief from her apron waistband and wiped the perspiration from her forehead.

"That woman." She turned back to the sink to finish washing the dishes while Elizabeth picked up the dish towel. "Every time she visits, I'm happy to see her go. But then I have to repent of my uncharitable thoughts."

"She is horrible," Elizabeth said, drying a plate and setting it on the shelf above. "I don't see why you let her talk to you that way."

Mamm sighed, then smiled at her. "Now you need to repent. Salome isn't horrible. I don't think she knows how hurtful her comments can be, but she can be caring and helpful at times."

"All right. I'm sorry. But she's as prickly as a porcupine." Elizabeth wanted to add more to her description of Salome but didn't. Even though the woman was part of their community and the bishop's wife, Elizabeth couldn't forget the years Salome had acted as if she didn't exist, only because she had married outside the church.

"Salome did bring up a valid concern, though." Mamm didn't look at her as she immersed a stack of bowls in the dishpan. "It's been two years since Reuben died. Have you thought about marrying again?"

Elizabeth swallowed, her mouth suddenly dry. Even though Reuben had left to join the Confederate army nearly three years ago, she still had nightmares about him. She couldn't imagine willingly putting herself at the mercy of another man.

"I am content now, Mamm. I don't really want to marry."

"What about children? A family?"

Elizabeth's head pounded. She forced herself to pick up the next bowl to dry and watched her hand rub the dish towel over the wet surface. She had never told Mamm about the baby she had lost. That baby would have been five years old now, nearly the same age as her nephew Ezra, Gideon and Ruby's son.

"I don't think the Good Lord wants me to have children."

Mamm was silent as she finished washing the bowls and turned to the big pot Elizabeth had brought the ham and beans in.

"We never know what he has planned for us."

Mamm's voice was soft, but sure and steady. Elizabeth wished she could have even half of her mother's faith, but she was sure her future didn't hold the pleasures of a family and her own little ones. The Good Lord might bless others in that way, but not a woman like her.

After the kitchen was cleaned up, Elizabeth said good

night to Mamm and took her empty pot out to the pony cart. Datt had seen her coming and was hitching up Pie. Jonas's friend Aaron sat on the edge of the porch, his crutches next to him. He scooted away from the steps as Elizabeth went down them.

"It was nice to meet you, ma'am," Aaron said.

With the light from the kitchen window behind him, he didn't look as much like Reuben as Elizabeth had first thought. His words were drawn out and slow, nothing like the Englischers Elizabeth was familiar with.

"Thank you." Elizabeth paused, trying to think of what Mamm would say to him. "I hope you feel at home in Weaver's Creek."

"Yes, ma'am, for the time I'm here."

"You don't plan on settling here, then?"

Aaron rubbed his leg, the one that ended just above his knee. It was an unconscious motion, as if the leg often pained him.

"I don't know yet what I'm going to do."

Datt tied Pie to the hitching rail and took Elizabeth's pot from her.

"There's a place for you here," he said, setting the pot in the cart. "There is always room for a Zook in the community."

Aaron didn't answer. Elizabeth untied Pie's reins as Datt went back to the barn.

"Wait." Aaron rose and took a step toward her. "What did your father mean? Is there something special about my last name?"

"It's a common name among the Amish. Datt meant that you would fit in here easily, if you wanted to."

"Grandpop was raised in Pennsylvania. He never had a good word for his Amish family."

"Then you are Amish."

He shook his head. "I'm not Amish. I'm not anything."

"But if your grandfather's family was Amish, then—"

Aaron pushed back on his crutches, turning toward the porch steps. "I'm not Amish. I don't care what Grandpop's family was."

He swung up the steps and into the house, leaving Elizabeth standing alone with Pie. She stroked the pony's neck, then climbed into the cart and started for home.

She had thought Aaron was just another man like Reuben when she first met him, but Reuben, as hard as he was, never let her see any weakness. Reuben couldn't admit any vulnerability. But in her brief conversation with Aaron, she had caught a glimpse of a sad and lonely man.

2

On Monday morning, Aaron stayed behind in the barn while Jonas went to work with his father and brother. The men would spend the day walking behind the harrow or cultivator as they drove teams of horses back and forth across the fields. A man needed two good legs for work like that.

It was no good feeling useless, though. Once he was alone, Aaron found a broom to sweep out the aisle in front of the horses' stalls where some grain had spilled. He leaned on one crutch and grasped the broom with his other hand, but the result was an awkward drag of the bristles through the dust.

Ineffectual and helpless. The familiar feeling had dogged him day and night for the last eight months.

Setting his crutches firmly under his arms, Aaron grasped the broom with both hands and pushed it from right to left, creating a satisfying track in the layer of dust and grain. Several sparrows that had been picking at the grain scattered, fluttered between the barn rafters, then settled on the barn floor again, well out of reach of the broom.

"That's right, little birds." Aaron moved to his left, set the crutches, and prepared to make another sweep. "Stay out of the way. I'm armed and dangerous."

Two of the birds hopped closer as he grasped the broom again, then flew away as he set the bristles for the next pass. But he reached too far and lost his balance. He remembered to twist his body to take the impact on his shoulder and rolled in the dust. He ended up facedown on the dirt floor, his crutches careening in opposite directions as he fell. The birds flew up to the rafters in a flurry of fluttering wings and panicked cheeps.

Aaron rose up on his elbows and brushed the dirt from his beard. He wasn't going to lie here feeling sorry for himself. No one had witnessed that dunderheaded move. He reached for the broom and leaned it against the stall gate. Next, he grasped the crutch that had fallen near his head, then used his foot to bring the other crutch close. Setting the crutches upright, he pulled himself up until he stood again, his arms quivering from the exertion. He wiped the sweat from his eyes and started again.

He put the crutches in their places under his arms and put his weight on his foot. Once he got his balance, he picked up the broom again. Little sweep. Adjust the crutches. Little sweep. Adjust the crutches. This simple chore was going to take all day. The birds peered at him from above, waiting for another chance at the spilled grain.

What he wouldn't give for a rifle and a day tramping through the western Tennessee woods. Alone and free. Dependent on no man.

With two good legs.

Adjust the crutches. Sweep.

"Is my datt in here?"

The woman's voice startled him as it echoed in the empty barn and he took another dive onto the dusty floor, landing on his shoulder.

Groaning, he rolled onto his back. Elizabeth stood over him, a frown on her face.

"Are you all right? I didn't mean to surprise you."

Aaron frowned back. "I lost my balance, is all."

"Let me help you," she said as she reached for one of his crutches.

"Leave it." His voice sounded harsh to his ears. Like Pa's voice. He took a breath and started again. "Leave it. I don't need your help."

Elizabeth stepped back. He picked up the broom and leaned it against the stall gate, then the crutches, one at a time. He sat up, then pulled himself to a standing position again, looking away from the young woman's face. Her soft and vulnerable face.

"Your pa's working in the fields with the others." Aaron leaned on his crutches as rivulets of sweat ran down his back. "What do you need?"

She chewed on her lower lip. Aaron stared at the floor to keep from meeting her eyes. In the short few weeks since he had left the hospital, he had learned to avoid eye contact. Most folks either looked at him with pity or revulsion, and he couldn't take either one. Especially from a woman as fine as this one.

"Something got into our henhouse last night and I need to close off the hole it made."

"You lose any chickens?"

"Four." She glanced at him, then lowered her gaze to the floor as if the sight pained her. "Whatever it was only carried off one and left the rest behind."

"Probably a weasel. They kill for sport."

She nodded. "That's what I thought. Or maybe a fox. And it will come back again if I don't get that hole closed off."

Aaron drummed his fingers against the handles of his crutches. If he had two good legs, he'd know what to do. Fixing a hole in a chicken coop was easy.

He gazed out the barn door, then at the woman beside him.

"How far is your house?"

"Just up the road a piece, less than a mile. An easy walk—"

Her voice broke off as she glanced at his crutches. Her face turned pink as Aaron gripped the handles to hide the exhausted shaking in his hands. Elizabeth's eyes narrowed as she continued to stare at his leg.

"Maybe I should wait for Datt or Jonas."

Aaron's face burned at the dismissive tone of her voice. "I can do it. I don't need both legs to fix a chicken coop."

A frown brought her pale brown eyebrows together. Her eyes reminded him of Ma. He looked away again.

"I can't ask you to do it. You might hurt yourself."

Hurt himself? All thoughts of her vulnerability fled at that challenge. He would fix her chicken coop if it killed him.

Aaron tilted his head toward the back of the barn where the wagons were stored. "We'll drive Jonas's wagon. And I'll need to borrow some of your pa's tools."

Doubt still filled her gaze, but she gave a swift nod. "I'll tell Mamm we're taking the horse and wagon. Datt keeps his tools in the workroom over there."

He found the tools he needed, and using one crutch, he was able to carry them to the spring wagon. Elizabeth wasn't back from the house yet, so he let himself lean on the wagon wheel long enough to get his breath back.

Maybe Jonas was right. Heading into the wilderness of the West was hard enough for a man in good condition. Somehow, he'd have to learn to use his one good leg and build up his strength at the same time. Starting with the chicken coop.

By the time Elizabeth returned, her expression still wary, Aaron had retrieved the crutch he had left in the workroom and managed to bring in Rusty, Jonas's driving horse. The harness had been beyond his ability, though.

"Couldn't you find the harness?" Elizabeth asked.

"I was just getting to it," Aaron said. He started toward the wall where the harness hung on pegs. He might be able to get it down, but he knew he didn't have the strength or balance to toss it onto Rusty's back. His shoulders ached just thinking about it.

"Mamm said you might have trouble with the harness." Elizabeth stepped past him and lifted it off the hooks. "I can do this."

"I can't stand by and let you do the work."

She glared at him. "You think I can't harness a horse?"

He glared right back. "You seem to think I can't."

She shifted the weight of the harness in her arms and walked toward Rusty. As she tossed it onto the horse's back, the straps tangled, leaving a messy heap. Rusty turned to look at her.

But she had gotten the awkward weight up there. That was more than he could have done.

Aaron watched her pull on one strap, and then another, but the horse's back was above her head. She was such a short little thing that she couldn't see what she was doing. That didn't stop her, though. She squared her shoulders and tried again.

"Do you want some help?"

Those firm shoulders slumped, then she nodded. "I guess I could use another pair of hands. I can't seem to get it straight. This horse is much taller than my driving pony."

Aaron went to Rusty's off side. He would need two hands for this task, so he leaned his crutches against the post behind him. His good leg was aching from the unaccustomed work already, but it held him up as he straightened the harness and arranged the straps so Elizabeth could fasten them from the other side.

By the time Elizabeth had backed Rusty into position in front of the wagon, Aaron could hardly stand. He put the crutches into the wagon, then readied himself for the jump and pull up to the wagon seat. Elizabeth was climbing onto the seat from the other side, so if he failed to make this jump, she would witness everything. He grasped the handles Jonas had installed on either side of the wagon seat and jumped up, trying to make the clumsy maneuver look as smooth as he could.

But he couldn't stop panting once he reached the seat and twisted himself around to face the front. His face burned, but was it from exhaustion or embarrassment? From the corner of his eye, he could see Elizabeth's frown.

What he didn't expect was her question.

"How long has it been since you lost your leg?"

"Eight months." Eight long months of constant pain and bed rest.

"So you're still getting accustomed to it."

"I suppose so." Aaron leaned his crutches against the seat and rubbed his bad leg. "The trip out here took more out of me than I thought it would."

"Have you ever thought about getting one of those wooden legs? I saw a soldier in Millersburg with one a few months ago. If he hadn't been limping, I never would have noticed it."

A wooden leg. Sure, he had seen them. The men who had gotten them looked whole again. The muscle on the side of his jaw began to twitch.

"Union soldiers can get them from the government, but they won't give them to us Rebs."

Elizabeth picked up the reins and clucked to Rusty. She was silent as they drove over the stone bridge and onto the road. Then she turned to him again.

"Why do you have to have someone give you one? Why not make your own?"

He stared at her, ready to say . . . what? One of the other prisoners in the hospital had talked endlessly about how the Federals owed the Rebs something for leaving them crippled like this, but he knew Washington didn't owe him anything. He was a casualty of war, that was all.

Aaron turned away from her and stared into the trees. A

casualty that left him only half a man. The war had stripped him clean, but he wasn't going to crawl into a hole and wait to die. Elizabeth's suggestion rang in his ears. Why not make his own leg? Then nothing could stop him from standing on his own two feet.

~~~~~

"One, two, three . . ." Katie counted the chickens as Elizabeth scattered cracked corn for them.

"I think you counted the red one twice." Elizabeth tossed an extra handful of corn toward the little reddish hen that was her favorite. The chicken had a distinct personality and always made Elizabeth smile. She was glad Prissy, as she secretly called her, had survived the marauder.

Elizabeth recounted the chickens in the yard as Katie went into the henhouse to count the ones still sitting on their nests. Elizabeth counted the flock three times and then joined Katie inside the little building.

"How many did you find in here?"

"Eleven," Katie said, reaching under a brown hen for the next egg.

"That makes twenty-five. They're all here again today."

"Whatever Aaron did to fix the hole in back, it has worked." Katie ignored the next chicken's complaints as she took an egg from her nest. "What do you think of Jonas's friend?"

Ignoring Katie's sidelong look, Elizabeth searched through the empty nests for eggs.

"He's all right, I guess."

"He's a single man." Katie got to the end of her row of

nest boxes and turned toward her. "I thought you might be a little more interested than you appear."

Elizabeth reached for another egg, but her stomach was quivering. She couldn't tell Katie why she would never be interested in any man. Not even her own sister Ruby knew the whole story.

"You know I don't plan on marrying again. Being a single woman suits me. I'm very happy."

Katie didn't seem to hear her. "Aaron Zook is an honest, hardworking man, according to Jonas. His missing leg doesn't keep him from helping around the farm."

"But there are some things he just can't manage with his crutches, like walking behind a plow or cultivator."

"That's true. But he repaired our henhouse, didn't he?"

Elizabeth gave in as she put the last egg in her basket. "You're right. He's a hard worker and pleasant enough to be around. But that doesn't mean I'm going to marry him."

"You don't have to marry him," Katie said as she fastened the henhouse door and led the way toward the house. "Just be willing to see the possibilities. Who knows? You just might fall in love."

As she said this, Katie twirled around to walk backwards up the path, grinning at her. Elizabeth met her irresistible happiness with her own smile. Katie had endured many months of waiting for Jonas's return from the war and she deserved the happiness that spilled from her like clear water from a pump.

"All right. I'll be open to what might happen."

"You never know what the Good Lord might have planned for you."

Elizabeth worked to keep the smile on her face. She might have made her peace with the church, but God was another matter. She didn't dare to think about what God would do to her after the years she had spent living a life outside of his will.

After the morning chores were done, Katie went to her sister's house while Elizabeth started toward the home place to spend the day with Mamm in her garden.

It was good to see Katie laughing again. Much had changed while Jonas had been gone. Katie's father had passed on, then in the autumn of 1863, her mother had also died. Since the news had come of Elizabeth's husband's death at Vicksburg, both friends were single and alone. And with her sister Ruby's marriage to Gideon Fischer, Elizabeth had left her husband's old, dark cabin and come to live with Katie. The two enjoyed each other's company in the pleasant little house in the Stuckeys' woods.

But with Jonas's return, Elizabeth's life was changing again. She had felt sorry for Katie during the long separation from Jonas, but whenever she considered the full and vibrant future Katie looked forward to with Jonas's return, self-pity closed in.

How she hated feeling sorry for herself! For sure, her marriage had been a mistake, but now she was free of Reuben. She shuddered, remembering her life before Reuben went off to join the Confederate army. The dingy cabin, the horrible odor of stale alcohol, the fear . . .

Elizabeth blinked her eyes, forcing the threatening tears away. Reuben wasn't part of her life any longer. That time was in the past. The war was over, Jonas was home, and life could get back to the way it was before the war.

She was free and content, wasn't she? And she meant to stay that way.

As she reached the road at the end of the lane, Elizabeth was surprised to see Jonas and Datt at the clearing across the creek where Jonas had planned to build a house before he had gone to war.

Jonas saw her and waved, so Elizabeth walked across the log bridge.

"Are you starting on your house again?" she asked. Aaron sat on a bench, out of sight of the road. If she had seen him earlier, she would have called out in Englisch, but Aaron didn't seem to notice her.

"It's about time to finish Katie's house, don't you think?" Jonas said as he met her at the end of the bridge. "We're figuring out how much lumber to order, and Datt has some ideas for changes to my original plan."

Datt smiled at Elizabeth, his tender look reminding her of the closeness they had shared before her marriage. "I had thought that Jonas and Katie would live in her house to begin with, but it turns out that there will be another couple using that house."

Elizabeth's stomach turned. "You mean the house Katie and I are sharing now?"

"You haven't heard? Katie's brothers decided that Young Peter Lehman should have it when he marries Katie's niece Margaret this summer. But you don't need to worry about where you live. Your Mamm and I always have room."

Swallowing, Elizabeth attempted a smile. "That's all right. I'll move back to my cabin. There's no reason to have it sitting empty, and I will enjoy living closer to Ruby and her family."

"Do you think it is wise for you to try to manage one hundred sixty acres on your own?" He stroked his beard. "If you want my advice, I think you should sell the farm and move home. If you want to live on your own, we can build you a house near ours."

Jonas grinned. "You could build near the woodlot and be our neighbors. Katie would like that fine."

Datt looked around the clearing as if he was measuring the space. "But first we need to make these changes to Jonas's plans. His original thoughts are fine for a young couple just starting out, but they'll want a larger house as their family grows."

"Have you talked to the ministers then?" Elizabeth asked.

Jonas shook his head. "Not yet, but I have confidence that they will give permission for us to marry."

"What will you do if they say you can't join the church?"

Her brother's face darkened. "I'm not sure yet, but we'll do something. Katie and I have waited long enough to get married, and I don't want to let anything stand in our way."

Datt's frown told Elizabeth how he felt about that idea. "We'll see what happens. Just don't be too quick to act."

Elizabeth glanced at Aaron. They had been speaking Deitsch during their conversation. He hadn't been listening but was examining a piece of wood about two feet long. He put one end on the ground, then stood next to it.

"Does that one look like it might work?" Jonas said in Englisch, walking over to him. Elizabeth followed.

"It might." Aaron sat again and handed the piece of wood to Jonas. "It's a solid piece of oak. I'll need to form some sort of socket in the top."

A wooden leg. Aaron was making a wooden leg. Elizabeth glanced at his pinned-up trousers.

"You'll want a cushion too," she said. "The man I saw in Millersburg had a pad between his leg and the wooden one."

"Elizabeth is right," Jonas said. "And you'll need a harness to fasten it on. A couple of the members in our community are harness makers. Perhaps they could help you design something."

Aaron's face took on a hopeful look that banished the empty expression in his eyes. Perhaps he needed nothing more than a goal and a plan to be useful.

"Harness makers? Grandpop taught me a little bit about working with leather, and I'd be beholden to them if they could teach me how to make such a thing."

"Dan Zook and his brother Ephraim run the business together along with their farm," Datt said. "Who knows? You might be related to them."

Aaron glanced at Elizabeth. "One of the many Amish Zook families? I don't think you'll find any of my relatives here."

"What if you did?" Jonas asked. "You don't have any other family. It would be a blessing to find someone to belong to."

Aaron's face closed again, making Elizabeth curious. It was possible that Dan and Ephraim Zook were related to him, but Aaron didn't seem interested in them at all. Was he so determined to remain independent that he'd even deny his own family?

3

Aaron looked forward to a quiet morning by himself on Sunday. After breakfast he went out to the back porch. The sun was coming up behind a covering of gray clouds. It would rain today.

The family was getting ready for church and their usual routine was hurried. Jonas came out on the back porch, dressed in black trousers and a snowy white shirt. He smoothed his hair down before settling his black straw hat on his head.

"You're not coming?" he asked as he tugged on the ends of his sleeves to smooth the creases.

"I'm not much for church going," Aaron said, easing back farther in the chair. "Haven't since Ma passed on. I'll just stay put." He didn't tell Jonas that he intended to go back to bed as soon as the family was gone.

Jonas peered closely at him. "Are you all right? You've been working pretty hard the past few days."

Aaron resisted rubbing his stump. "I'm a bit tired. Those

months in the hospital took more out of me than I thought they would."

"I've heard that a man can lose more strength by lying in bed than anything else. But you came pretty close to death a few months ago. You need to build up your stamina. Give it some time." He leaned against the porch rail, dusting it with his hand first. "I wish you'd change your mind about staying home this morning. Spending the day worshiping the Lord might be just what you need."

Just what he needed? A sudden memory of Sunday mornings by Ma's side at their country church at home brought moisture to his eyes. Aaron rubbed it away. He was tired, nothing more.

"Y'all eat there?"

"Sure. After the services we eat together. Not a big meal. In the summer it's usually cold roast and bread, along with pickles and other such things. And desserts, of course. Usually pie."

Aaron's mouth watered even though he had just finished breakfast.

"But the preaching is in German," Jonas went on. "You probably wouldn't understand too much of it."

"Grandpop made sure I understood German. He used it enough that I picked it up. I can make out most of what y'all say."

Jonas stood up, dusting off the seat of his trousers. "It sounds like you're talking yourself into coming to church."

"I don't have fancy duds to wear." Aaron glanced sideways at Jonas's clothes.

"These aren't fancy, although they are special for the

Lord's Day. But you're a visitor. No one will expect you to dress like us."

Aaron ran his fingers through his beard. It might be worth sitting through the preaching to get to the meal. If he stayed here, he'd have to rustle up his own grub. And it wouldn't be as if he didn't know anyone there. He had met most of the community at Jonas's welcome-home party.

"I'll go with you." Aaron ignored Jonas's grin.

"I'll hitch up the spring wagon."

A number of folks had already arrived at the farm just past Elizabeth's and Katie's house when Jonas drove the wagon into the yard. Abraham and Lydia had insisted on walking, and Aaron saw that there were only a couple other buggies.

"Where's the church building?" he asked Jonas.

"We don't have one. We meet in homes, like the Amish have always done. Each family in the community hosts the church service twice a year. Today it's Karl Stuckey's turn."

Aaron looked for faces he knew and saw Elizabeth standing with some other women. Katie nodded to Jonas and smiled.

"We'll wait out here until everyone has arrived," Jonas said in a quiet voice. "We use the time to prepare ourselves for worship."

He led the way to a group of men standing off to the side. The group was a subdued contrast to the other night. No one spoke more than a quiet greeting.

Just after Abraham and Lydia had joined the gathered community, another buggy arrived. The horse was black and spirited, but the man driving the shiny rig held the reins with confidence. He pulled the horse to a stop in the middle of the crowd. Abraham stepped forward.

"Welcome, stranger. Can I help you?"

The man smiled. "The name is Solomon Mast." He flashed a smile at the crowd. "New in the area. I just bought the old Patterson place and moved in this week from Lancaster County in Pennsylvania. Neighbor Amos Beiler told me where the community was meeting for worship today, so I thought I'd join you."

Aaron's feet didn't move as the men around him stepped closer to the newcomer. The man's voice plucked at his memory, taking him back to a night in Virginia, smoke hanging in the dark air between the tents of the camp. He shook his head. It couldn't be the same man.

"You're welcome, brother," Abraham said. "We are just about to go in to worship." He signaled behind him and one of the older boys ran forward to take the horse and buggy to the barn.

"Denki," Solomon said. "I look forward to getting to know all of you."

As the man's gaze scanned the crowd, he paused when he saw Aaron. His eyebrows lifted as if questioning his presence, and he met Aaron's gaze. Instead of the open, honest expression Aaron had come to expect from Jonas's family and friends, Solomon Mast's face tightened, his eyes narrowing and his full lips pressing into a thin line. Then, as if a towel were whisked away, the smile returned, and the man's gaze continued around the gathered group. Had it been a look of recognition? Or only surprise at seeing a non-Amish man in the group?

Then Jonas nudged Aaron. It was time to go into the house. Rows of benches lined the large open room with an aisle between them. The women and young children sat on one side and the men on the other. Aaron and Jonas took their seats on the back bench, while Solomon Mast followed Abraham right up to the front. Aaron frowned. They might both be visitors, but Solomon showed the stark difference between them. He acted as if he belonged here and Aaron did not.

~~~~~~~~

Elizabeth helped serve the fellowship meal after church, but her thoughts were on today's visitors. Solomon Mast had appeared in their midst like a fresh breeze on a warm day. He sat with the ministers and Datt for the first seating of the meal, and his voice rose above the other conversations.

"The Patterson farm is eighty acres," Solomon said, answering someone's question. "It's good land, but less than forty are tillable at present. The rest is poor and stony, but it will be useful for grazing cattle."

Elizabeth carried a bowl of sauerkraut to the table and set it down in front of Bishop Amos. Solomon smiled at her, making her the center of his attention for a moment. Elizabeth felt her cheeks grow warm as she moved down the table to place a second bowl in front of Jonas and Levi Beiler at the other end. Aaron sat with them and smiled his thanks to her.

The conversation at the other end of the table continued. "Do you have a family, Solomon?" Preacher Amos asked.

The man's face grew downcast. "Sadly, no. I am a widower. My wife passed away and our only child perished with her." He paused as the other men expressed their sympathy. "But it has been several months since her passing, and I am ready to start again. That is why I moved here to Ohio." He glanced at Elizabeth, then turned his attention back to the men. "This is a new beginning for me in a new community. I must thank you for your kind welcome to a stranger."

"Are you in need of any help on your farm?" Gideon Fischer, Elizabeth's brother-in-law, asked.

Solomon shook his head. "Patterson had already done the spring planting, and he sold me the equipment and livestock along with the land and buildings."

"I hadn't realized Abel Patterson was planning to sell out," Gideon said. "I spoke with him a few weeks ago."

"He told me he had decided to go back to New York to live with his son. I met him in the land agent's office in Millersburg where I went to inquire about land for sale." Solomon smiled at the men around him, his white teeth gleaming. "I suppose you could call the meeting the Lord's providence. We settled the matter there and then."

Elizabeth went to the kitchen to fetch another plate of bread. When she came back, the men were still discussing Solomon's business.

"Gideon, is it?" he said, turning to her brother-in-law. "You said you had spoken to Patterson recently. Does that mean that we're neighbors?"

"My farm is nearby," Gideon said, "but Elizabeth's land is between us. She owns one hundred sixty acres, eighty on the west side of the Berlin Road and eighty on the east side." He nodded toward Elizabeth as she set the bread on the table. "This is Elizabeth Kaufman."

Solomon turned his warm smile on her. "Elizabeth, I am happy to meet you. So, you and your husband will be my closest neighbors."

Elizabeth felt her cheeks warming again. "My land is your neighbor." She couldn't keep from returning his smile. "I don't live on the land, and my husband has passed away."

"We will have to become better acquainted, then."

"I'm sure we will." Elizabeth turned and nearly ran for the kitchen. Her sister Ruby, Gideon's wife, and Millie Keck, Salome Beiler's married daughter, were there, along with Mamm. All of them stared at her.

"What is wrong?" Millie asked, jiggling one of her twin babies in her arms. "You look as if you're running away from a wolf!"

Elizabeth laughed at the image Millie's words portrayed. "Don't be silly. I was just thinking of something, that's all."

"I saw you talking to that new man." Millie rocked the fussing baby back and forth. "Where is he from? What is he doing here?"

"Girls, we don't want to gossip," Mamm said, slicing another loaf of bread.

"He was very open about his business as he spoke with the men," Elizabeth said. "He has bought Abel Patterson's farm and intends to settle here."

"And his family?" Ruby asked.

"There is no family. He's a widower."

"That is interesting," Millie said, grinning. "A widower in the community. I'm sure he'll be looking for a new wife."

"He can look all he wants," Elizabeth said, reaching for Millie's son. He settled in her arms and stared up at her, his fist in his mouth. "There are plenty of young single women for him to court, between our community and the neighboring ones." She smiled at the baby and touched his nose. "Which baby is this one, Millie? I can't tell them apart."

"That's little Amos. But don't think you're going to change the subject. What about Solomon Mast?" She sighed. "I can see the wedding now."

"What wedding?" Ruby asked, laughing at Millie's dramatic expression.

"When Elizabeth marries Solomon, of course." Millie laughed along with her. "Don't you think they belong together?"

Elizabeth handed little Amos back to his mother. "Don't be silly. I don't even know the man. Save your wedding plans for someone else."

"I think they're well suited, with his land right next to hers," Millie said as Elizabeth escaped out the door. She didn't wait to hear Ruby's reply.

When it was the women's turn to eat, Elizabeth found a seat at the table between Mamm and Ruby. As the men had finished their meal, they had drifted toward the barn where they could stand out of the light rain and visit. Some were admiring Solomon's buggy as he pointed out the red-painted details on the undercarriage. He laughed often and even the soberest of the men joined in. Such a contrast to Reuben, who would never gather with any of the men in the neighborhood except Ned Hamlin.

Aaron and Jonas had not made themselves part of the

group. They sat together on a bench under a tree talking with Gideon, but Aaron's attention wasn't on either man. He was watching Solomon. Solomon didn't seem to notice, but then Elizabeth saw him glance in Aaron's direction. His handsome face paled, then he shifted his stance so that his back was to Aaron. Aaron frowned, still staring at the group of men, fingering his long red beard.

What was that all about?

———

Levi Beiler took a deep breath of the fresh evening air as he stood at the top of the hill, just before the road dipped into the Weaver's Creek valley. The afternoon showers had moved on, leaving cool weather behind for the rest of the Lord's Day.

He often stopped in this spot near Elizabeth Kaufman's old house to enjoy the beauty of the farms and woods with the creek winding through like a thread. Tonight, the creek was golden as it reflected the lowering sun, and off to the east a rainbow graced the sky. A familiar longing twisted his heart, though he barely noticed it after so many years. If only . . .

Levi shook his head. He had no reason to be discontent. At twenty-three years old, he finally had a comfortable, respectful relationship with Father. And the farm was doing well enough to support his parents and himself. Millie, his younger sister, was married and happy. At least, he assumed she was. Any woman would be happy, as busy as she was with her six-month-old twins.

Most satisfying of all was the freedom he now had to

study the scriptures and other church writings to his heart's content. Father even discussed what he was reading with him on occasion.

No, he had no reason to be discontent, except that a man should have a partner. Adam had Eve. Father had Mother. Jonas had his Katie. If only there was someone he could share the joys of this life with. Even though Paul had written that it was better for a man to be alone . . . except he also wrote that it was good to marry . . .

Levi started down the hill. He mustn't forget his errand. Solomon Mast's appearance at the church meeting this morning had taken everyone's attention and Levi hadn't been able to have his talk with Abraham.

He found the older man alone in the barn, finishing up the milking.

"It's an easier job now that you only have one cow, isn't it?" Levi leaned on the top rail of the cow pen.

Abraham glanced at him, then picked up the pail of milk and poured it into a can. "It is. I've tried to convince Lydia that we don't need even this one, that we could get our milk from Samuel, but she won't hear of it." He patted the cow on the rump and sent her back out to the pasture. "What brings you by?"

Levi grabbed the milk can and followed Abraham to the springhouse between the barn and the house. "I wanted to talk to you about the next ministers' meeting this afternoon at church, but I didn't get an opportunity. It's going to be in Wayne County again this year."

"I had heard," Abraham said, closing the springhouse door after Levi set the can in the cool running water. "I also heard that the last two meetings, in Pennsylvania and Indiana, were dominated by the change-minded faction."

"That's exactly right. That is why as many conservative leaders as possible are meeting here in Holmes County the week before the general meeting in July."

Abraham's gaze was piercing. "It sounds like they're ready to pit one side against the other. That isn't a peaceful way to solve the differences."

Levi followed Abraham to the porch. "Even though many hold out hope that there can be a reconciliation, I don't see how there can ever be the unity we've enjoyed in the past. The change-minded faction is determined."

"So are the traditionalists." Abraham settled into a chair and Levi joined him. "I hate to see it, but these controversies have been brewing for many years."

"Sometimes I think a schism in the church is inevitable."

Abraham sat silently for a few minutes, then heaved a sigh. "You'll be going to this meeting?"

"I'll go to both of them with Gideon. I want to observe, even if I'm not allowed to vote on the issues. I'm curious to see how the change-minded group accepts our position."

"You think they will object?"

"The conservative leaders want to state our position in a unified way and present it in written form so that their meaning can't be mistaken." Levi rubbed the perspiration off the bridge of his nose. "But I'm afraid the change-minded ministers won't pay much attention to them. They dismiss their brothers as old fashioned and afraid to try new things."

"We will have to wait and see how it plays out." Abraham

rose from his chair. "The end is in the Good Lord's hands, and he knows best."

A thump sounded from inside the house, followed by a pause, then the sound of the kitchen door opening. Jonas came out on the porch, along with his Englisch friend. As Abraham went inside the house, Levi greeted Aaron with a nod. He had been surprised but pleased to see the stranger at the church meeting this morning.

"Aaron," Jonas said, keeping his Deitsch slower and more distinct than usual. "This is Levi Beiler. You've heard me mention him."

"Several times." The man grinned as he shook Levi's hand. "I remember seeing you at the church service this morning."

"Did I hear your last name is Zook? You must be related to Dan and Ephraim."

Aaron's grin disappeared as he shook his head. "Not that I know." He sat on the top step, resting his crutches on the edge of the porch.

Jonas laughed and clapped his hand on Levi's shoulder. "Everyone who meets him asks him that. I think it would be good if we found out that Aaron was related to the Zooks here. It doesn't matter who you are, knowing you have family around is important."

Aaron rubbed the stump of his leg.

"You don't have family back home?" Levi wanted to pull back the words as soon as they were out. He didn't know this man well enough to prod him with a personal question like that.

Jonas lowered his voice. "Aaron's father and grandfather died during the war. He has no one else."

Levi moved to the porch steps and sat next to Aaron. "It would be good for you to find out if you have family here. Dan told me his father is coming to Ohio for the ministers' meeting next month. He lives in Lancaster County in Pennsylvania but will be moving the rest of the family out here to live near Dan and his brother, Ephraim. He might know if you have any family connections."

"I don't know. I might not be here next month." Aaron had switched from struggling to speak in Deitsch to Englisch.

Levi glanced at Jonas.

"I thought you had decided not to go west," Jonas said.

"Yeah, well, I haven't decided for certain yet." He picked up a pebble from the step and threw it out into the twilit drive. "I'm not sure I'm ready to put down roots anywhere." He picked up another pebble and rolled it between his fingers. "Every time I stop moving, memories catch up with me."

"Those memories will fade eventually," Jonas said. "I've heard that men can recover from the effects of war."

"Not when reminders show up when you least expect them." Aaron tossed another pebble. "Like that Solomon Mast this morning. He reminds me of someone. Someone I'd rather forget."

In the east, the evening star shone in the darkening sky. Fireflies blinked on and off in the meadow while silence followed Aaron's words.

After long minutes, Jonas sighed. "Promise you won't head west until you've healed," he said. "It hasn't been long enough since your injury for you to recover fully."

Aaron looked down. Levi followed his gaze to the pinned-up trouser leg. He had always admired Jonas and they had been good friends, but Jonas had traveled through a valley with Aaron that he couldn't imagine. Perhaps it would be best if the stranger just moved on like he said he wanted to. A friendship this close with a non-Amish fellow could pull Jonas further away from his home than the war had.

The most important task for Jonas right now was to join the church and get on with the life he had planned with Katie. He needed to put the war and Englisch ways behind him.

4

After the Monday morning chores were done and Katie had gone to visit her sister-in-law Lena, Elizabeth tied her bonnet strings under her chin. Ever since Datt had told her that Young Peter and Margaret would be moving into this house she was sharing with Katie, Elizabeth had been restless. It was true that she was welcome at Mamm and Datt's house and could easily move back into the bedroom she had shared with Ruby as they were growing up, but she had left nearly fifteen years ago now. Would it be so bad to move to the log cabin where she had lived while she was married? She hadn't been back since she left to set up housekeeping with Katie after Margaretta had passed on nearly two years ago.

Leaving the laundry to finish drying on the line, Elizabeth walked down to the road. But as she passed the home farm and turned up the hill leading toward Reuben's farm, her steps slowed. Perhaps she would stop and visit with her sister Ruby first. After all, she would be passing the Fischers' farm.

Elizabeth interrupted her thoughts with a quick shake of her head. She would visit with Ruby after she took a look at the cabin. It was no use putting off the unpleasant task once she had determined to do it.

She hurried past the lane leading to Ruby and Gideon's house and climbed up the hill. When she could see the cabin, she stopped, forcing herself to look closely instead of turning her head away like she usually did when she passed this way. The walls leaned farther into the slope than she remembered, and the roof was covered with moss. She took a few steps closer, putting a trembling foot on the overgrown path that had once led to the front of the cabin. The door hung open. One of the leather hinges had finally rotted through. Walking up to the door, she pulled on it gently and it swung open a bit farther. The table was still in its place but was littered with dirt and half-eaten pinecones. The bed frame in the corner was bare, the ropes that had once held the mattress hanging loose. The rest of the cabin was in shadow and a rustling noise came from the darkness in the far corner.

The last time she was here, Ruby had been with her, helping her pack her things to move to Katie's house. Ruby had always filled the cabin with life and light, but now the old memories had crept back with the neglect. Elizabeth's head throbbed as her mind ran in a direction she couldn't bear, and she backed away, pushing the heavy door closed with all her strength. She clasped her stomach. She wouldn't get sick. She wouldn't. Reuben was dead. She was free.

She took a deep breath and walked around to the back of the cabin. Her garden was overrun with weeds and the chicken house had blown down in a storm. It must have happened last winter, because she remembered it was there the last time she had seen the cabin, her home for so many years.

Not home. Home was a place of love and joy, where folks made you feel welcome. Reuben's cabin had never been her home. Elizabeth turned her back on it and headed down the hill to Ruby's.

Five-year-old Ezra and his two-year-old brother Daniel were in the shaded front yard playing in a sandpile, but when Ezra saw Elizabeth, he ran to her.

"Guess what we're doing," he said, his feet planted in front of her as if he dared her to try to walk past him. "Guess."

"Only if you give me a hug first."

Elizabeth opened her arms and he fell into them, squeezing her waist in a hard, quick hug, then pulled away. He took her hand, tugging her toward the sandpile. Elizabeth longed to hold him close, but he was never still long enough to satisfy her. Every time she looked into his face, she wondered . . . had her child been a boy? Would he have been as active and full of life as her nephew?

"We're building a farm," Ezra announced before she could make her guess. "Daniel is building the lanes and I'm planting the fields."

The boys had plucked leaves from the surrounding bushes and Ezra had planted them stem down in neat rows. Daniel's lanes wobbled between the fields, wherever he pushed his piece of wood to make a flat road.

"It's a fine farm." Elizabeth knelt at the edge of the sand. "What crops are you growing?"

"That's corn, and that's oats, and that's barley, and that's wheat." Ezra pointed as he named the fields. "We're going to plant beans next. Then there will be a meadow and Daniel will put his animals in it."

Daniel looked up. "Cows and horses." He stood up. "I get them."

Both boys ran toward the house. Elizabeth followed them, letting herself into the kitchen. Ruby looked up from rolling out a piecrust on the kitchen table.

"I thought I heard someone talking to the boys. What brings you this way today?"

Elizabeth sat at the table and watched Ruby roll the dough with short, sure strokes. "I went up to the farm. I thought I might be able to fix up the old cabin to live in, but it's a mess."

Ruby finished rolling out the crust and eased it into a pie plate.

"You never liked living there alone," she said as she lifted the plate and cut the overhanging edges of dough. The spiral fell back to the table.

"I know, but I need to find somewhere to live. Katie and Jonas will be married soon, and the Stuckeys have planned for Margaret and Young Peter to live in Katie's house after their wedding."

"So, you need a house." Ruby fetched a pan from the stove and poured the red fruit filling into the pie.

Elizabeth took a deep breath. "Rhubarb?"

"With strawberries." Ruby checked the oven's temperature. "It's Gideon's favorite." She gathered the dough scraps into a ball and started rolling out the top crust for the pie. "But back to your house. You won't really move into that old cabin, will you? Talk to Datt. Perhaps we could build you a new house on your farm."

"Datt suggested selling Reuben's—" She stopped herself. "My farm. He says I can move in with the folks, or they could build a house for me on the home farm."

"That sounds like a good solution to your problem." Ruby positioned the top crust over the pie and settled it into place.

Elizabeth watched as her sister put the pie in the oven and brushed the flour off her hands, as confident as Mamm in every motion. She was happy.

The thought was startling. Elizabeth's mind went back to the days before Ruby and Gideon married. Her sister had been pleasant enough to be around, but she hadn't been happy. Marrying Gideon had given her a husband to love and a ready-made family. The arrival of Baby Lovinia almost a year later had given Ruby even more confidence, but now it was combined with a joyful peace that Elizabeth watched with envy, tinged with fear for her sister. She knew what men could become when they thought no one was watching.

"I don't want to give up my independence," Elizabeth said, pushing those thoughts aside and giving an answer Ruby would approve of. "If I sell the farm, I won't have anything of my own. I'll go back to depending on Mamm and Datt again."

Ruby poured a cup of coffee for both of them and set one in front of Elizabeth before sitting down.

"There's nothing wrong with that, is there?"

"You're the one who always told me a woman should be able to support herself."

"And I still think that." Ruby stirred some honey into her cup. "But being able to support yourself and doing it when it isn't necessary are two different things. You're a widow, but you don't have to be alone. If you don't want to move back to the home farm, you could get married again."

A sick knot twisted in Elizabeth's stomach, but she put a smile on her face. "Who would I marry?" She forced a laugh. "I'm not going to grab a man off the streets in Millersburg."

Ruby laughed with her. "Nothing like that. But there's Levi Beiler. He's still single, and definitely ready to get married."

"He's a lot younger than I am. Besides, I doubt if Salome wants me for a daughter-in-law." Elizabeth shuddered, remembering the tone of Salome's voice when she had mentioned that very thing to Mamm not too long ago. But Salome had been right to let the idea go. She would never be good enough to satisfy that woman.

Ruby tapped her forefinger on her lips, thinking. "Aaron Zook is single, and any friend of Jonas might be a good prospect."

Elizabeth pressed her lips together and shook her head. "If I ever marry again, my husband will have to be a member of the church. I'll not make that mistake again."

"Perhaps Solomon Mast is the answer. We need to get to know him better, but he seems like a good Amish man. Solid and secure."

Elizabeth turned her cup between her hands. The warmth felt good on her suddenly chilled fingers. Solomon was handsome and outgoing, but he probably wouldn't look twice at a woman like her. She certainly wasn't the new wife he would be looking for.

"He'll most likely snatch up some pretty young girl. I don't think he'd be interested in me."

Ruby sipped her coffee. "I'll keep looking. There has to be a man out there for you somewhere."

Elizabeth reached across the table and took Ruby's hand. "Don't. I'm not planning to marry again. I don't ever want to be at the mercy of another man."

"Not all men are like Reuben," Ruby said, her voice low. "There are good men too."

Elizabeth's eyes filled as Ruby squeezed her hand. She didn't deserve a good man.

———

By Wednesday, Aaron had the wooden leg fashioned to his satisfaction. He smoothed his hand along the straight length, checking for any stray splinters. It still looked more like a piece of wood than a leg, but it should do. He had hollowed the top like a bowl to give his bad leg a secure rest, then he had whittled the remaining log down until it resembled a peg. Carving an actual leg with a foot had been his first vision, but that was beyond his skills. And he appreciated one advantage to this design. It was lighter than if he had tried to duplicate his missing limb's shape.

Since the day was overcast and drizzly after a night of heavy rain, Jonas had offered to drive him to Dan Zook's in the afternoon. The cool, damp air made Aaron's leg ache.

"I'm happy you will finally be getting to know Dan," Jonas said, breaking the silence of the quiet drive.

"I didn't meet him at church, did I?"

Jonas shook his head. "They had some illness among the

children in both families last Sunday." He grinned. "But I told him about you, and he's convinced that you're related to each other."

"I doubt that we are. Grandpop told stories about a brother, but no other kin."

"So, you don't know your grandfather's family?"

"Never met them, and from his stories about his pa, I'm not certain I'd want to."

"Family is important." Jonas leaned back in the wagon seat. "Even when I was out East with the army, I knew my parents and the rest of my family were keeping me in their prayers. And home . . ."

His voice faded. He swallowed and then continued.

"Coming home wasn't to see the buildings and the farm, but to see the people. Katie, of course, but also my parents, my brother and sisters, the church family. That's what makes a home." Jonas turned the horse onto another road that angled toward the east from the one they had been on. "I know you lost your house in Tennessee, and your father and grandfather. That makes it even more important to find any other family. What if Dan turns out to be a cousin you never knew you had?"

Jonas's words brought back memories of the events that had propelled Aaron into joining the army. Grandpop had been killed trying to defend his home and property from a Yankee raiding party, and then Pa, never in his right mind since Ma had passed on, had been killed early in the war, taking a foolhardy chance trying to avenge Grandpop. With their deaths, the last vestige of home was destroyed. He was alone and adrift in the world.

Aaron pulled his mind back from the edge of that dark abyss. "My family is gone. Clinging to some imagined sense of attachment to a stranger isn't going to change that."

"But what if it isn't imagined? What if it's true?"

Aaron snorted. "They're still strangers, ain't they?"

Jonas whistled a bar of "Dixie," then grinned at him. "They're only strangers until you meet them."

The roof of a large barn rose above the trees, and before long Jonas drove the horse into the barnyard. The house was nearly identical to the Weavers' home, painted white to match the barn. A garden had been planted between the house and the road, and across the farm lane was a smaller building that matched the barn and house, with a sign over the door. The words were German, but Aaron recognized the name. It was the same as his own. His mouth went dry. Knowing there were other Zooks around was one thing, but reading his name on the sign . . . he couldn't deny that it felt good to see it.

A tall man that looked close to Aaron's age came out of the shop to greet them. He spoke to Jonas in Pennsylvania Dutch, his words running together too quickly for Aaron to follow, but his eyes often drifted to Aaron as he spoke. Those eyes . . . they were Grandpop's eyes.

When Dan spoke to Aaron, it was in Englisch. "Jonas tells me you know some harness making."

"A bit. My grandfather taught me how to repair our mule's harness when I was a youngster, but not much else."

"Come into the shop. We'll see what we can do."

Jonas took the wooden leg and they both followed Dan into the harness shop. Aaron breathed in the various scents of leather, tannin, and neat's-foot oil. Scents that were sharp and familiar. If he closed his eyes, he could be back in the barn in Tennessee, watching Grandpop work the oil into the old mule's harness.

Dan motioned for Jonas to set the wooden leg on his workbench. "Let's see what we have here."

He examined the leg, using his hands to explore every inch from the supporting saddle to the peg leg.

"That's fine work. Not a splinter anywhere." Dan looked at Aaron. "Did you have any ideas about how to hold it on?"

"I modeled this after one I saw while I was still in the hospital. The man had a cloth belt with laces that fastened around his leg above the knee, then leather straps on either side sewn to that. The straps were fastened to the wooden leg near the top."

Dan nodded. "We have a piece of canvas we can use for the belt, and the leather straps should be easy enough. Will you be able to work on it with me so we can be certain it fits properly?"

"How long do you think it will take?"

"A few days." Dan started sorting through a bundle of leather scraps, then grinned at Aaron. "It will give us an opportunity to get acquainted and figure out how we're related."

Jonas returned home, leaving Aaron with Dan as they got to work. As Dan talked, his face was animated. Every expression reminded Aaron of Grandpop, as if he were with a younger version of the man who had raised him. The man who had refused to talk about his father but had entertained the young Aaron with tales of his boyhood escapades during the quiet winter evenings by the fire.

"Tell me what you know about your Zook family," Dan said as he sorted out straps that were approximately the same length. "Where do they live?"

"Grandpop said he grew up in Pennsylvania, but I don't know if any of his family still lives there. He had no brothers or sisters."

"Do you know where in Pennsylvania?"

"All I know is that it was in Lancaster County, but it was a long time ago. Grandpop was near ninety years old when he was killed, and he said he left home when he was barely old enough to grow a beard."

Dan took an awl from his workbench and started tapping out the stitching guides along the edge of the leather. Aaron took a second strap and another awl and followed suit.

"*Dawdi*—my grandfather—was about the same age as him, then. He passed on last fall." He measured out some thread and started coating it with beeswax. "My datt and stepmother still live in Lancaster County, but in his last letter Datt wrote of moving out here now that Dawdi is gone. He would know more than I do about the Zook relations. We'll have to ask him when they arrive next month."

"So, you and your brother moved out here together, but your father stayed in Pennsylvania. What made you decide to move to Ohio?"

"We had heard about the good farms out here and talked about making the move, but then Datt married a widow with her own children, and Ephraim and I decided it was time to head west. Tobias and Elise, our stepbrother and stepsister, needed Datt's attention after being without a father for several years." Dan took his strap and Aaron's and started sewing them together with the waxed thread. "We've been here for six years. The land is better than the farm in Pennsylvania, and we've got a good Amish community here, so Datt decided to join us."

"You must be a close family." A memory trickled into Aaron's mind. A mother. A father. Grandpop. Happier times.

"I suppose you could say that," Dan said, concentrating on his stitching. "We write every week even though we haven't been able to visit the rest of the family since we moved out here." He grinned at Aaron. "It will be good to see them all again."

Aaron watched Dan finish the seam, his strong hands tightening each stitch before going on to the next one. In profile, the resemblance to Grandpop was even stronger. It was possible they were related, but what difference would that make? Dan didn't need him. He had a family that he loved. He didn't need a tagalong shirttail cousin trying to fit himself into a home here.

He would move on when the time came.

***

Solomon Mast rose early on Friday morning. After two days of steady rain, he frowned at the clear light of sunrise as he stood on his front porch with a cup of black coffee in his hand. The rain had kept folks home and had given him time to plan his next move. The better weather might bring unwanted callers.

Patterson had built his house on the highest point of his land, giving Solomon a good view of the valley to the south and the creek that wound past the tidy farms. Weaver's

Creek, they called it. He drained the cup of coffee and grimaced at the bitterness. He spat out the coffee grounds that had been mingled with the last mouthful.

When he had stopped by the land office in Millersburg earlier in the month, he had spent hours examining the map of the county and had settled on German Township because most of the farmers were Amish. Solomon liked the Amish he had run into since he left the Shenandoah Valley two years ago. They were as peaceful as the Mennonites he had grown up around, but much more placid. Like sheep, they didn't act until the entire community agreed on a matter. And like sheep, they were trusting of anyone as long as he acted like one of them.

Sunday, his first introduction to the folks of Weaver's Creek, had gone well. They had been friendly and accepting, just as he had expected. They welcomed him as one of their own, but he hadn't missed the clucks of disapproval when old Abraham Weaver had inspected the red trim on his new buggy.

"Buggies are new around here," he had said, "but that red trim stands out. You say it's allowed in your old district?"

Solomon had painted over the glossy red paint with dull black on Monday morning.

He sat in Abel Patterson's willow rocking chair and leaned back, his gaze on the land across the Millersburg Road. Hearing that the farm belonged to the widow Elizabeth Kaufman hadn't surprised him. He had learned that information at the land office. But finding out that she was young and lovely was a welcome bit of information he had tucked away. He had taken the Patterson place because of the widow across the road, and her beauty just made his plans more desirable.

Settling back in the rocking chair, Solomon rested his heels on the porch rail. The widow's land was one hundred sixty acres, divided into two parcels. Added to the eighty acres he got from Patterson, he was on his way to a respectable-sized farm, but just a small place compared to Abraham Weaver's holdings. The number of acres in the Weavers' names had turned his gut into a twisting mass as he had traced the borders on the map. He needed that land. It should be his. It would be his. His heels thudded on the porch floor as he stood to get another look at his neighbor's land.

Patience. He batted at the word as if it were a wasp circling his head. Patience? He had no time for patience. The land was his.

He took a deep breath, his gaze still on the land across the road. No mistakes this time. Move slow. Don't rush. Make them trust you.

Movement on the road to the east of the Patterson place drew his gaze. A spring wagon pulled by a single horse. A young man and an older woman. He watched the horse turn into his farm lane.

"Callers." The very thing he had expected when the morning had dawned so fine. He turned around and cracked open the front door. "Dulcey!"

The young woman appeared in the hall leading to the back of the house, her dark skin blending into the shadowed interior of the house.

"Get yourself down into the cellar and stay put. Someone is coming and I don't want them to see you yet."

The girl disappeared like a shadow and Solomon closed the door. He shook his arms, letting his hands hang loose for a moment, then took a deep breath. As he let it out, he stepped into the man his visitors expected to see. Well-to-do Amishman Solomon Mast, new to the community and pleased to be part of it.

The young man driving the rig had a fair complexion with pink skin that looked prone to sunburn. The woman with him looked old enough to be his mother. Solomon searched through the faces in his memory. Sally? Sarah? Not quite.

The woman waved to him as the young man brought the wagon to a stop at the bottom of the porch steps.

"I'm glad we found you at home," she called, rising to her feet before the wagon came to a complete halt.

With the sound of her grating voice, the name came to him.

"Salome Beiler, isn't it?" Solomon stepped off the porch to help her step out of the wagon. He glanced at the driver. "And Levi? Did I remember correctly?"

Salome's smile was broad. "You did. Levi is my son. I wanted to call on you earlier this week, but the weather didn't allow it."

"Won't you come in? I have coffee on the stove."

"Ach, *ne*." Salome waved him off. "I know you're living alone, so I brought some things over for you." She signaled Levi and he jumped down from the wagon and brought a basket from the rear. "Only a few baked goods and a pot of soup. Just enough to give you some of the comforts of home."

"I appreciate it," Solomon said, reaching for the basket. The fragrance of freshly baked bread drifted through the morning air.

"Levi can take it into the kitchen for you." Salome peered around him to the front door. "And it wouldn't be any trouble for me to fix a fresh pot of coffee for you."

"That won't be necessary," Solomon said.

As he took the basket from Levi, Salome slipped past him and started up the porch steps.

Levi gave him a sheepish grin and shrugged his shoulders. "Very few folks find it easy to keep Mother from extending hospitality when she sets her mind to it."

Solomon fought to keep his face pleasant. "What a charming trait, and so appropriate for a woman of her position."

At Levi's raised eyebrows, Solomon mentally gave himself a kick. No Amishman talked like that. He took the basket into the house, Levi following him. Salome was in the front room.

"Abel Patterson left all of his belongings?" she asked.

"He was in a hurry and sold it all to me." He pushed past Salome, hoping Dulcey had followed his instructions and left no evidence of her presence. "The kitchen is this way."

As he set the basket on the table, Salome took charge. Whisking off the covering towel, she brought out two loaves of bread, a pie, and a covered iron pot wrapped in a cloth. She unwrapped the pot and set it on the stove, then stirred the morning's fire and put more sticks on to bring it up. She moved the coffeepot to the front of the stove and opened the lid, peering into the dark interior.

"Tsk, tsk." She shook her head and poured the remainder of the contents into the slop bucket. "I'll make some fresh coffee and we can visit while we have some pie." She turned to Solomon. "I hope you like peach pie. I made it with some preserves from last summer. Now sit down and we'll have a nice visit to get acquainted."

Solomon's smile was genuine as he took a seat at the kitchen table next to a resigned Levi. He might not have wanted callers this morning, but Salome Beiler was just the type of person to give him the information he needed without even realizing what she was doing.

He gave Salome his most charming wink and picked up his fork as she set a plate in front of him. "Now then, tell me all about my new neighbors." He cut the point off the triangle of pie. "Start with the Weavers."

As he listened to Salome talk, he savored the sweet peach syrup and flaky pie crust. Yes, Salome was a perfect fit for his plans.

5

A week after his first day of working with Dan Zook, Aaron strapped on his new wooden leg, ready to begin his new life. He stood next to his bed, testing the weight on his leg. The stump was still tender, but the pad Lydia had made for him helped distribute the pressure. He took a step, adjusted the laces on the cloth foundation, then took another careful step. Finally, he straightened up, stretching to his full height.

He grinned, catching sight of himself in the small mirror hanging on the washstand. He looked normal again. After nearly a month in Weaver's Creek, eating Lydia's good cooking and working outdoors, he was gaining strength. His color was better, his cheeks ruddy above his red beard rather than pale. The new leg would take some getting used to, and he'd need to use a cane to help with balance for the rest of his days, but for the first time since that fateful battle near Richmond, he could look himself in the eye.

"You look like a man again," he said to his reflection,

keeping his voice low. "And from now on you'll act like a man, not a wounded animal."

He took a step closer to the mirror, but a sharp pain stopped him. The stump was still too tender to put his full weight on it for very long. With a sigh, he grabbed his crutches and went downstairs to breakfast.

"I hope you won't mind being on your own today," Jonas said as they went out onto the porch after the meal. "I'm meeting with the ministers this morning and Datt's coming with me."

"Are they going to decide if you can join the church or not?" Aaron stopped and adjusted the laces again. It would take some time to get used to this contraption.

"They'll discuss it. They have some questions to ask me, and I hope they'll decide to let me join. Everything is at a standstill until we hear their decision."

"What if they decide against you?"

Jonas shook his head. "I hope it doesn't come to that."

"What work needs to be done?" Aaron tapped his new leg. "I'm able to do much more now that I have this."

"Before this meeting was scheduled, I was going to fix a broken board on Katie's porch. Do you think you could do that?"

"No one could do it better." Aaron looked up the road toward the house Katie and Elizabeth shared. "I'll have to drive up there."

"The horse and wagon are available, and the tools are in the workshop. Do you need help hitching up Rusty?"

"I think I can do it." Aaron had a flash of memory of the last time he tried to harness the horse. "But stick around.

I'll try to do it myself before you leave and let you know if I need help."

As Jonas went back into the house to finish getting ready for his meeting, Aaron went to the barn, using his new leg as much as possible instead of the crutches. If it were anyone but Jonas, he would never ask for help, but Jonas was different. He had seen Aaron at his worst, when he had been near death and delirious with fever but hadn't abandoned him. In fact, their friendship had grown stronger.

Rusty was standing just outside his stable door in the morning sunshine and came right away when Aaron called him in. Through the door, Abraham's bull stood in his pasture. The big animal grazed with the sun on his sides, absorbing the morning rays.

Aaron patted Rusty's neck. "You know you'll get oats when I call, don't you?" He poured a cup of oats into his feed bin and fetched the brush.

His new leg held him up well enough as he groomed Rusty, and Aaron reveled in the new strength in his arms as he lifted the harness from its place on the wall and carried it to the horse. He had to walk slowly, but he kept his balance during the few steps between the wall and where he had tied Rusty, even turning around without falling.

Aaron had settled the harness on Rusty's back and was beginning to buckle the straps when Jonas came into the barn.

"It looks like you're doing well without my help," Jonas said, standing off to the side while Aaron worked.

"The new leg makes a big difference," Aaron said, reaching under Rusty's belly for the final strap and fastening it. "I can keep my balance and use both hands at the same time. I think I'll need help with the wagon, though."

Once Rusty was hitched to the wagon, Jonas fetched the toolbox and some lumber from the workshop while Aaron boosted himself onto the wagon seat, adjusting his jump to accommodate the weight of the wooden leg. Jonas stowed the toolbox in the back and Aaron clicked his tongue at Rusty. As the horse headed out of the barn, Aaron fingered the lines in his hands. He hadn't driven in nearly a year and he had missed this live communication with the horse through the reins. He drove across the bridge and turned onto the road.

The drive was pleasant with the early morning sun low enough that the shadows were still fresh with the night's cool air. Birds sang in the trees and Aaron spied a wild turkey hen with her brood scurrying across the road ahead of him.

A tune came to him. It was a hymn from his childhood, long forgotten until he had heard the boys in the camp singing it around the fires at night during the war. He hummed it for a few bars, then whistled it as Rusty turned into the drive leading to Katie and Elizabeth's house. The tune stuck with him as he hopped down from the wagon seat and tied Rusty to the hitching rail. He pulled the toolbox from the back of the wagon and carried it to the porch, using one crutch for balance.

The front door opened. Aaron had hoped it would be Elizabeth to greet him, but instead it was Katie. When she saw him, her smile turned to a disappointed frown.

"I thought Jonas was going to fix the porch."

"Sorry," Aaron said. "Plans got changed so you're stuck

with me." He grinned at her. "I know that isn't as much fun for you."

Katie blushed, her pink cheeks turning red. "What is Jonas doing that's more important than fixing our porch?"

"He said he had a meeting with the ministers this morning." Aaron set the toolbox on the porch next to the broken board. "I guess he thought that was important enough."

A happy smile covered her face. "That's for sure. I had hoped they would meet this week. We've waited a long time."

"Are you sure Jonas is worth it?" A familiar, nearly forgotten, teasing note colored his voice.

"Of course, he is. That doesn't make the time pass any faster, though." Katie's smile didn't fade as her gaze went past him, down the drive toward the unfinished house on the other side of the creek. "I'd wait my whole life for Jonas if I had to."

She stood there, unaware of him or anything else, lost in her thoughts. Jonas had told Aaron about Katie, but until he came here and witnessed the bond the two of them enjoyed, Aaron hadn't realized how strongly Jonas's life was tied to her. Yes, to the farm, his family, and the community too. But Katie was Jonas's home.

As Katie went back into the house, Aaron got to work. He pried up the broken board, then hammered out the nails and straightened them. Going back to the wagon, he found a board the right size and tested it on the porch. A little trimming, then some sanding, and the new board would fit right in.

Humming as he worked, Aaron sat on the top step of the porch. Without thought, the words to the song formed themselves and he sang softly, remembering Ma's voice singing this same hymn.

> "Rock of ages, cleft for me,
> Let me hide myself in thee . . ."

Aaron stopped, the board in one hand and the sanding block in the other. This little house surrounded by pines reminded him of the cabin where he had grown up. Had Ma called upon her God when she was in her final affliction, that terrible day when she breathed her last? He let the sanding block rub along the grain of the board, continuing the song.

> "Let the water and the blood,
> From thy wounded side which flowed,
> Be of sin the double cure;
> Save from wrath and make me pure."

Grandpop had never called upon the Lord, but Ma had spent hours holding Aaron on her lap, teaching him about her Lord Jesus Christ and what she called his saving grace. The same Lord who had abandoned her to her fate and Aaron to a life without her.

He pressed his lips together and rubbed harder.

"Don't stop singing."

The voice came from behind him, but he recognized it. Elizabeth had come out onto the porch and he hadn't heard her. He was losing his soldier's awareness.

"I got to the end of the verse," Aaron said, not looking at her.

"Then sing the next one. It's a lovely tune." She sat on the step next to him.

He turned the sanding block and started the next verse.

> "Not the labors of my hands
> Can fulfill thy law's demands;
> Could my zeal no respite know,
> Could my tears forever flow,
> All for sin could not atone;
> Thou must save and thou alone."

"That's a beautiful thought," Elizabeth said, sitting with her chin in her hand watching the trees at the edge of the yard. "The words are talking about Jesus, aren't they?"

"Probably. It's a song my mother liked to sing."

"So, you sing it to remember her?"

Aaron nodded. "It's about all I remember of her." He turned his mind to the memories of her last day and night as she gave birth to the sister he had never known. "She passed on when I was a youngster."

"But she believed in the Lord?"

"I suppose she did. She tried to teach me, but it didn't stick. Didn't help her much, either."

"Why do you say that?"

Aaron ran his hand along the new board. No splinters. He'd give it a coat of paint, then nail it into place after it dried. He looked at Elizabeth, who still waited for an answer to her question.

"Where was her God when she was in the agony of childbirth? Where was he when she cried out to him for help? Nowhere. She died and that was it."

Elizabeth's face was thoughtful.

"You're not going to argue with me?"

She shook her head. "How can I?" Her voice dropped to a whisper. "He turned his back on me too."

Elizabeth rose from her seat with a jerk and disappeared into the house. Aaron's sanding block slowed, then stopped as he turned to look after her. Grandpop had always told him that the Amish were high and mighty, bragging about their special place in God's eyes, but Elizabeth didn't seem to be like that at all. Her whisper . . . maybe he wasn't meant to hear it . . . but her whisper betrayed a brokenness as deep as his own.

Levi slipped in the front door of his family's home and sat in a chair near the door, close enough to observe Jonas's meeting with the ministers without interfering.

"There has been no precedent on this issue that I can think of," Wilhelm Stuckey said as he opened the meeting. "Jonas was not a baptized member of the church when he took up arms, nor did he join the army out of a sense of discontent or anger."

"But he did join the army, something that goes against the deepest ingrained teaching of the church. Jesus Christ himself showed us the way to live, and loving our enemies is paramount." Father paced as he spoke, just as he did when preaching on Sunday mornings, his left hand fisted behind his back and his right hand punctuating his sentences in the air.

Abraham Weaver leaned back in his chair. Gideon, the third minister, sat with his fingertips steepled beneath his chin, his eyes closed in thought. Jonas perched on the edge of his chair, looking from one man to the other as they discussed his fate.

"The precedent exists," Gideon said, his eyes still closed. His voice was strained, and Levi felt the anguish he was experiencing at deciding Jonas's fate. "During the American Revolutionary War, members of the church that supported the rebellion against the established government never rejoined the fellowship of the church."

"But that doesn't address Jonas's case." Wilhelm looked at Father with a hard gaze. "I say that if he can assure us that he didn't act in a war-like manner while he was in the army, then we should welcome him into fellowship."

Father, silent for once, stared at Jonas, then resumed his pacing.

"Amos, what questions would you ask him?" Abraham's voice stopped Father and all the ministers looked at him. "What would satisfy your requirements?"

"First of all," Father said, taking his seat, "we need to be clear about whether his actions ever harmed another man."

All three men looked at Jonas, who didn't meet their gaze but stared at the floor.

"There were times when I was required to fire my rifle. However, I aimed above the soldiers' heads and didn't intentionally kill or wound any man. I can't say that the bullet spent itself without causing harm, but I'm not aware if it did so."

Wilhelm cleared his throat. "So, you did not knowingly take the life of any man, but you were involved in fighting a battle?"

Jonas nodded. "Before I was transferred to the medical

corps, I was in several battles as a soldier. I found a way to make myself useful by treating the wounded and pulling them from the heaviest part of the fighting. Then, at the Battle of Fredericksburg, I was captured by the enemy."

Father stopped his pacing and faced Jonas. "Jesus taught that sin is not only in the committing of a deed, but also in the contemplating of the deed. During these battles and after you were captured, what thoughts filled your mind? Did you hold animosity toward your fellow man?"

"No. I felt . . . pity. Remorse at the situation I was in. Horror at the evil that overtakes men during a battle."

Levi saw a slight shudder pass through Gideon, the only other one in the room who shared Jonas's experiences. Gideon had told Levi of the part he had played in the war when he had been forced to work as a teamster. He had also told him about the agony he experienced when his inaction caused the death of a young soldier.

Gideon addressed his question to Jonas. "Was there ever a time when you could have prevented an act of violence, but didn't?"

"Not that I know of. I tried to save the wounded, Federals and Rebels alike."

Father resumed his pacing. "If I have the facts clear, after you were released by your Confederate captor, you were transferred to service in the medical corps, where you spent the rest of the war in acts of mercy. Is that correct?"

"For the remainder of the war I served in field hospitals and most recently at a hospital in a prisoner of war camp. I did my best to bring comfort to the wounded and dying."

"But you were still a member of the army."

Jonas nodded, his eyes on the plank floor beneath his feet.

Clasping his hands together, Father turned to Abraham and Jonas. "If you would wait outside, we will discuss this matter among ourselves."

Jonas led the way out of the room and Levi followed him. Abraham brought up the rear as they walked to the shaded area in front of the barn, out of earshot of the discussion taking place inside the house.

Abraham sat on a bench near the barn door and leaned against the wall. The late morning air was warm and humid.

"What do you think, Datt?" Jonas asked, keeping his gaze on the house. "Do you think they will support me?"

"I can't say." Abraham stroked his beard.

Levi's thoughts drifted back three years to the night Jonas had left to join the army. Had his friend's actions been foolish? Perhaps. But he had kept his brother Samuel from suffering a worse fate.

"What will you do if they refuse to bring you into the fellowship?" Levi asked. They both watched the house for any sign of a conclusion to the deliberations.

"I've had a lot of time to think about this," Jonas said. He sat next to Abraham on the bench. "For three long years I've wondered what would happen today. If they decide against me, I will still marry Katie. We'll join a Mennonite church, or a Dunker congregation. We would still be part of our families, just not the church."

Abraham laid a hand on his son's knee as if he could call him back. "Don't forget that Katie has joined our church already. Would you have her turn her back on her membership vows?"

Jonas drew both hands over his face. "I hate to put her in the position of deciding between me and the church, but it's up to the ministers now."

"Ne." Abraham patted Jonas's knee. "It's up to the Good Lord. We will pray that the ministers listen to him."

A bumblebee buzzed in the clover near the barn door. It stopped on one purple flower, making it sway up and down, and then moved on to another, landing heavily. Levi watched it search each part of the blossom for the nectar within. By the time the bee had flown away to a new hunting ground, the front door opened, and the three ministers came out.

Levi followed Jonas across the barnyard, then fell back to keep pace with Abraham. He searched the three faces. None of them met Jonas's gaze as he walked toward them. They stood on the porch, no one talking.

They caught up to Jonas at the foot of the porch steps. Father glanced at his fellow ministers, then at Jonas.

"We have decided that we need more time to pray and discuss this matter. We will also confer with other ministers from around the country next month when they gather for the ministers' meeting in Smithville. Until we come to an agreement on our decision, Jonas is welcome to continue worshiping with us as he has always done."

So, there was dissent among the ministers. Jonas's shoulders slumped.

Levi stepped close to Jonas. "Everything will turn out all right."

The other men said their farewells and left, the Stuckeys in their spring wagon and Abraham and Gideon walking home together. The two paused on the road, waiting for Jonas to join them.

"You think it will?" Jonas's face was stony. "No decision at all is worse than refusing to let me become a member. Now everything will be delayed more weeks before they decide against me."

"You don't know what the final decision will be."

"Don't I?" Jonas scrubbed the back of his neck with one hand. "I knew the night I left to take Samuel's place in the draft that this would be waiting for me when I came home. If the church wants to turn me away, Katie and I will be all right. We'll find a community that will accept us. But this isn't the way I wanted our lives to be."

Levi swallowed the lump in his throat. "Don't do anything rash. Wait until the ministers make their decision."

Jonas sought Levi's gaze and held it. Years of friendship stood between them, shimmering like heat rising from the barn roof on a hot summer day. Levi fought the urge to grasp Jonas's arm. To hold him fast, pull him back from the edge.

"I'll wait." Jonas rolled his shoulders. "I need to do everything I can to stay in the church for Katie's sake."

He gave Levi a nod, then turned for home, joining Abraham and Gideon on the road.

On Friday morning, Elizabeth and Katie left the house early to help Mamm in the big garden at the home farm.

"I love our little house," Katie said. "The pine trees whisper in the wind, and the shade keeps the place cool in the summer. But there isn't a sunny place anywhere."

"No spot for our own garden, that's for sure." Elizabeth kicked a stone to the side of the road. "But you Stuckeys have that big garden for the family, and our family has this one." She grinned at Katie. "I guess this is the year that you are part of the Weaver garden."

Katie blushed. "By harvesttime Jonas and I hope to be married. I'm glad to be able to put up what garden produce I can before then."

"And we're glad to help you." Elizabeth smiled at the friend who was like a sister already.

Mamm was hard at work with her hoe when Elizabeth and Katie arrived.

"Is Ruby coming today?" Elizabeth asked, stopping to train a stray bean stalk onto the trellis Mamm had erected when they planted the beans last month.

"She said she'll be down later. Roseanna brought word that she is pickling eggs this morning, but she'll come down when she's done."

"Pickling eggs?" Katie took a hoe from the pile Mamm had brought out to the garden. "Her hens must be laying well."

Elizabeth picked up her own hoe and started at one end of the corn row. The little shoots were almost hidden in the weeds that had sprung up since last week. May was always the month to fight weeds in the garden. By June the plants would be tall and full enough to shade the ground beneath them and keep the weeds from growing as well. She worked steadily as Mamm and Katie visited, but she didn't pay attention to their conversation. The combination of the bright sunshine, the earthy odor of the garden, and the call of the red-winged blackbirds along the creek transported her thoughts to many childhood days of hoeing weeds. She had hated the task then, but now that she was older, it was a joy. A quiet respite from the busyness of life.

A movement on the other side of the pasture fence caught her attention. It was Datt's bull, Samson. Datt had raised him from a calf, but Elizabeth hadn't seen him for a long time. Datt had been keeping him in the far pasture, away from the cows. This spring the bull had grown to his full size and looked like a brute instead of the sweet yearling she remembered.

"Mamm, is Samson supposed to be in that pasture?"

Mamm shaded her eyes and watched Samson walk along the fence as if he was looking for a weak spot.

"He must have broken through his fence again. Abraham needs to sell him. We have no need for a bull, and he's getting too big for the men to handle. I'll let your datt know he got out again at dinnertime."

The bull raised his head and looked in their direction.

"Here comes a visitor," Mamm said, turning to see what Samson had noticed. "It looks like Solomon Mast."

"Is Datt in the barn?" Elizabeth put her hoe down. "I'll go fetch him."

"Ne, he's out in the fields."

Mamm dusted off her hands and walked to the farm lane and Elizabeth joined her. Solomon drove his horse over the stone bridge and into the farmyard and smiled at them as he pulled his horse to a stop.

"Good morning, ladies." He touched the brim of his hat.

Elizabeth looked at her feet to keep from staring. The

various Amish communities had different customs, but she had never heard any Amishman greet anyone like that.

"Abraham is out today," Mamm said. "You'll find him if you follow the farm lane west along the creek."

Solomon stepped out of his buggy. "I didn't come to see Abraham. I had hoped to find Elizabeth here."

"Me?" Now she didn't worry about staring. Solomon's face was as pleasant as she remembered, with dark eyes set wide and a ready smile. White teeth gleamed above his beard.

"Do you mind? Perhaps we could go for a little walk?"

Elizabeth wiped her hands on her apron, sure that garden dirt clung to them. "I'm busy right now. The garden needs to be hoed."

"Katie and I can get along without you for a few minutes," Mamm said, turning back to her work. "Take your time."

"Well then." Solomon indicated the lane leading along the creek past the house. "Shall we?"

He set the pace, walking slowly between Elizabeth and the creek. She strolled next to him, waiting for him to begin.

"I hear that you are a widow."

"That is right."

"And you have heard that I lost my wife a few years ago."

Elizabeth glanced at him. "I have heard that."

"I thought"—he caught her gaze and smiled—"that since we're both alone, perhaps we should learn to know one another, to see if we're compatible."

"You are very new in the area. We don't know you yet."

"That's true. But I wanted to see how you felt before any other beau has a chance to snatch you away."

He wiggled his eyebrows as he said this, and she laughed.

"I don't think there is any danger of that. I don't intend to marry again."

Solomon stopped walking and grasped her hand. "Perhaps I can change your mind."

She held his gaze. His eyes were clear and open, his smile friendly. Elizabeth pulled her hand from his grasp and continued along the lane. "Tell me about yourself. Where did you live before you came to Ohio?"

"In Lancaster County, in a small community outside Ephrata. I settled there soon after my wife passed on, but after two years I still hadn't found the right woman to share my life, so I decided to try farther west."

Elizabeth watched his profile as he spoke. His voice had caught when he talked about his wife passing away, but he showed no other emotion.

"Why did you choose Weaver's Creek?"

"Because of Abel Patterson. He had a farm to sell and I was looking. The situation was providential."

"Providential?"

He smiled. "God's providence. All good things come from God."

Elizabeth stopped at the gate in the fence between the farmyard and the wheat field. Feathery green growth covered the field, undulating in the gentle breeze. She had heard that phrase before, that all things come from God. Good as well as bad. Was it God's providence that brought Solomon Mast to Weaver's Creek? Could it be that God was giving her a second chance to make a marriage that was pleasing to him?

Across the field, coming toward them along the lane, Aaron drove the farm wagon. Solomon opened the gate as he approached. Aaron drove through, then pulled the horses to a halt.

"Solomon Mast, isn't it?" Aaron asked. He made no move to climb down from the wagon seat.

"That's right." Solomon stepped close to Elizabeth, close enough for their shoulders to touch. "I recall seeing you at the meeting on Sunday, but I don't think I heard your name."

"Aaron Zook. I think we might have met before," Aaron said, his voice hard. "A few years ago? In the Shenandoah Valley?"

Solomon chuckled. "What would an Amishman be doing in the Shenandoah? We have no communities there."

Aaron's eyes narrowed and Elizabeth felt Solomon stiffen. Why was Aaron being so rude?

"I need to get to my work in the garden," she said. "Are you going back to the barn, Aaron?"

He shook his head, but his gaze didn't leave Solomon. "Abraham needs to borrow a tool from Gideon, but I can give you a ride back to the house, if you would like." His blue eyes shifted from Solomon to Elizabeth and softened. "You needn't walk if you are in a hurry."

Elizabeth glanced at Solomon. She didn't want to abandon him in the middle of their walk. "I'll go back with Solomon."

Aaron slapped the reins on the horse's back and went on, but twice he turned around to look at her.

"That was a strange question for him to ask." Solomon took her hand and tucked it around his elbow as they started walking back toward the house. "He doesn't seem to be Amish. Where is he from?"

"Aaron is from Tennessee. He and my brother became friends during the war."

His arm tightened under her hand, but his face was calm and relaxed. They were nearly back to the house and Solomon's buggy.

"I hope you've given some thought to my proposal. I think we could become very good friends." He untied the black horse from the hitching rail. "Shall we go for a drive on Sunday afternoon? Just the two of us?"

Elizabeth shook her head, her hands growing clammy. She took a step back. "It wouldn't be proper. I mean, to ride in your buggy alone with you." She had learned her lesson many years ago. Before they had been married, Reuben had always urged her to come with him alone, but a woman alone with a man was too vulnerable.

A frown appeared for a second, so briefly that Elizabeth couldn't be sure she had even seen it.

"You are right, of course. Perhaps you have a friend or a sister who could accompany us?"

Bells clanged in Elizabeth's head. She shook them away, but the warning persisted. Would the memory of Reuben always affect her this way?

"I wouldn't want to leave the fellowship early. Maybe . . ." She licked her lips. "Maybe another time."

She turned and strode toward the garden, searching for her abandoned hoe through clouded eyes. What was wrong with her? Solomon was a good man, a member of the church, friendly and solicitous . . . Her hoe struck deep into the packed dirt and ripped out a dandelion. And that was the problem. She didn't deserve a man like him.

85

6

On Sunday, Aaron slipped into the back row of benches just in time for the service to start. Jonas had already taken his seat near the front next to Levi, but Aaron didn't want to draw attention to himself by thumping up the aisle. Folks stared at him enough as it was.

He looked around the room as the first hymn started. The congregation sang slow, drawn-out songs in a chant that sounded nothing like the hymns Aaron had heard before, and the words were in high German rather than the Pennsylvania Dutch he was more familiar with. He hummed along, not bothering with the words as he tried to identify the folks he knew from the backs of their heads.

On the women's side he found Elizabeth's sister Ruby easily. Her red hair floated in light tendrils around the edge of her kapp. Next to her were her daughters and Lydia. Samuel Weaver's wife, Anna, was next with her daughter. Aaron had seen them often at the Weavers' farm. And then came Elizabeth, sitting very still, her eyes closed as she sang, her expression a slight frown, as if she was concentrating on the words.

The singing ended and the song leader announced the next hymn, *Das Lobleid*. This was the one he was beginning to learn since the congregation sang it at every worship service. The song was a praise to God, and Aaron let the words surround him, singing along when there was a phrase he remembered. He watched the back of Jonas's head five rows in front of him. Jonas would nod as one word, which followed several notes, ended and the next one began. It was just enough of a cue to allow Aaron to keep up.

But then at the third verse, the man sitting three rows ahead shifted in his seat, blocking Aaron's view. Aaron frowned and tried to lean to the left, but he was between two strangers and couldn't move far enough. All Aaron could do was wait until the other man shifted again. He stared at the back of the man's head. Straight black hair, smoothed against the head with the imprint of the hat band visible . . . Every thought of the church service and the song fled Aaron's mind. He had seen that head before. He blinked.

"Got any more information for me?" the lieutenant had said. The night was dark, the air filled with the smoke of a hundred campfires.

"Sure enough." That voice. Smooth as if it had been run through a grease bucket. "The Yankees are in Winchester, but they're gettin' ready to come this way."

"How about the provisions?"

"The Dunkers have banded together to hide their stores." The voice chuckled. "But I know right where they are, just a few miles from Staunton. I can show you on the map."

Coins clinked together as Aaron looked around the tent flap. The lantern in the tent showed the spy clearly, but only the back of his head. His straight black hair, shining in the light, smoothed against his head with the imprint of the hat band visible . . . a man dressed in the plain clothes of the farmers in the valley. He held out his hand and the captain dropped the coins into it.

The song ended and Aaron blinked again. As the leader called out the number of the next hymn, Aaron stared at the back of the head. Solomon Mast's head. But why would an Amishman have been in the Shenandoah Valley during the war? And why would he sell information to the army? He had to be mistaken. It couldn't be the same man.

After the services were over, the men arranged the benches for the fellowship meal. Aaron found a place at the table between Jonas and Dan Zook. Ephraim sat across from them.

"When do you expect your father and the rest of the family to arrive?" Jonas asked Dan as he buttered a thick slice of bread.

"Datt wanted to be here in time to attend the early meeting before the ministers' meeting begins next week," Dan said. "So, we expect him any day now."

"Does he have a place to live?"

"Dan and I have their house nearly built," Ephraim said. "Between us, we have more than enough farmland for all three families."

Levi sat down on the other side of Jonas. "We will certainly welcome them to the community. Will it be your parents alone, or do you have younger brothers and sisters?"

"Datt remarried several years ago," Dan said. "Our stepmother was a widow and brought her two children to the family." He looked at Ephraim, his eyebrows raised in a question. "Tobias was eighteen when they married, if I remember correctly."

Ephraim nodded. "And Elise was fourteen. So, they are twenty-four and twenty now."

"And both of them are coming to Ohio?" Levi asked.

"That's what Datt indicated in his last letter," Dan said. "I thought Tobias would be married by now, but from what Datt says, he's anxious to establish his own home out here in Ohio." He chuckled. "It sounds like he'll be looking for a wife."

"Is your father a harness maker, also?" Aaron asked, concentrating on the Pennsylvania Dutch words.

"He's the one who taught us the trade," Dan said. "I was thinking that it might be good for you to keep learning. You already know quite a bit about it, and it is a skill that you don't need both legs to do."

Aaron took another slice of bread and laid a piece of ham on it. "I don't know. The community isn't large enough for so many harness makers. Besides, I'm not sure how long I'll be around here."

Ephraim pushed his plate away and leaned across the table toward Aaron. "Even if you don't stay in Weaver's Creek, the harness trade is one you could do anywhere. You should learn from Datt while you can. He has a lot of experience that he'll be happy to pass along."

Taking a bite of his sandwich, Aaron let Ephraim's words settle in. He had never considered that he would be a tradesman. He had spent the years before the war hunting, fishing, and trapping. He had always planned to go back to that life once the war ended, but that was out of the question now. Even in the settled hills of western Tennessee, he would find it impossible to make a living with only one leg. He'd be at the mercy of every bear and panther in the forests, and even more so in the West. He'd heard tell of giant bears out there with grizzled shoulders that could kill a man with one swipe of their paws.

A trade would provide a living, if he could stand being in a workshop all day long. And he enjoyed the feel of leather between his fingers. Dan had said he had a talent for stitching even seams. He had felt welcome and at home in the harness shop when they were constructing his wooden leg. It was something to think on.

The men's conversation continued without him as the others prepared to leave the table to make room for the women and children. Solomon Mast got up from his seat at the end where he had been sitting with Bishop Amos and Abraham. Instead of accompanying the other men outside, Solomon made his way toward the kitchen. He leaned against the doorframe, talking with the busy women in the crowded room. Whatever he said made the women laugh, and then he stood aside to let someone through—it was Elizabeth. Her face blushed pink as she went past him, her hands full of clean plates and a smile on her face.

Solomon watched her walk away, and his gaze caught Aaron's. His smile widened, then he looked back at Elizabeth's figure. Aaron's eyes narrowed. In any other place, he would accuse Solomon Mast of taking liberties with a woman, watching her like that. But the Amish had different ways. Ways he wasn't familiar with. Perhaps if two adults were courting, the man was freer to show his attraction in public, asserting his claim.

Somehow, that thought left a sick feeling in Aaron's stomach.

"Solomon Mast is watching you." Millie's voice held a teasing lilt. She was washing the dishes after the fellowship meal while Elizabeth and Katie dried them.

Elizabeth frowned as she dried the cup in her hands. "You must be mistaken. Why would he pay any attention to me?"

Katie nudged Elizabeth with her elbow. "Because you're a young widow and he's a widower. What could be more normal than the two of you becoming a couple?"

Elizabeth glanced behind her. Solomon smiled when he saw her looking, his expression warm and friendly. She turned back to her friends.

"Nothing is going to come of it. He's becoming acquainted with the people in the community, that's all."

Millie giggled. "I think he wants to become acquainted with one particular member of the church, and that's you. Don't look now, but he's coming this way."

Katie grabbed a dry dish towel and concentrated on wiping the next cup while Millie suddenly started scrubbing a plate. Elizabeth felt the warmth of someone close behind her.

"Would you care to take a short walk with me?"

Solomon's breath stirred the hairs on the back of her neck, causing Elizabeth's stomach to flip. She turned around and took a step back as he towered over her. His dark eyes twinkled as he smiled at her, and the scent of something rich and woody played in the air between them.

"I . . . I have to finish drying the dishes." Elizabeth concentrated on the snowy white front of his shirt. "I can't leave the work to Katie and Millie."

"Go ahead," Katie said, taking the forgotten towel from Elizabeth's hand. "We're almost done. Millie and I can finish up."

"You have no excuse then." Solomon stepped aside, indicating that she should lead the way.

Elizabeth kept her gaze on the floor in front of her as she made her way through the front room of Wilhelm Stuckey's house and out into the yard. From the comments she overheard, all the women noticed what was happening. A creeping red heat started at her neck and went upward.

"Where does this path go?" Solomon asked, pointing to the trail through the pine woods.

"It goes to our house. The one Katie and I share."

"Was your husband one of the Stuckey family?" Solomon strolled beside her along the dirt trail.

"Ne. I live with Katie Stuckey. At least I do until she and Jonas marry."

"Then you'll live there alone?"

Elizabeth glanced at Solomon's face, but only saw mild curiosity.

"I'm not certain where I'll live yet. The Stuckeys are giving the house to Young Peter Lehman when he marries Margaret Stuckey later in the summer."

"You own a farm, don't you?"

"My husband owned the farm that borders my father's

and brother's land. I had thought of moving back to the house there."

"That old cabin?"

"You know the cabin?" Elizabeth stopped and looked at him. "So, you knew I owned the farm all along."

Solomon chuckled and kept walking, forcing her to catch up. "I admit it, I asked your brother-in-law about you. But only because I was curious about my neighbor. You wouldn't consider living in that cabin in the shape it is now, would you?"

Elizabeth shuddered. "I don't think I could live there again even if it was in decent shape."

"You didn't enjoy living there?"

His eyebrows were raised, but his question sounded more like a comment. How much about her marriage would she divulge to a stranger?

"My husband was difficult." As Solomon nodded in understanding, Elizabeth decided that was all the explanation he needed. "Datt has talked about building a new house for me, but he wants me to live on the home farm, closer to the rest of the family."

The path opened into the yard of the little house she shared with Katie. Solomon strolled past the chicken coop and the clothesline.

"So, this is the house you live in now?"

"Ja, with Katie." He stood in the center of the yard, his hands clasped behind his back, looking at the house. Was he waiting for an invitation to come inside?

"It's a fine little house," he said, walking around to the front. "Well built and solid. The log walls are quaint." He stepped onto the porch and turned around to watch the chickens scratching in the dirt along the path.

Elizabeth waved a hand toward one of the chairs. "Would you like to sit down?"

He smiled and a wave of relief washed over Elizabeth. His smile meant he was happy and enjoyed being with her. Could it be that he would choose to court her? She had never been the center of any man's attention, except Reuben's.

"Do you mind if we sit here and talk?" Solomon took off his hat and fanned his face. "We were interrupted the other day."

Solomon sat in Katie's rocking chair near the door and Elizabeth slid past him to take her seat in the corner of the porch. He leaned back in his chair and pulled on his coat to straighten it.

Once he was settled, he smiled at her again. "How long were you and your husband married?"

Elizabeth's mouth went dry. "Reuben and I were married for almost thirteen years before he passed away."

"No children?"

The memory of that young life stirring under her heart brought tears to her eyes. She looked away from Solomon and blinked them away. "We weren't blessed in that way."

His eyes narrowed briefly. She had said something wrong. He would leave if she couldn't steer the conversation back to a more positive topic.

"I suppose you're right. Some couples never do have children." He rocked in the chair. "I've gotten the feeling that your family thinks it was a good thing when your husband didn't come home from the war."

"He . . . Reuben . . . wasn't Amish. My family didn't approve of my marriage."

"But you're a member of the church?"

"I wasn't baptized when I married him. That came later, after he was . . . gone."

Solomon leaned forward in his chair, a warm smile on his face again. "You had said you don't intend to marry again when we talked before. Is there anything that would change your mind?"

Elizabeth forced herself to look into his eyes. Open, friendly, serious. There was nothing in his manner or his speech that reminded her of Reuben. Life with him would be gentle. Predictable. The way an Amish couple was supposed to live. She pushed her caution away and let a smile pull the corners of her mouth up.

"I don't know. Perhaps, if I got to know you better."

Solomon's smile turned into a satisfied grin. "That's easily done." He took her hand. "I think you are a lovely example of what a fine Amish woman can be, and I think you will make the perfect wife for me."

Elizabeth's heart pounded as he stroked the back of her hand with his thumb. He knew about Reuben—it seemed he knew as much about her as her own family did—and he was still interested in her. She caught her bottom lip between her teeth and searched his face. Perhaps he was the man she should have married in the first place. She smiled into his brown eyes.

"I would like to spend time with you, to get to know you better."

His grin widened. "Wonderful. Tomorrow? You can come

to my house and see where you will be living. We'll have a picnic lunch on the front porch."

"Where I'll be living?" Elizabeth withdrew her hand, the caution coming back with full force. "I didn't say I would marry you."

"Not yet, you haven't." Solomon rubbed his hands together. "But you need to see what I can offer you. Please come tomorrow, sometime in the morning."

Elizabeth paused. Up until she met Solomon, her mind had been closed to the possibility of a future marriage. Closed to putting herself under the power of a man again. But here he was, the man of her childhood dreams come to life. She pushed past that warning bell again. Solomon would be a son-in-law her parents could be proud of.

"Ja," she said, smiling at him once more, "tomorrow will be fine."

As Elizabeth stood to walk back to Wilhelm Stuckey's place, Solomon took her hand and threaded it through the crook of his arm. She was slender and quiet. Not nearly as meek as he would wish, but that would come in time.

Meanwhile, she was coming around. Agreeing to come to the house tomorrow was a stroke of luck. They would be alone, but it was too soon. Too early to press his advantage. That was the mistake he had made back in Pennsylvania. That girl had been just flirtatious enough to fall easily into his hands. As the only child of wealthy Amish parents, she would inherit everything from her father. But his error had been to assume the girl's parents would be eager to marry her off once they learned she had been compromised.

Elizabeth, though, was as cautious as a doe in an open meadow. He had to be careful not to frighten her away. From what he could tell from the talk about her dead husband, she had reason to be reticent. That was all right with him. He only had to win her trust and she would be his.

"Isn't that beautiful?" Elizabeth had stopped in the path, her hand still in the crook of his elbow, looking into the pine branches above them. Solomon looked up but didn't see anything. Was she daft?

"What did you see?"

"Didn't you hear it?" Elizabeth resumed walking, still watching the branches above them. "It was a cardinal calling."

"Sorry." Solomon stroked the back of her hand. "I was paying more attention to you."

She blushed at that. This woman wasn't used to compliments. Solomon filed that information away.

"We're almost back to Wilhelm's farm," she said. "Denki for the walk."

"We don't have to end it so soon." Solomon kept her hand tucked in close. "It's still early. Is there another path we can take?"

"Maybe another time. I don't want to miss visiting with my friends. I will see you tomorrow, close to noon."

He let her hand slip away. When they reached the edge of the farmyard, Elizabeth started walking faster, leaving him behind as she hurried to join the other women. One glance behind her told him all he needed to know. She regretted leaving him.

Solomon watched her until she disappeared into the group of women and he couldn't distinguish her kapp from the others. Amish women all looked the same, except that Elizabeth was pleasant to look at all around. Walking away was especially enjoyable as her skirt swayed with every step. Yes, he could get used to that.

"Well, my fine fellow," he said under his breath, "you've lucked into a good spot here. A willing widow, one hundred sixty acres of land nearly yours, and more to come."

He scanned the groups of folks resting in the shade while they visited. A crowd of children played a game close to where the women had gathered, their laughter piercing the afternoon quiet. Solomon made his way in the other direction toward a group of men that included Abraham Weaver. Elizabeth's father. He needed to get on the old man's good side.

Nodding to Gideon, Solomon took a seat next to him, one that the one-legged man, Aaron, vacated when Solomon entered the circle. Solomon felt the other man's stare as he hobbled to the edge of the group and leaned against a tree, but he chose to ignore it.

"Well, Solomon, are you getting settled in?" Abraham asked. Several of the other men leaned forward to hear his answer.

"Without any problems." Solomon included the whole group in his smile as he spoke to Abraham. "The house is in fine shape and the livestock are in good health."

"Abel sold his livestock to you as well as the farm?" one of the men asked. Solomon thought he might be one of the Weavers.

"The farm equipment, also. He didn't want to take anything with him, and it saved me from having to search out the necessary items." Solomon kept his voice calm to smooth over the suspicious wrinkles on a few of the foreheads. "He was traveling by train, so he only took his clothes and other personal things."

"I still think it's strange that he didn't stop at our place to say farewell," the younger Weaver said.

Gideon shrugged his shoulders. "He must have been in a hurry. Or perhaps he stopped by when you weren't home."

Solomon jumped in to stop the speculations before they went too far. "He told me that he received a telegram and had to act quickly. Most likely, he didn't have time to say goodbye to his neighbors."

That Weaver, Solomon thought it might be Samuel, still looked suspicious, so he changed the subject.

"The corn looks to be growing well." He nodded toward one of the older men. Lehman, if he remembered right.

The man took the bait. "Ja, for sure. It's a fine year for corn. Growing well and leafing out already."

"Don't start building new silos yet," said another man. One of the ministers. "Take heed, lest you fall into the error of counting your bushels before they're harvested."

"Come now, Amos," said Abraham, "let's enjoy a good crop while it lasts. If it keeps up this way, we'll have plenty of work to groan over come harvesttime."

The other men chuckled, and Solomon joined in.

"How is Abel's crop doing?" Abraham asked Solomon. "He purchased a new seed drill last year and was hoping it would increase his yield."

Solomon made a mental note to examine the machinery in the barn and try to figure out which one was a seed drill.

"The corn looks good to me," Solomon said. "The seed drill must have worked the way he wanted it to."

Silence followed his statement, then he remembered.

"Any one of you is welcome to borrow it next spring, come planting time. It's there and waiting."

The men murmured their thanks, then the subject changed to breaking horses and Solomon relaxed. He noticed movement out of the corner of his eye. Aaron was making his way around the outside of the circle, then stopped when he got to a tree in Solomon's line of sight. He hadn't met this man before he came to Weaver's Creek, as far as he knew. Solomon stared back, trying to fit the man's face into his memory, but he would never have forgotten that dark red hair and piercing blue eyes. Eyes that watched every move he made.

Solomon shifted in his seat so he wasn't looking directly at him, but Aaron shifted again so that he could see him out of the corner of his eye. This was irritating. If the man knew him, that could be the end of his plans. But he had never been to Ohio and had never been in an Amish community except the one in Pennsylvania.

Could it be that this man had seen him in Virginia? Solomon pushed the thought out of his mind. Impossible. Even if he had, nothing could be proven. It would be one man's word against another's.

But the one-legged man still stared at him as if he could see right through him. Solomon shifted again. He would have to confront the fellow, find out what he knew, and then take care of it.

7

As the afternoon drew to a close, Aaron was relieved to see that Solomon left with the rest of the families. A few of the young people stayed behind to prepare for something Jonas called a Singing.

"It's for the singles to get to know each other and have fun together," Jonas said. "Sometimes young folks come to our Singing from other districts or we go to theirs. We look forward to it."

"Will you be going?" Aaron noticed that the young men staying behind were quite a bit younger than either he or Jonas.

"Ne, not me. I'm too old. And besides, I've already found my Katie."

Jonas looked across the farmyard to the house where Katie was saying goodbye to her friends. Elizabeth was with her, empty dishes in her hands. Abraham and Lydia had already left, walking down the lane toward the main road.

"I suppose we should be going," Aaron said. "I can walk all the way, but I'm slow. You can go on ahead of me."

"I won't leave you behind, but I'm going to walk Katie and Elizabeth home first. Come with us, and then we'll walk back together from there."

During the short walk along the path to the cabin in the woods, Katie and Jonas fell behind, leaving Aaron and Elizabeth to lead the way. Giggles drifted in the late afternoon air from the couple behind them, and Elizabeth grinned.

"I hope those two are able to get married soon," she said. "Katie is miserable on the days when she can't see Jonas. Is he the same?"

"Not that I've noticed." Aaron was using only one crutch and had to concentrate on each step. "Although he does look in the direction of that house he's building more than he needs to."

"Katie tells me she acts that way because she's in love."

Aaron had no response. Being in love was far outside of his experience. The women he had known never lingered in his mind.

Elizabeth stopped in the path, looking into the branches where a cardinal was calling, establishing his territory to all who could hear.

"Isn't that lovely?" she asked.

"One of the prettiest calls in nature," Aaron said.

They both listened for another minute, then Elizabeth walked on, humming to herself.

"Have you ever been in love?"

Aaron glanced at her. "What?"

"I was just wondering. When a man falls in love, is it the same for him as when a woman falls in love?"

"I wouldn't know."

"Well, a woman in love spends all her time thinking about the one she loves. She imagines talking to him and what she will say, and she tries to understand everything he's doing and saying." Elizabeth plucked a dandelion that was growing along the path. "Take Katie. She does nothing but talk about Jonas. Their house, their plans, if he needs his hair trimmed, what he ate for dinner, what their wedding will be like. You would think she has no other interests in the world."

Aaron longed for the companionable silence he usually enjoyed when he was with Elizabeth.

She continued. "And a woman will also speculate about new men that she meets, wondering if he might be the right man for her."

"Do you mean that Katie is thinking about someone else?"

Elizabeth laughed. He couldn't remember hearing her laugh before. "Katie would never do that."

They had reached the house, and Elizabeth led the way around it to the front porch. She skipped up the two steps, then sank into the chair nearest the door with a sigh. Aaron watched her. She couldn't be talking about herself. The sick feeling in his stomach was beginning to act like an old friend. Elizabeth was smiling, looking at . . . He turned his head to follow the direction of her gaze. Nothing. She was smiling at nothing.

Women.

"I'm going to start for home. When Jonas gets here, tell him I'll see him there."

Elizabeth nodded absently.

Aaron picked his way down the lane toward the road. It was a gentle slope, but he hadn't mastered going downhill yet. Even with the crutch helping him, he was unsteady. He was nearly to the main road when he caught a whiff of tobacco smoke. He stopped as Solomon Mast stepped out from behind a tree.

"I thought you'd come this way," he said, his voice friendly. He extended his right hand. "I'm not sure I caught your full name."

Aaron took his hand. Where Aaron's hand was hard and sinewy from working in the harness shop the past few weeks, Solomon's was as soft as a clerk's.

"Aaron Zook."

"I'm sure you know I just moved to the area from Lancaster County." He stepped closer to Aaron. "I've noticed you watching me. Are you trying to warn me away from Elizabeth?"

His eyes narrowed as he spoke, and he watched Aaron's face. Aaron kept his expression neutral but watched Solomon's eyes in return.

"I thought we might have met a few years ago, in the Shenandoah Valley."

The other man's pupils widened, although nothing else in his expression changed. "I've never been to the Shenandoah. Isn't that in Virginia?"

"Yes." Aaron switched to Englisch. "I was there with Heath's division during the war."

"You're not Amish, then? I didn't think so." Solomon's Englisch words echoed with the soft, rolling accent of the Blue Ridge.

Aaron adjusted his crutch. "Your voice betrays you. I know a Virginian when I hear him."

Solomon chuckled. "You have a good ear. My family was originally from Virginia, but when our Amish community dwindled, my parents moved to Pennsylvania. That was many years ago, when I was still a boy."

Could Aaron have been mistaken? The voice, the manner, even the tobacco scent all told him this was the spy from the Shenandoah Valley, but he had never seen that man's face.

Solomon's smile remained, but his expression grew hard. "So, what is a non-Amish Zook doing here in Ohio?"

"Jonas Weaver is a friend. I came this far with him."

"You have no interest in his sister, then?"

"What if I did?"

The smile widened and the voice lowered. "I'd tell you to move on. You have no place here. You're an outsider that will never be part of the community." He pulled a pair of fine leather gloves from a pocket inside his coat. "On the other hand, I am the perfect husband for Elizabeth. I will be able to support her well, and she will have a good standing in the church with me as her husband. None of the folks here can claim the kind of heritage I can. Especially you."

Aaron's fists clenched.

"And if you try to tell anyone I said any of this, I will deny it. Think, Aaron Zook." He reached over and tapped Aaron's forehead. "Who will they believe? A war veteran who is only half a man, or me, a successful farmer and member of the community?"

Solomon tipped his hat to Aaron, then walked away to the horse and buggy he had left waiting on the main road.

Solomon's words echoed in Aaron's mind with the beat of the horse's trotting hoofs. *Half a man. Half a man.* That's exactly what he was. Half a man who would never be able to support himself or . . . He threw the crutch on the ground.

Or find a woman who would ever look at him with anything but pity.

⁓

Before Ruby left for home on Sunday afternoon, Elizabeth had made her promise to spend Monday morning with her. Mamm had agreed to care for the little ones, and Elizabeth set out with the pony cart on Monday morning to pick up Ruby and take her along to Solomon's house.

She hadn't slept at all the night before. The memory of Solomon's deep brown eyes twinkling at her warred with her better sense. One minute her imagination would have him embracing her with the gentle, protective comfort of her feather bed, and the next she would be fighting off his attentions in the nightmare that often visited her dreams. Then she would sit up in bed, sweaty and nauseous, unable to go back to sleep until she had woken up fully, paced around her small bedroom, then crawled back into bed for another fitful hour or two.

"It's just silliness," she said to herself as she turned Pie onto the stone bridge. "I'm letting my imagination take me places that I don't belong."

The pony shook his head and trotted faster when he saw the open barn door.

"Not today, Pie." Elizabeth turned him toward the hitching rail in front of the house. "No lounging in Datt's barn for you."

Ruby slipped out of the kitchen door before Elizabeth

could tie the pony to the rail, waving Elizabeth back into the cart.

"Mamm has little Lovinia occupied for the moment," she said as she took her seat. "If the baby sees me leave, she will cry until we are out of sight. This way, all she knows is that she's with her *grossmutti*."

"And she has the other children to keep her company, too." Elizabeth backed Pie away from the house, then turned him toward the road again.

"You never told me where we are going today. If we're going into town, I'll need to stop by the house and get my shopping list."

Elizabeth shook her head. "Not that far. It would be too much for Pie." She paused. Now, in the light of day, it seemed silly to have asked Ruby to come with her. "Solomon asked me to come to his house this morning and have lunch with him."

"Are you certain I'm not going to be in the way?"

"Not at all. I know better than to be alone with a man." Elizabeth forced a smile. "What would Salome say?"

That brought a laugh from Ruby. She knew how Salome's rumors spread, better than most others. Elizabeth's hands grew sweaty on the reins. Ruby would also understand that Salome's rumors weren't the only thing she was cautious about. She had learned her lesson about putting herself in a compromising position with a man.

"I'm glad we have these few minutes alone," Ruby said as Pie walked up the slope past Reuben's old cabin. "I want you to be the first to know, after Gideon, of course."

Elizabeth shook herself out of her morose thoughts. "What is it?"

"I'm expecting another little one, sometime before Christmas."

Ruby had blushed a bright red and her face shone. Elizabeth was happy for her. Really. She gave her sister a hug, letting go of the reins. Pie's walk slowed as he reached the turnoff at the top of the hill.

"That is wonderful news, Ruby."

Tears blurred her vision. She fumbled for the reins she had dropped and started Pie off again, down the road toward Millersburg and Abel Patterson's place, Solomon Mast's new farm. But Ruby knew her too well.

"I know—" Ruby broke off and put an arm around Elizabeth's shoulders. "I know you wanted your own children with Reuben. I'm sorry that he died before—"

"Don't." Elizabeth interrupted her sister. "Don't even think about it. That is all in the past." She took a shuddering breath, then tried to smile. "It's all right. Maybe someday I'll meet someone, or maybe not."

Maybe Solomon . . .

Ruby spoke Elizabeth's thoughts out loud. "Maybe Solomon Mast is the one for you. He couldn't stop watching you yesterday afternoon."

"That's why I wanted you to come with me today. Sometimes I think he might be a good husband, but I don't trust my own judgment. And I don't trust myself alone with any man. I don't want to end up with another Reuben."

"Solomon isn't anything like Reuben." Ruby squeezed her shoulders again. "And I'll keep you from being charmed into doing something you don't want to do." She grinned. "Solomon is very good looking, isn't he?"

"Too handsome for me. Why would he even look at me twice?"

"Because you are a very beautiful woman. Both outside and on the inside, where it counts."

Elizabeth drew a shuddering breath again as Abel's big brick house came into view. Ruby knew her as well as anyone could, but she didn't know about the black pit of sin and despair that hid itself from her family and friends. If anyone knew, they would hate her. Cast her out from the church and their lives. But if she was lucky, no one would ever know. Especially Solomon Mast.

"Look," Ruby said, shading her eyes with one hand. "Solomon is on the porch waiting for us."

Elizabeth shook her head. "Waiting for me. He doesn't know you're coming."

"Well then, I will be a nice surprise for him." Ruby didn't look the least bit worried.

When Elizabeth drove up to the hitching rail on the gravel drive, Solomon met them at the bottom of the porch steps. It could have been only in her imagination, but she thought she saw a frown cross his face. But when he caught Pie's bridle and looped the reins over the rail, he was smiling at both of them.

"Welcome to Fairacres," he said, extending a hand to help Ruby out of the cart, and then Elizabeth. "I didn't expect to see you, Ruby. I thought you would be busy today tending to your little ones."

"Mamm is happy to take care of them this morning so I could accompany Elizabeth."

"You didn't need to go to the trouble." Solomon smiled

at Elizabeth, his eyes twinkling, just like in her dream. "We would have gotten along just fine on our own."

As Solomon led the way up the steps, Ruby said, "I didn't know Abel Patterson had named his farm."

"I had that privilege." Solomon stopped on the top step and let his gaze sweep around the farm, finally resting on Elizabeth. "The countryside around here is very fair, and I thought my farm should reflect that."

Ruby, standing behind Solomon, caught Elizabeth's eye and raised her eyebrows. Elizabeth knew what she was thinking, that naming a farm was a fancy thing to do. But she supposed Solomon knew best.

"After all," Solomon said as he led the way to some willow chairs on the wide porch, "once Elizabeth and I marry, we will join our farms together. My eighty acres added to her one hundred sixty will create a grand farm, and one worthy of the name Fairacres."

"I haven't yet said that I will marry you," Elizabeth said. She sat next to Ruby in a willow seat large enough for two.

Solomon's smile didn't change. "That will come in due time. You will soon see that my ideas are good for both of us."

A young woman in a simple dress with a handkerchief tied around her head came out of the house carrying a tray. Her skin was darker than any person Elizabeth had ever seen, even among the few freed slaves that lived in Millersburg.

"Thank you, Dulcey," Solomon said in Englisch. "You can set the tray here on the table. And as you can see, I have an extra guest for luncheon. Bring another plate and silverware."

The woman didn't look up but put the tray down and fled back into the house.

Elizabeth exchanged glances with Ruby again.

"Who is Dulcey?" she asked.

"She is my housekeeper and cook. I found her in Millersburg, and since she was looking for a job, I brought her here."

"She doesn't look very happy," Ruby said.

"She has had a hard life." Solomon's face grew sad. "She was born in the Deep South. Mississippi, I think. How she ended up here I don't know. But until the end of the war, she was a slave."

The woman came out to the porch again with the plate and silverware, then started laying out the items for a picnic, setting three places and bowls of cooked minced chicken with slices of bread, cold potatoes, and strawberries. A covered basket came last, with the mouthwatering scent of fresh biscuits rising from it. She turned to go back into the house, but Ruby stopped her.

"Aren't you going to have lunch with us, Dulcey?"

Dulcey glanced in Solomon's direction, her gaze still lowered.

Solomon chuckled. "Dulcey will be happier in the kitchen, won't you?"

Dulcey nodded and disappeared. Once she was gone, Solomon bowed his head for the silent prayer. After a very short time, before Elizabeth had finished her own prayer, she heard the clank of a spoon in a serving dish. Solomon was helping himself to the food.

"Once we're married," he said, "Elizabeth won't have to tie herself down with dull chores. Dulcey will take care of everything."

Elizabeth had been reaching for the glass of water in front of her, but at Solomon's words, she stopped.

"We Amish don't employ servants, Solomon. Surely you know that. Dulcey would be a great help with the house-work, but I wouldn't think of letting her do it all. I would work together with her. We could become great friends, I think."

Solomon's smile only grew wider. "What a kind thought. With everything you say, I am more convinced that we are meant to be together." He beamed at Ruby. "I know I have much to learn about living in your more conservative district, but I intend to make my home here, with a lovely wife by my side."

He turned his gaze to Elizabeth when he said the last phrase, and her heart melted. This man was nothing like Reuben and seemed to have her best interests in mind. Could she get used to living in such a big house, with a hired woman to help her? Her mind flitted ahead to children filling the house, days spent working by Dulcey's side, and Solomon coming home in the evening, caressing each of the little ones on the head and leading them all in family worship after their supper. Perhaps Dulcey would also find a husband who could work on the farm. Their children would fill the house to bursting. How blessed could she be?

"What are you smiling about, my dear?"

Elizabeth focused on him, her imaginary life still very fresh in her mind. "I was just thinking about how beautiful the weather is today."

Solomon reached over and took her hand in his. "It is a perfect day, isn't it?"

Clouds moved in on Monday afternoon, providing a respite from the bright late-May sunshine, but not the heat. Aaron wiped his arm across his sweaty brow before he grasped the end of the beam he and Jonas were lifting into place. This one was the center beam and the support for the attic loft Jonas was putting in his house. He and Jonas held it in place as Abraham slid the support post under the center. When they were finished, Aaron sat on an upended log in the middle of Jonas's future kitchen to catch his breath.

"It's beginning to look like a house," Jonas said, stepping back and looking up toward where the rafters would be placed next. "There were times when I never thought I would finish this house."

"I always knew you would finish it." Abraham took a drink of water from an earthenware jug and passed it to Aaron. "Even when the first house blew down in the storm, I didn't give up hope. You're a man who finishes what he sets out to do."

Aaron passed the jug to Jonas and looked around the spacious ground floor of the house. Jonas had often told him that thoughts of Katie and their unfinished house were what kept him going through the long nights in the army hospital. He had to agree with Abraham. Nothing would stop Jonas once he set his mind to something.

"What about you, Aaron?" Jonas sat on a pile of sawn lumber and took a drink of the cool water. "You aren't still thinking of going west, are you?"

Aaron shifted on his seat, easing the pain in his leg. Jonas was known for following through on his plans. Could he do any less? "It's what I've been planning, ever since my home was destroyed. With nothing to go back to, I figured I'd head out that way once the fighting was over." He rubbed his leg. "I never figured on this, though."

"I wish you would decide to settle here," Abraham said as he sat next to Jonas. "You fit in well, and there's always work for a skilled harness maker."

"I'm not sure I'm what you'd call skilled."

"Dan says you have a natural talent. It's a good, steady job for a man looking to make a home somewhere."

He could always settle in some little town out where no one had ever heard the name Zook. Out where it didn't matter if you were from Tennessee or Pennsylvania. Out where a man's worth was based on what he could do, not who his kin were.

Aaron rubbed his leg again. The muscles cramped every once in a while, and he didn't think anything of it, except that out west his leg would be the first thing folks saw. Everywhere he went, he would have to prove himself. Something a whole man wouldn't need to do.

"Why is Mamm taking care of Ruby's children today?" Jonas asked, taking the conversation past where Aaron had dropped out of it.

"Ruby is spending the day with Elizabeth. Lydia said Elizabeth told her Solomon Mast had invited her to see his house and farm."

"Is he thinking about courting her?" Jonas asked.

Aaron looked from Jonas to Abraham. "He can't," he said. "He isn't—" Aaron stopped himself. Solomon just might be Amish. Just might be who he said he was. "He isn't the right man for her."

Abraham leaned his elbows on his knees. "He appears to be a good Amish man, in spite of a few unusual ways. But he's trying to fit into the community. I heard that he asked to be considered for membership in the church."

Aaron's insides coiled, but he had no evidence for his suspicions. It was his word against Solomon's, and he might be wrong. But if he was right, Elizabeth had no business being near him.

"I just have a bad feeling about him, that's all." Aaron took another drink of water. If Solomon was the man Aaron suspected him to be, Elizabeth needed to be warned, and he was the only one who could do it.

After supper, Aaron walked up to Elizabeth's house. All afternoon he had waged a war with himself, what he should say to her and how. He had no claim on her. Nothing gave him the authority to put his stick in her fire. If she wanted Solomon to court her, he couldn't say anything about it. But he'd give warning to anyone about to step into a rattler's nest, whether he knew them or not.

He was being a friend. That was all.

Elizabeth was sitting on the front porch working on something with her knitting needles, rocking and humming to herself. The same song Ma had always sung about the Rock of Ages. She hadn't seen him yet as he stood in the evening shadows under the pines. A soft wind blew through them, sounding like the sea on the Virginia coast, catching Elizabeth's kapp strings. As he watched, one blew over her shoulder, but she didn't notice. She kept rocking and knitting, the evening sun landing on her face every time the chair went forward. He didn't blame Solomon Mast for wanting her.

He continued toward the porch steps until she finally saw him approaching.

"Is that you, Aaron? I didn't see you coming."

"You were busy wool-gathering."

"I was thinking about my day. I saw that a lot of work got done on Katie's house. Did you help Jonas today?"

"Ja, I did." Aaron tried to think how he would say what he needed to say in Pennsylvania Dutch but gave up. He switched to Englisch. "I heard you and Ruby went to Solomon's this morning."

Elizabeth gathered up her knitting and put the needles and yarn in a basket at her feet. "Solomon invited me to see his house and farm. It's a lovely, large house."

Aaron tapped his crutch on the hard-packed earth studded with gravel. "So, you liked his place?"

"It's still very Englisch. Abel Patterson left all of his furnishings, and they're quite fancy. Too much for my taste, but Solomon likes it. He says all the houses back East are filled with upholstered furniture and pictures on the walls."

Aaron snorted. "Not all of them."

"Solomon also said that I could choose which things to keep and which to sell after we're married."

The percussion of mortar fire wouldn't have left him more numb than her statement did. "Is he . . . is he courting you?"

"He wants to." Elizabeth looked beyond him to the dark blue sky between the pine branches. "I haven't told him he could yet."

"Don't let him. He isn't the man for you."

Her gaze skewered him in his place. "What does it matter to you?"

"It doesn't." Aaron pulled on his beard. Why did it matter? "Except you're the sister of my friend, and I want to look out for your welfare."

"And you think I'm in some kind of danger?"

The image of Solomon's smiling face yesterday afternoon flashed through his mind. The face might have been pleasant, but the man's voice held a threatening edge. He knew what kind of man Solomon was, but he had no evidence, and without proof, Elizabeth would never listen to him.

"You might be. Solomon might not be the man he appears to be. There's something about him."

Elizabeth laughed. "Are you sure you're not just jealous?"

"Why would I be jealous? That would mean that I think of you as more than my friend's sister." He couldn't meet her eyes.

"I meant that you're jealous of Solomon. He is everything you're not. He's an upstanding member of the community, a successful farmer. He has property and a house—"

"And I have nothing."

Elizabeth stood, picking up her basket of knitting. "You have what you have. But Solomon belongs here."

She went into the house, leaving him standing there, the words she didn't say hanging between them.

"And Solomon is a whole man." He said the words softly, but he couldn't keep the bitterness out of his voice. "A whole man with a home to offer any woman that appeals to him."

He turned and started the slow, halting walk back to the Weavers' farm, making his way down the lane and onto the main road. Elizabeth was right. He didn't belong here. Nothing was more obvious. He should pack up tomorrow and head west. Head toward whatever was waiting for him out there. Except . . .

Elizabeth had lit a lamp inside the house and a light gleamed through the pine branches. He couldn't leave. Not as long as Elizabeth was in danger. He might not be the man for her, but he'd die before he saw her wed to Solomon.

8

On Wednesday, the last day of May, thirty-four men from
Amish communities as far away as Indiana in the west; On-
tario, Canada, in the north; and Somerset County, Pennsylvania, in the east began arriving in Holmes County. Levi met
the train in Millersburg and drove the men to the farm where
the meetings would be held. The mood of his passengers was
solemn but determined.

"They can't ignore us this year," one man said, a minister
from Elkhart County in Indiana.

"If they don't listen to our needs, I see a split in the church
coming." The second man was close to Father's age, with
curly black and gray hair framing his round face.

A tall man Levi recognized from the first meeting that
had been held in Wayne County three years earlier shook
his head. "I don't know why those who want these changes
don't join the Mennonites or form their own church. Why
do they have to make all of us accept their modern ideas?"

Then the man sitting next to Levi on the wagon seat, a

man older than anyone Levi had ever seen, gripped the top of his cane. He turned as far around as he could to address the ministers in the back of the wagon.

"We must remain true to the old ways. If we stray, we stray from God himself." He faced front again and tapped Levi's foot with his cane. "You listen to what I say, young man. We can't leave God behind in the quest for progress."

"I agree," Levi said. "The church must hold on to Scripture, above all."

The old man nodded with satisfaction and rode the rest of the way in silence.

On Thursday morning, the first day of discussions began. Levi stood outside the crowded house with Jonas and Aaron, trying to hear the proceedings. But even though he listened as closely as he could, he only heard every third or fourth word that was spoken in the meeting. Finally, he gave up and sat on the porch step next to Jonas.

"What do you think they'll decide?" Jonas asked.

"They've already decided it. They want to write down their position in an official paper to present at the ministers' meeting next week. Right now, they're discussing who should be the one to do the writing."

Aaron chuckled. "The more men there are to discuss something, the longer it takes."

"There's someone else coming," Jonas said, looking down the road. "An emigrant wagon."

The three of them walked to the road to greet the newcomers.

"We're looking for Weaver's Creek," the driver said.

"You're nearly there," Levi said. "Keep going down this

road about three miles. Is there someone in particular you're looking for?"

"Dan and Ephraim Zook."

"You must be their father. They've been expecting you." Levi reached up and shook the man's hand.

"I'm Casper Zook. This is my wife, Rosina." He lifted the cover of the wagon. "Come on out. There are young folks out here you'll want to meet."

A young man about Levi's age pulled back the wagon cover and jumped out. "Name's Tobias," he said, then he reached up to help a girl out of the wagon. "And this is my sister, Elise."

She was beautiful. A shy smile, blue eyes, and a dark red dress that was neat and clean in spite of riding in an emigrant wagon. Levi swallowed. Then she glanced at him and her cheeks grew pink. She looked away again and that lovely face was hidden in the depths of her bonnet.

Jonas stepped forward. "I'm Jonas Weaver, and my friends are Levi Beiler and Aaron Zook."

"Zook?" Casper looked closely at Aaron. "You don't look much like any of the rest of us Zooks."

Aaron's face was as red as his beard. "I was told that I take after my mother's side of the family. They were Scotch-Irish."

Casper's eyebrows rose. "Scots-Irish? Not Amish? I'd like to hear your story when we have more time, but right now I'd like to see my sons. Can you direct us to their farms?"

Levi glanced back at the house. He hated to leave, but nothing much would happen today, and he couldn't let this opportunity to get to know Elise better slip out of his hands.

"I can show you. I need to get home, and the Zook farms are on the way."

Jonas nudged his arm with an elbow. "Why don't you ride with the Zooks? Aaron and I can follow with your spring wagon." He grinned and shifted his eyes toward Elise and back at Levi.

"We'd be pleased to accept your help," Casper said. "Come on up here and take the reins."

Levi climbed up to the tall seat of the wagon and lifted the reins. The tired horses shook their heads as if to say they thought they had gone far enough.

"It's only a mile or so to Ephraim's farm." Levi started the horses, conscious of Elise standing in the wagon bed, looking out between him and her datt . . . close enough to touch. He swallowed.

"The boys have written about their life here. They praised the fertile soil, the rolling hills, and the strong community." Casper watched the scenery as they traveled along the road toward the Zooks' farms on the northern edge of the Weaver's Creek district. "That's one reason we decided to come out here to join them."

"I'm glad you came." Levi swallowed again. "I mean, we're glad you're here. Dan and Ephraim are welcome members of our community. They're becoming well known around the county for their harness making."

"So, tell me about this Aaron Zook. Where is he from?"

How could he explain the situation?

"Jonas worked in a hospital during the war. Aaron was one of the patients there and came home with him after the war was over."

Casper fingered his beard. "So, Aaron was a soldier?"

Levi nodded. "He wasn't raised Amish and joined the army when the war started. He said he did it after his father and grandfather were both killed in the fighting."

"Zooks fighting in that terrible war." Casper shook his head. "I wouldn't have believed it, but many strange things have happened during the last years."

Tobias, standing in the wagon bed next to his sister, said, "Look! That has to be Ephraim's barn. It's exactly as he described it in his letters."

"That's right," Levi said. "We're almost there. Dan's is just beyond it, down the road."

Casper leaned forward and Levi jiggled the horses' reins to get more speed out of them. They picked up their pace, and as soon as they turned into Ephraim's lane, Tobias jumped out of the back of the wagon and ran toward the house. Levi pulled the wagon to a stop in the farmyard, and Casper climbed down, then helped Rosina. Levi jumped down from the seat and went around to the back of the wagon, hoping he wasn't too late.

Elise stood in the back of the wagon with an expectant look on her face. When Levi came close, he held out his arms, and she grasped his hands as she dropped to the ground. He held her hands in his for the briefest of moments, and she looked up at him, her blue eyes mirroring his own. The same shade of blue. She smiled, then went to join her mother. Levi's hands tingled as the spring wagon drove up.

"Levi." Jonas tapped his shoulder with the buggy whip. "Are you all right? Or have you been bitten by a bug?"

Aaron grinned, sitting next to Jonas.

"It's nothing." Levi started to climb up into the seat of his spring wagon. "We'll let the Zooks get on with their reunion."

"Wait a minute." Jonas stopped him. "She's looking at you."

Levi frowned. "It isn't fair to tease me."

"I'm not teasing. Look behind you."

He turned, expecting to see the Zook family ignoring everyone but themselves, but Jonas was right. Elise was watching him until she saw him look. Then she ducked her head, her face hidden again by her bonnet. A roaring started in his ears. He had heard of someone falling in love at the first glance at a pretty face, but he had always thought that was just silly girls' chatter.

He had been wrong.

~~~~~~

The Sunday after the Zook family arrived was a non-church day. Aaron enjoyed the relaxed off Sundays, but Ma had taken him to church every week, down in the hollow where the preacher lived next to the sawmill. Even though Jonas had tried to explain the value of the fellowship time and rest the community enjoyed on these quiet days, Aaron still had the feeling they should be in church. Maybe it was the memory of that fiery preacher's voice, echoing in the little frame building. Whatever the Amish believed, Aaron knew that Tennessee preacher would find fault with neglecting the meeting two Sundays a month.

On the other hand, he enjoyed the relaxed atmosphere of the farm after the morning chores were done. The family lingered over breakfast, and then Abraham read from his big Bible. The language was high German rather than Pennsylvania Dutch, but Aaron could now understand most of what was read after weeks of being immersed in the language. On this Sunday, Abraham read the Twenty-Third Psalm. Aaron was surprised that he remembered the words in Englisch and could recognize them in German. He must have been no more than five years old when Ma helped him memorize those words, but he hadn't thought of them much since she passed away.

Afterward, he joined Jonas and Abraham on the front porch. The side porch was where Aaron sat most often, right off the kitchen and mud room. The front porch seemed to be saved for summer Sundays. Facing north, it was shaded all day long, with the westerly breezes ruffling the leaves of the morning glory vines Lydia had planted to break up the afternoon sun's rays.

Abraham dozed in his chair woven from willow twigs while Jonas fidgeted in the seat next to him.

"I'm going to see what Katie is up to today," he said as he finally rose.

"I wondered what was taking you so long."

Aaron grinned as Jonas gave him a playful slap on the shoulder on his way to the porch steps. As he headed toward the lane that would lead him across the stone bridge toward Katie's house, Aaron relaxed in his chair.

Stretching his leg out in front, Aaron's eyes closed as he listened to the bees buzzing in the flowers. He couldn't remember such peace. Not since the war started. Rest. No worries. Nothing to tug him away, nothing to hold him back.

His thoughts drifted to Elizabeth. Should he worry about her? She seemed so vulnerable when it came to Solomon. She was like a dove, unaware and unafraid, being stalked by a fox.

That thought pulled his mind out of the drowsy place it had gone, then the buzzing bees and gentle breeze lulled him back until Lydia opened the front door.

"Abraham." Her voice was soft, reluctant to wake him up.

Aaron sat up just as Abraham lifted his hat off his face. "Ja, what is it?"

"We have visitors. The Zooks are coming."

Abraham stretched as he rose from his seat, then went to greet the Zook family. Aaron followed, curious about these relatives who weren't really related. Sharing the same last name with Dan and Ephraim had come to feel ordinary while he had been working with Dan in the harness shop, but the thought they might be family was just wishful thinking.

He stood back as Abraham greeted Dan and Ephraim and their families and was introduced to Casper and Rosina, and Rosina's children, Elise and Tobias. Lydia stepped forward then, inviting the women to join her in the kitchen. Dan's and Ephraim's children ran off to play in the little house near the barn that Abraham had built for his grandchildren. The men followed Abraham back onto the porch, and Aaron leaned against the porch rail as the men sat in chairs.

Half listening to the conversation, Aaron watched the Zook men. They looked like any other Amish fellows, and certainly nothing like him. But they also looked a lot like Grandpop with their round faces and wide-set eyes. The mannerisms were similar, too, giving Aaron the feeling that they could have been sitting on the front porch of Grand-pop's cabin in the Tennessee hills.

Then Dan turned to him. "How is your new leg doing? Does the harness work the way you wanted it to?"

"Ja, for sure it does." Aaron showed where the harness was strapped onto his leg outside his trousers. "The details you suggested, like using soft leather for the side next to my leg, work fine. It doesn't slip at all."

Casper was closest to Aaron and leaned closer. "That's fine stitching. Dan, is that your work or Ephraim's?"

"It's Aaron's. He knows quite a bit about harness mak-ing."

The older man looked up at Aaron. He was about the same age as Pa had been when he died.

"Who taught you, son?"

"My grandpop. He did harness making off and on, when-ever someone would pay."

"And you're from Tennessee, you said."

Aaron nodded, wondering what the man was thinking.

Casper looked at his sons, then back at Aaron. "There's a story in our family, about my datt's brother. Years ago, back before the second war with England, Datt's brother had a row with his father and ran away. He was never heard from again."

Abraham leaned forward. "That's a tragedy. What do you think happened to him?"

"We never knew. My father, Heinrich was his name, had been very close to his brother as they grew up. He told me that there was something about him that was worrisome. He was a rebellious child, and it only grew worse as he got older. He got so he was against everything the family stood for—their faith, the work they did, even eating together as a family. He was only sixteen years old when he left home."

"I've never heard this story, Datt," Ephraim said.

"By the time I married, and you boys came along, we had stopped talking about him. I think the memories just hurt my father too much. I know he never forgot his brother, though. I was named after him."

Aaron's mouth went dry. The reason for Casper's story began to become clear.

"Did anyone ever try to find him?" Abraham asked.

"My grandfather never stopped looking for him. At first, they thought he had gotten lost in the forest. There were some that said the Indians had taken him captive." Casper ran his hand over his face. "There was even a report from a trader that he saw a young man living with an Indian tribe in western Pennsylvania, and the description matched Datt's brother. To my grandfather's death, he hoped that his son would return."

"You think," Aaron started, but he couldn't think of the Pennsylvania Dutch words. He started over in Englisch. "You think your father's brother might have ended up in Tennessee."

"Now that I've met you, I think so. He knew harness making, and he could have a grandson about your age."

He swallowed. "Grandpop's name was Cap, not Casper."

Casper smiled. "That's a short name for Casper. My grandson is called Cap." He stood. "And your father's name?"

"His name was Henry. Grandpop said he named him after his brother."

"Henry is the Englisch way to say Heinrich. He named his son after my father." Casper's eyes filled with tears in spite of his widening smile. "It couldn't be, could it? That we would find the answer to the mystery here in Ohio?"

Dan grinned. "The evidence seems to point that way. What do you think, Aaron?"

Aaron ran his hand over his face, suddenly aware that it was the same gesture Casper had made a few minutes ago. Talking with him . . . it was as if Grandpop had come back to life as a younger man. "It sounds like it could be possible. I never thought Grandpop's family in Pennsylvania would still remember him."

"Remember him?" Casper shook his head. "You never forget family. No matter how long it's been since you've seen them. Uncle Casper's place in the family has been empty for years, but now we have an answer."

"The Lord works in mysterious ways," Abraham said, his smile as wide as Casper's. He called into the house for the women to join them.

Once Rosina heard the story, she walked over to Aaron and pulled on his shoulder until she could reach his cheek. She kissed it softly. "Welcome to the family, Aaron."

"Almost like the Prodigal Son," Dan said, shaking Aaron's hand.

It was too much. Aaron reached up to wipe away the tingle that Rosina's kiss had left, but she stopped him.

"That's a mother's kiss, young man. And a mother's kiss lasts forever."

He heard an echo in his memory. Ma, happy to see him and pleased with the results of his first hunting trip with Pa.

She had taken his face between her palms and kissed him on the cheek. He felt too grown up for that and wiped it away with his hand.

But Ma had laughed. "A mama's kiss lasts forever. No wiping or washing will ever make it disappear."

She had been right. He could still feel that kiss. He grinned at Rosina, and then at Dan. He didn't know what to say. But he knew—knew in his heart—that Casper must be right. All the pieces fit. This was the family Grandpop had left behind so long ago.

Then Ephraim hugged him, laughing. "Look at you! You'd think you never had a family before."

Aaron returned Ephraim's hug, then hugged Tobias before Casper wrapped his arms around him in a tight, strong grip and held him, as if to make up for all the lost years.

Ephraim was right. He had never had a family like this before.

9

"Did you hear the news?" Katie asked.

It was Tuesday morning and Elizabeth was ironing the dresses they had washed and dried the day before while Katie folded the rest of the laundry.

"Only that the ministers' meeting has started. Several of the men from our district have gone up to Wayne County this week."

"Not that. The news about Aaron and the Zooks."

Elizabeth shook her head in reply, concentrating on ironing out a stubborn wrinkle.

"It turns out that Aaron is a long-lost cousin of theirs."

Giving up on the wrinkle, Elizabeth placed the iron back on the stove to heat again. Katie was quick to share every rumor she heard, especially if it sounded like good news.

She smiled at Katie's earnest face. "How can they know if they are related or not? Are you certain this isn't just more gossip?"

"I heard it straight from Jonas, and he heard the story

from his father. You know Abraham wouldn't spread any news unless he is sure it's true." Katie pulled the basket of dish towels closer. "Jonas said Aaron's grandfather was the brother of Dan and Ephraim's grandfather. Aaron's grandfather left home when he was still a boy, and the family never heard from him again."

Elizabeth picked up the second iron and tested it. Just right. She tackled the wrinkle again. "And they think Aaron's grandfather is that boy? How do they know the two were brothers?"

"That's what is so wonderful about this whole story. Dan and Ephraim's grandfather named his son after his brother who had run away, and Aaron's grandfather named his son after his brother too. The family names are what told them that Aaron belonged to them."

Elizabeth put the iron back on the stove and adjusted the skirt so the next wrinkled section was ready to work on. Aaron was a difficult person to learn to know, but she had seen the wistful expression in his eyes when he spoke of his mother, as if he missed having a family in spite of acting like he didn't need anyone. What did he think about the idea of belonging to the Weaver's Creek Zooks?

A knock on the front door interrupted her thoughts. Katie went to answer it, and Elizabeth heard her talking to someone. She moved the coffeepot to the front of the stove to prepare for their visitor, but Katie came back into the kitchen alone, carrying an envelope.

"It was Mr. Stevenson, from the sawmill. He had been to Farmerstown and he said Mrs. Lawrence asked him to deliver this letter for you. It had been waiting at the post office for a few weeks, waiting for someone from Weaver's Creek to fetch the mail. He said it looked important."

Elizabeth took the envelope and sat in a chair at the table. It was larger than any envelope she had ever seen and had official-looking printing on it.

"Hoben, Williamson, and Turner. Attorneys at Law. Vicksburg, Mississippi," she read aloud, then looked at Katie. "What could it be? Why would a lawyer contact me?"

Katie sat across the table from her. "You won't know until you open it." Her eyes glowed with excitement. "Maybe it has something to do with Reuben. Wasn't he in Vicksburg when he passed away?"

Elizabeth turned the envelope over and smoothed the sealed flap. Katie was right. It might have something to do with Reuben, or the new wife he had married during the war, or the son they had had together. Touching the letter brought life to her memories. Unwelcome life. What would opening it bring?

"Don't you want to know what it says?" Katie drummed her fingers on the table. "It might be good news."

"It could also be bad."

"You won't know until you open it."

Katie handed her a knife and Elizabeth slit the envelope. She took out the letter and unfolded it. The script was large and bold, and at the bottom was a notary's seal embellished with gold.

"It looks official." Elizabeth tried to make out the Englisch words, but the writing was too different from the German script she was familiar with.

"What does it say?"

"I'll have to find someone who can read it. Perhaps Datt can."

"Abraham went to the meeting with the rest of the men." The coffeepot started boiling and Katie rose to pour two cups. "Do you think Aaron could read it?"

"I'm not sure." Elizabeth recognized her own name but couldn't make out the rest of the writing. "Solomon could. He seems to have more experience with Englischers. He could read it and also tell me what it means."

Katie grinned. "Are you sure you aren't just making an excuse to see him again?"

Her face heating, Elizabeth folded the letter and put it back in the envelope. "Of course not. I just think he might be the best person to ask. I can't wait too long, either. That gold seal means that the letter is important."

The letter's weight pulled at Elizabeth's mind as she finished the ironing, fixed a small lunch for the two of them, and cleaned up the kitchen. What could it say? Letters like this one changed folks' lives.

Reuben had received one several years ago, soon after they were married, and had taken it to a lawyer in Millersburg. The lawyer said Reuben had inherited some money from his father in Philadelphia.

Elizabeth gave the kitchen shelf a final wipe with the dish towel before rinsing it in the last of the rinse water and hanging it up to dry.

That money had been enough to pay the mortgage and then some, Reuben had said. She never found out what happened to the rest of it, but that letter changed Reuben . . . for a time. He was kinder and easier to live with until the following winter when the money was all gone. Then he had blamed her for spending it, or hiding it, but Elizabeth suspected he had lost it at the gambling house he frequented.

She stopped, tapping pursed lips with her finger as she considered. Should she go to a lawyer in Millersburg first like Reuben had? If Datt was home, he would advise her. But all the men had gone to the ministers' meeting, except a few. Solomon was the only Amish man she could think of to ask.

Was it proper for her to call on Solomon alone? Katie had gone to Lena's after lunch to help the Stuckey women prepare for Margaret's upcoming wedding, and Mamm had gone to Wayne County with Datt. Ruby wouldn't be able to go with her in the afternoon during the children's nap time. She could go by herself. It wouldn't hurt anything. And she wouldn't be alone with Solomon, not with Dulcey there.

The sun wasn't far past its noon zenith when Elizabeth had hitched up and was on her way. The letter crinkled from its spot in her waistband, reminding her of the importance of this errand. All was quiet in the farmyards she passed, and she kept Pie at a trot until they started rising out of the valley. She slowed him to a walk until they crested the top of the hill.

She watched Solomon's house grow out of the surrounding fields as she approached. Pie shook his head and she loosened her tight grip on the reins. He had sensed her sudden misgivings.

"You can trust Solomon," she told herself. Pie's ears swiveled to listen to her voice. "He has always been kind to you. Besides, Dulcey is there. You won't be alone with him."

The red brick house seemed taller than before, leaning

toward her as if it were a cat welcoming a mouse to dinner. She shook her head, clearing her vision. It was just a house. There was nothing for her to fear.

She tied Pie to the hitching rail and walked up the wide porch steps. She lifted the iron knocker on the door and let it fall with a sharp tap. After a moment, Dulcey answered the door.

"Hello, Dulcey." Elizabeth smiled in a way that she hoped would let the young woman know she wanted to be friends. "Is Solomon at home? I need to speak to him about something."

Dulcey didn't meet her gaze but backed away to let Elizabeth into the hall.

"Masta Solomon, he's in the study. I'll fetch him straightaway."

Dulcey knocked softly on a door that led from the hall, then pushed the door aside and slipped into the room. Elizabeth looked around at the tall seat with hooks for hats and capes, the table with a vase of flowers on it, and the narrow carpet in the center of the floor. She wondered when Solomon would dispose of Abel Patterson's fancy furnishings to make the house more comfortable. She missed the simple lines of her parents' home.

Muffled voices came from the room Dulcey had called the study, then the doors slid open and Solomon walked through, a smile on his face.

"Welcome, Elizabeth. This is a surprise."

Elizabeth pulled the letter from the envelope and handed it to him. "I received this letter today but had trouble making out what it says. I hoped you could help me."

Solomon glanced at the letter, then at her. "Why don't we go into the front room to discuss this." He gestured for her to lead the way.

Elizabeth went into the dim sitting room. The shades were drawn against the bright afternoon light, and the room was crowded with furniture. She sat on a chair with a horsehair seat and waited for Solomon to read the letter all the way through.

His expression changed from interest to a frown, then he looked at her again.

"This letter says there is a woman in Mississippi who is claiming ownership of your land."

"You mean my husband's land."

"This letter says that Reuben Kaufman is the husband of Melanie Kaufman. This law firm is making inquiries on behalf of Mrs. Kaufman and her young son." He laid the letter on the table next to Elizabeth's chair and looked at her, his eyes narrowing. "I had understood that you are the widow of Reuben Kaufman, but this letter claims that you were his sister. What is the truth, Elizabeth?"

A familiar sense of helplessness washed over Elizabeth. It was as if Reuben were alive, accusing her of her sins from across time and space. She swallowed, then took a deep breath. *He is dead. He is dead. He can no longer harm me.*

Elizabeth stood, reaching out to him as if her touch could convince him of the truth. "My husband betrayed me by marrying this other woman while we were still married. But I am Reuben's widow. He must have never told this woman in Mississippi that he was married to me, and she assumed I was his sister."

Solomon turned his back on her and stared out the window that was obscured with lace curtains. His rigid back told her everything she needed to know. He didn't believe her.

⌒

Solomon straightened his shoulders, aware that the woman behind him was scrutinizing every movement. Had she lied to him? If she had, then the entire community had agreed with the story.

His mind tried to tie the evidence together with this new information, but it didn't make sense. According to the county land records, the land was owned by Reuben Kaufman's widow Elizabeth. Elizabeth was the daughter of Abraham Weaver. It was the first step in his quest to gain control of the valley.

But now there was another claimant.

Solomon clenched his fist. Another silly woman thinking she could claim his land. The answer was clear. He needed to confirm that Elizabeth's ownership of the land was secure and immovable.

"This other claimant." He turned back to the woman standing in the center of his sitting room. "Were you aware of her?"

Elizabeth nodded. "Someone came to the farm with the news of Reuben's death. He had assumed I was Reuben's sister since Reuben had married this other woman in Mississippi." Her face grew pink and she rubbed the end of her nose in a gesture that reminded him of a young child. "I didn't correct him. I was—" Her cheeks flamed red. "I was only relieved to hear that Reuben wouldn't be coming home."

Solomon read through the letter again. "It will be simple enough to clear this up. We will send a copy of your marriage certificate to this lawyer, and this woman's claim will be worthless."

"I don't have a marriage certificate."

"You must. When you get home, look among your things."

She shook her head. "I don't have any papers."

Was she lying again? Or was she just stupid?

"You have the deed to the farm, don't you?"

She shook her head again. "My husband didn't tell me anything about his business, and I never found any papers. No deed, no marriage certificate. Nothing."

Solomon threaded his fingers together. Shaking her senseless as he longed to do wouldn't achieve anything. "Then we will look for them. You will search your cabin, and I will pay a visit to the county courthouse in Millersburg. You must establish your ownership of that property or all our plans will be ruined."

Elizabeth chewed on her bottom lip. "What plans?"

He smiled in the way that he had learned disarmed people and gave him what he wanted. He took both of her hands in his.

"Our marriage. Our future. Our family's future. Uniting our properties will help us provide for generations to come."

She blushed, her eyes turned down and a smile on her lips. His smile stretched wider. He had found her weak spot. A family. Children and grandchildren. He could ask anything of her now.

Taking a step closer, he released one hand and lifted her chin with his finger. "You know I lost my dear Anna in childbirth along with our child. I look forward to being blessed with a house full of children."

"I had heard that you still grieve for her, and I can . . . imagine the pain of losing your child, also. Reuben and I were . . . we never had . . . children."

Her voice caught, betraying her emotion, and the thrill of easy prey coursed through him as her eyes glistened. Unrequited longing. Her hopeful expression fed his instincts.

He licked his lips. "But first, before we can move forward with our plans, we need to establish that you are the rightful owner of your farm."

"Reuben's farm."

Her soft voice barely registered in his hearing. He chose to ignore it.

Solomon took her shoulders and steered her toward the door. "You go and search the cabin. Men hide important papers in strange places sometimes. Perhaps he hid them under a stone in the fireplace or in the loft. Check everywhere they could be hidden."

"I will." She turned to look at him. "What will happen if we don't find them?"

"Don't worry about that. I'll take care of everything." He pushed her into the front hall. "You just look in the cabin."

She frowned, making her even prettier. "What should I do if I find them?"

He patted her back. "Bring them to me. I'll take care of everything. But don't say anything to anyone else. This lawyer may have an agent working here, and we don't want them to learn information that would put us at a disadvantage."

Her frown softened into a puzzled look. Pretty and naive

enough to trust him. His favorite type of woman. "You can rely on me, Elizabeth. I have experience with these matters and I only have your best interests at heart."

She gave him a nod as he prodded her closer to the door that Dulcey held open for her.

Elizabeth grasped Dulcey's free hand and spoke in Englisch. "Thank you, Dulcey. I look forward to visiting with you sometime. I would like to learn to know you better."

Dulcey didn't answer but closed the door as Elizabeth walked out to her cart.

"What was that all about?" He glared at Dulcey.

The skinny girl backed against the door, still holding the knob with one hand. She shook her head.

Suspicion left a metallic taste in his mouth, feeding his need for release.

"Have you talked with her before?"

Dulcey shook her head, her eyes tight. "No, Masta, not once. I don't know why she spoke to me like that."

Solomon reached for the buggy whip he kept in the umbrella stand next to the door. His heartbeat pounded in his ears, strong and steady. He could already see the welts the whip would bring on Dulcey's bare legs. Red stripes, each one crossing the other until the blood flowed freely in rivulets against the dark skin.

"You must have encouraged her. Smiled at her?"

He stepped closer and Dulcey's knees buckled, casting her prostrate on the floor in front of him.

"I swear, not once. I don't never look at her."

Solomon reached down to lift her skirt above her knees, exposing the evidence of previous days and weeks of satisfying his lust for blood on her. Then a thought crossed his mind and the whip dropped from his hand, forgotten. Elizabeth's interest in talking to Dulcey could be used to his advantage. He grabbed the slightly built girl's arm and lifted her to her feet.

"I have something for you to do." She was shaking and flinched when he reached to straighten the kerchief on her head, his hand gentle. "I want you to talk to Elizabeth the next time she visits. Invite her into the kitchen for coffee. Offer her something to eat."

Dulcey cast a sideways glance up at him. "Why?"

"She'll tell you things she would never tell me. Ask her about her farm and her life. Find out everything you can and then report to me."

His servant didn't answer but looked at the floor. He shook her, still holding her by the arm.

"Do what I say, or you'll end up back in that saloon where I found you. You remember what that was like, don't you?"

She nodded.

"Now go and lay out my regular clothes, and make sure you've brushed my coat. Then hitch up the buggy. I need to go to Millersburg."

As she disappeared up the stairs, Solomon picked up the buggy whip and put it back in its place. Dulcey would obey him. She was always compliant.

Late Tuesday afternoon as Aaron was walking home from Gideon's farm, he heard a cart coming behind him on the road. He glanced back, preparing to make his way to the edge of the graded dirt track, but then saw Elizabeth turn her pony cart into her farm. He changed direction and headed up the hill, using his new cane to steady his steps. Whatever Elizabeth was doing at the old cabin, she might need some help.

By the time he arrived, the pony was tied outside the cabin. Aaron walked to the door and looked in just in time to see a ceiling beam give way in a shower of dirt and old leaves.

"Elizabeth!"

"I'm all right."

Her voice came from the loft above, or what was left of it.

"What are you doing up there?" Dust filled the air in a cloud, obscuring everything.

Elizabeth coughed. "I'm looking for something and thought it might be in the loft." She coughed again. "What brings you here?"

"I saw you turn into the farm from the road and thought you might need some help."

The dust started settling and Aaron picked his way through the debris covering the floor. Elizabeth was standing on a second beam, keeping her balance by holding on to the rafters. He leaned on his cane.

"It looks like you might need some help getting down. How did you climb up there?"

"There is a ladder. It was leaning against the beam that fell."

Aaron found the ladder under the broken beam and pulled it out. Setting his cane aside, he maneuvered it upright and leaned it against the remaining beam. Elizabeth grasped the top, then started down.

"How did you avoid falling when that beam gave way?"

Elizabeth reached the floor and tried to wipe the dust from her skirt. "I was between the two beams when I heard it crack. When I jumped toward the wall, it fell, but I had reached the second beam. I'm glad it didn't break too."

Aaron looked around at the old cabin. He had seen some shacks in west Tennessee, but not many in as bad shape as this one was.

"You used to live here?"

Elizabeth looked around at the mess, crossing her arms with her palms cupping her elbows. "It was in better condition then. After Ruby and Gideon married, I moved into Katie's house. I thought about moving back here once, but I've realized that even a good cleaning wouldn't make this a place I'd want to live in."

"You could tear it down and build a new house here."

She snorted. "It needs to be burned down."

Another cloud of dust rose up as part of the beam settled farther toward the floor.

"We should get out of here. Something else may fall."

"Not until I find what I'm looking for."

"I can help. What is it?"

"Some papers. I've never seen them in here, but Solomon said they must be somewhere. This is the only place Reuben could have kept them."

Aaron grimaced at the mention of her husband. Jonas had told him little about Elizabeth's marriage, but from the information he did give him, Aaron knew he wouldn't want to meet the man.

"What kind of papers?"

Elizabeth shifted her gaze away from his, chewing on her

bottom lip. "Solomon didn't want me to tell anyone, in case the lawyer in Mississippi finds out. But I could use your help." She shrugged her shoulders. "I'm looking for the deed to the farm, our marriage certificate. Important documents."

Aaron's stomach twisted. Why did Solomon want her to find papers like that? And what did a lawyer have to do with it? But he wasn't going to leave her alone to look. Another part of the old cabin could fall down at any time.

He waved away the swirl of dust motes hanging in the air between them. "Did he keep the papers in something? Like a leather pouch or a metal box?"

"I don't remember ever seeing them, but he did have a metal box. He never let me see what was in it."

"But you don't know where he kept it."

She shook her head. "The only time I saw it was—" She bit her lip. "I was sick, and he thought I wasn't watching him, but I still don't know what he did with it."

"I have some time this afternoon. I can help you look."

She hesitated. "You won't mind? As you can see, it's going to be a dirty job, and we might not find anything."

"Let's start at that corner and work our way around."

Aaron prodded at the dry chinking between the logs in the corner while Elizabeth pulled the bed frame away from the wall.

"So, Solomon suggested that you look here?"

Elizabeth peered up the cold chimney. "He said he would look through the records at the courthouse in Millersburg, but he thought Reuben would have kept the papers here."

"Why is Solomon looking for them?"

"Because of the letter." She was standing on the floor of

the fireplace with her head inside the chimney and her words were muffled.

"What letter?"

She stepped out of the fireplace and started examining the mantel. "I received a letter from a law firm in Mississippi asking about any property Reuben might have owned in Ohio."

"Why would a southern lawyer be interested in Reuben's property?"

Elizabeth coughed again. "Let's go outside for a few minutes while the dust settles."

Aaron grabbed his cane and followed her into the bright afternoon sunshine. She drew a bucket of clear water from the well and they both took a drink, then sat on a bench someone had placed in the shade of a tree long ago. Elizabeth sighed deeply and gazed at the cabin.

"My husband was a cruel man." Her voice was even. Flat. As if she were telling him about the weather.

"Jonas told me a bit about him."

"Reuben joined the Confederate army early in the war and was in Vicksburg for more than a year. While he was there, he married another woman. They had a son."

Disgust for this man Aaron had never met rolled over him in a wave. Both Grandpop and Pa had taught him that women were to be protected, nurtured, and cherished. Women were strong and capable, but their job of bearing and raising children made them even more precious. The thought of this man turning his back on Elizabeth . . . Aaron resisted the urge to take her in his arms and settled for laying his hand on top of hers.

"I'm sorry."

She looked at him, her eyes wide. Tears glistened in the corners.

"You believe me?"

"Of course. Men can be stupid creatures, only thinking of themselves. If it had been me . . ." He let his words trail off. If Elizabeth had been his wife, he would have done everything in his power to come home to her.

"I took the letter to Solomon because it was written in Englisch. I got the feeling he didn't believe me at first. In fact, he insisted that I had to find a certificate of marriage to prove that I was Reuben's wife."

Aaron's jaw clenched. "You should have brought it to me. I could have read it for you."

She pulled her hand out from under his. "I didn't think you would be able to read it. The script was very fancy, and the letter was full of long words I couldn't make out. I knew Solomon had had dealings with the Englisch and he would know what to do."

"Solomon isn't the man you should be going to for advice. Abraham will be home in a few days. Wait to see what he says."

"I can't wait that long. The letter took several weeks to arrive. I know the lawyer is waiting for an answer." She chewed on her lower lip, still watching the cabin. Finally, she looked at him, a smile on her face. "I had better start looking for those papers again. Solomon thinks they are very important."

"Did he say why?" Aaron rose to follow her back into the cabin.

"He said we needed to prove that I am the rightful owner

of the farm, although I don't know why he is so insistent. If this other woman needs money to support herself and her child, I would give the property to her. It doesn't mean anything to me. If Solomon and I marry, we could live very well on his farm."

Aaron halted as Elizabeth continued into the cabin. Marriage to Solomon would be the worst mistake of Elizabeth's life, if he was right about the man. As bad as Reuben had been, Aaron knew Solomon would never give Elizabeth the life she longed for. Men like that never considered anyone else when they made their plans.

10

Elizabeth found herself standing near Salome Beiler on Sunday morning before church. It was pleasant weather on this second Sunday in June and people lingered outside Simeon and Hannah Keck's house, waiting for the service to start.

"Tsk, tsk, tsk," Salome said, shaking her head. "I never thought I would see a minister act like that."

When Elizabeth saw what Salome was looking at, she covered a grin with her hand. Gideon had purchased a buggy for his family and had driven it to church. The black sides shone in the bright sunlight.

"We all voted on whether to allow buggy driving on Sunday, Salome," Mamm said from the other side of Elizabeth. "For families with several children or for older folks, driving a buggy makes it possible for them to attend the church meeting. Too many stay home when the distance is too far for them to walk."

"I didn't vote for it." Salome crossed her arms.

"No one at the meeting objected." Mamm's voice was

strong and steady. Elizabeth admired her for keeping her temper, even in a disagreement with Salome.

"I knew everyone was against me."

"Solomon Mast drives a buggy to church, but I've never heard you complain about him."

Salome sniffed. "Solomon Mast is different. He is a good Amishman."

Elizabeth kept her gaze on the ground. What would Salome think if she knew that Solomon had practically asked her to marry him? Elizabeth stifled a giggle. She might be speechless, given her opposing opinions of the two of them.

"We are equal in the eyes of God." Mamm's voice held an edge, as if she was warning Salome to watch what she was saying.

"Ja, ja, ja." Salome started walking toward the house. "I know, Lydia. You needn't bring it up again."

Mamm chuckled softly.

"What was that about?" Elizabeth asked.

"I decided that the way to stop Salome's thoughtless comments was to remind her that she is no better than anyone else." Mamm smiled. "It has made bearing her company more pleasant."

Elizabeth followed Mamm toward the house, falling behind a little as she watched the buggies arrive. Solomon hadn't driven up yet and Elizabeth hoped he wasn't going to miss the worship service. Finally, just as she reached the door, she saw his black horse turn into the farm lane. She had only seen him once since he had asked her to look for the documents proving her ownership of Reuben's farm.

When he learned that she hadn't found them yet, his frown was enough to bring a quick apology.

"I'm sorry. I'll keep looking."

"See that you do." His voice had growled. "We don't have anything to discuss until you find those papers."

"I won't stop until I find them."

Then he had caught her chin in one hand, grasping it hard enough to leave a red mark. "I know you won't."

He had patted her cheek and gone into the house to talk to Datt.

Elizabeth hadn't liked how hard he had held her chin, but he didn't know how strong he was. That was the only problem. Solomon would never deliberately hurt her.

She slipped into her place on the bench next to Ruby and her family just as the first hymn was announced. While they sang, Solomon walked in and took the last spot on the bench on the men's side, directly across the aisle from her. He didn't look her way but opened a copy of the Ausbund and joined in the singing. As the service progressed, Elizabeth tried to catch his eye, but his gaze remained on the front of the church.

After two of the sermons were done and Gideon was rising to deliver the third one, Ruby leaned over to whisper, "I need to take Lovinia out to change her. Would you watch the boys for me?"

Elizabeth nodded and held her arms out for Daniel. He climbed into her lap, sleepy as they drifted toward the end of the service. Ezra took his mother's place between Roseanna and Sophia and watched his father.

Gideon started his sermon.

"I will be speaking on the twelfth chapter of Hebrews, the first and second verses."

The pages of the Bible rustled in the quiet room as he turned to the passage. As Gideon read the verses, Elizabeth heard them as if they were birds' wings beating a soft thrum on her heart. When he reached the phrase "the sin that so easily besets us," she thought of how a crow will struggle to fly away from the smaller birds that attack it when it comes too close to their nest. She knew what it was to be beset by sin. Nothing had ever been able to remove that dark stain. She could almost feel the sharp beaks picking at her, attacking her, never letting her forget.

Then Gideon read, "'Looking unto Jesus, the author and finisher of our faith.'" Elizabeth didn't hear the rest of the verse. She had heard about Jesus all through her life, but had she ever looked to him?

Gideon finished reading and closed his eyes for a brief minute. When he opened them, he talked about the stain of sin and how there was nothing in one's own power that could remove that terrible curse. Elizabeth found herself nodding in agreement.

Then Gideon said, "But there is an answer. God has provided the way for you to be free of your sin."

Elizabeth leaned forward over Daniel's sleeping body, but his next words were lost when Ruby came back and pushed past Elizabeth to take her own seat. After Ruby had sat down again, holding a sleeping Lovinia, Elizabeth happened to look across the aisle and caught Solomon watching her. He nodded at the sleeping boy in her arms and smiled.

A warm wave of delight washed over Elizabeth and she

returned Solomon's smile. His message had been clear. He liked seeing her with her nephew in her arms. Solomon turned back to the front of the room and Elizabeth leaned down to kiss Daniel's sweaty forehead. Someday, perhaps soon, she could be holding her own child in her arms. A child that was wanted and loved, not rejected by his father.

She stroked Daniel's cheek, dreaming of that day, until Gideon's voice stopped speaking and the ministers stood to close the service. Whatever she had missed of Gideon's sermon didn't matter anymore.

After the fellowship meal, Levi joined the other men standing in the doorway of the large bank barn. The doors were swung wide at both ends of the building and the gentle breeze cooled the shaded bay. The rafters in the open haymow tossed the men's voices back to them in soft echoes.

"What did you think of the ministers' meeting last week?" Simeon asked. "I wanted to go, but I had a cow about to calve and couldn't leave."

Abraham lifted his eyebrows. "A heifer?"

"Healthy as I could ask for. She's out there with her mamm now." Simeon pointed out the far door at a brown cow and calf in the meadow. The calf was nearly hidden by the tall grass.

Gideon leaned against the doorframe. "The meeting went like I expected."

"You mean they ignored us," Caleb Lehman said. "The tradition-minded men had drawn up a fine document stating our views and they didn't even discuss it."

"At least they read it," Levi said. "I never expected it would be discussed."

"It's as if they mean to drive us out of our own church," Gideon said. "I fear the split that started in Indiana will spread to the rest of the communities."

Casper Zook pulled at his beard. "The change-minded folks are the ones leaving and they will never come back. They're adopting new worldly inventions as fast as they can."

"Photographs and lightning rods," said Caleb.

"Holding political office," Simeon added.

"Building churches and holding Sunday schools," said Solomon.

"What is so bad about Sunday schools?" Aaron asked. He looked around at the men. "Other churches have them."

"Sunday schools are acceptable if they are done carefully and don't take the place of the parents' instruction," Abraham said. "My main objection to them is that they separate families when the children are still at a tender age. But we don't adopt changes only because other churches have. We are called to follow God's direction, not the world's. And especially not the churches of this world."

The men were silent for a few minutes. Levi watched the folks gathered in small groups in the shaded yard behind the Kecks' big farmhouse. The children played a game of tag while their mothers watched. Older women sat in a circle under the biggest tree listening to something Lydia was telling them. The older boys huddled near the pasture where the horses were grazing, furtively glancing at the group of older girls gathered at the kitchen door.

Levi grinned. Not too long ago, he and Jonas and the others would be pretending to watch the horses while keeping a close eye on the girls. Now most of their group were married as well as those girls. He and Jonas were the only bachelors left from their group of friends, and he hoped Jonas wouldn't remain unmarried for long. Father and the other ministers had discussed his situation at the end of the ministers' meeting in Wayne County. Levi hadn't heard the results of that discussion yet, but Father needed to tell Jonas what they decided before anyone else did.

His gaze slid over to the group of young women, many of them girls when he and Jonas had idled their Sunday afternoons away with the fellows. Some were married, some not. None of them had children old enough to play tag with the others. It didn't take long for him to find Elise. She sat next to Millie, with one of the twins on her lap. She laughed at something Millie said and her face was as joyous as a lark's song. Even though her smile wasn't aimed at him, it found a target and wound itself around his heart.

"What do you think, Levi?" Gideon asked.

Levi felt his face heat as the others waited for his answer.

"I'm sorry. I missed what you were talking about."

"Too busy watching the scenery," someone said, and the others chuckled.

"What will you do if the change-minded faction decides to leave the church? Should we try to force them to stay?"

He cleared his throat. He wasn't asked to share his opinion very often. "You can't force someone to go against their conscience, even if you think they're wrong. If we try to force them to remain united to us, the only result would be discontent and complaints. I think we should approach their decision the same as when an individual leaves the church. If they are sinning, we need to shun them until they repent." Levi wiped the trickling sweat from his forehead as the men nodded in agreement. "But I'm not convinced that they are sinning. We have a difference of opinion regarding certain things, but those things are contrary to our traditions, not the teaching in the Bible."

"Even when they take photographs?" Solomon crossed his arms. "Isn't that a graven image?"

"I've heard some say that," Levi said. He spoke carefully so he wouldn't be misunderstood. "I don't think a photograph is breaking the second commandment. When you read through the commandments in the Bible, it is clear that God is forbidding us from worshiping idols, especially images we might try to make of God. But a photograph or an engraving, capturing a moment in time in a visual way, is innocent. It is only the sin in our own hearts that is a danger when we are tempted to use it as an object of our worship."

Perspiration prickled on his back as he looked around the circle of men. He had never spoken at such length before in a group like this, with men listening who were older and wiser than he was. Their faces were thoughtful. Some were nodding in agreement.

"Well said, Levi." Casper Zook smiled at him. "That was a prudent answer and one we should remember. The change-minded group are still our brothers in Christ, no matter what we may think of their actions."

The conversation continued as Levi left the group. The sight of Elise's face . . . had it given him the courage to speak his mind like that? He searched for her among the women, but the seat next to Millie was empty.

He walked down to the house to get a drink and found her next to the well. She was trying to pump some water for herself and hold the cup under the waterspout at the same time.

"Can I help you?" The question sounded silly to his ears. Levi nearly ran back the way he had come.

Then she smiled at him. "If you pump it, I'll fill the cup and we can both have a drink."

He worked the handle until the water began to flow. It filled the small tin cup to the brim and spilled over onto the grass at their feet. She laughed and his heart squeezed.

"Are you enjoying your new home here?"

She nodded and handed the cup to him. "The other girls are very friendly. I've been invited to stay for the Singing tonight, and Datt has said I may." She smiled. "I hope you will be staying also."

Levi smiled back. He was too old to go to the Singing and hadn't attended for several years. But if Elise was going, he wouldn't miss it.

"Only if I may walk you home afterward."

She blushed a pretty shade of pink. "I would like that."

He handed the cup back to her. "Then it's all arranged."

Their fingers met around the cup and she dropped her gaze to the ground.

"Elise—" Levi stopped. What should he say? He didn't know her well enough to ask if she felt the same as he did. "Elise, I hope no one else will ask to take you home."

She looked at him again. "Even if someone else does ask, I'll tell him he's too late. I'm already walking home with the finest man in the church."

Levi's face burned, but it was worth all the embarrassment to hear her say those words.

⁓

Even though no work was done on Sunday, certain chores were necessary. Aaron had started doing the Sunday evening chores a few weeks ago to give Abraham a rest, and he found he enjoyed it. Taking over the Sunday evening responsibilities was little enough compared to what Jonas and his family had done for him.

He took the stool from its hook on the wall and placed the milk pail under the cow's udder. She was an old cow and used to the morning and evening routine. She turned to look at him as he milked, strands of hay sticking out on each side of her mouth.

"You're all right, Bossy, you know I'll take good care of you."

The milk pinged in the pail until he had milked enough to cover the bottom. Aaron leaned his head against the cow's flank, taking in the comfortable fragrance of fresh milk and sweet hay. Even the odor of manure couldn't overpower the pleasant aromas of the barn but settled underneath it like a rich foundation.

The barn cats had heard the sound of milking. One twined itself around his ankle while the others sat in a circle, watching him. They knew he would pour a little fresh milk into a pan for them when he was done, but a few sat up on their haunches, begging for an early taste. He aimed one of the teats in their direction and squeezed. The big gray cat was an expert and caught the entire stream in its mouth. The black-

and-white one tried to bite at the milk and ended up covered with white drops. Aaron chuckled as it quickly cleaned its face before the drops disappeared.

He stopped in surprise. When was the last time he had laughed? The cow stomped a foot in protest, and he started the rhythmic milking again. He hadn't felt this comfortable and settled since . . .

Aaron thought back. Not at all while he was in the army. Every day he had lived in anxious fear that death would strike without warning. That the next artillery shell or musket ball heading his way would be the last one he would ever hear—if he heard it at all. And during the long days between battles, he lived as the other soldiers did. Bitter, angry, and hungry. Cold in the winter and hot in the summer. Nothing brought joy, even though he had tried nearly every diversion available.

Even the weekly church services he attended failed to satisfy his longings. He had sat in the back, in the shadowy edges, watching the preacher's face lit by a half-dozen campfires circling him. He had gone for the music. The hymns the men had sung reminded him of home. The home he had known before Ma died.

Closing his eyes, Aaron let his cheek rest against the soft flank as if it were Ma's bosom. If he listened closely, he could hear her singing to him. But when he opened his eyes again, it was still all gone. Destroyed. He was the only one left.

Not the only one. He smiled. The Zooks had taken him in as if they had known him from the time of his birth. Even though none of them had known Grandpop, they had accepted him for the old man's sake, and for Casper's father's sake. Both men gone, but their memories lived on in their descendants. Aaron whooshed out a breath. It was hard to get accustomed to, but he had a family. Dan and Ephraim were his cousins. Their children were part of him, carrying on a legacy he only knew from Grandpop's stories.

Grandpop had never returned home to his family, but Aaron had that chance. He could plant himself among the Zooks and others from the church, if he wanted to.

That was the problem. What did he want? He couldn't go home, and he couldn't see what was ahead. Anything beyond now was a shadowy haze.

He finished the milking, poured the cats' milk into the pan, then set the pail next to the door, covered with a towel and ready to take to the springhouse.

Leaning against the doorframe, he watched the sun lowering into a bank of clouds in the west, lighting the sky with colors so vivid he longed to grasp and hold them. The children were playing near the barn in the little playhouse Abraham had made for his grandchildren. Ezra and Daniel chased each other in and out while the older ones tried to catch the fireflies that were beginning to appear as the twilight cast its glow.

Aaron's breath caught. This . . . this was what he wanted. Not a western town where he would be a nameless stranger. Not a world where every day was a fight for a few pennies to survive. He wanted a life with a family. With children who hunted for fireflies, and a wife . . . He swallowed, casting his gaze back into the barn where the horses waited for their supper. A useless dream. No woman would marry half a man. The shadowed interior of the barn revealed the same future he saw for himself. Nothing. No answers anywhere.

The horses were gathered at the back door of the barn,

waiting to come in for their evening feeding. The team of big draft horses needed grain, even after a day of rest. Tomorrow would bring another long day of work for them. Aaron undid the clasp that held the gate closed and then started pouring the measures of grain into their feedboxes. One for each horse.

The children's voices grew louder. At first, Aaron thought they were playing a different game, but then he heard the shouts for help. He dropped the grain scoop and hurried outside. When he saw five-year-old Ezra in the pasture with Abraham's bull, he ran for the fence, thrusting himself forward with his good leg and pivoting on his wooden peg. He scrambled over the fence and dropped on the other side.

The bull didn't look his way. The beast must have broken through the fence again. His attention was on the boy in front of him. Ezra stood about ten feet away from Samson and too far away from Aaron. The big beast shook its head and grunted.

"Ezra." Aaron kept his voice calm as he slowly got to his feet. "Don't move."

"I didn't know Samson was in this pasture," Ezra said, his voice quivering. "I thought it was empty." The bull raked at the ground with one hoof.

"Don't talk." Aaron swallowed, watching the bull. "Just stand still."

Aaron took a slow step toward the boy. The animal cast one glance his way, the red eye rimmed with white. Aaron stopped and licked his dry lips. Ezra was frozen in place, his gaze locked on the bull. He had to make sure the boy would be able to follow his directions.

"Ezra, look at me."

The boy pulled his gaze away from the bull and turned a pale face toward Aaron.

"Can you take a step backward? Just one step. Very slow."

Ezra lifted his left foot and put it behind his right heel. As he moved, the bull grunted again and tossed its head.

Aaron tried to judge the distance between him and Ezra. He only had one chance, and when he acted, the bull would charge. Just beyond Ezra was a shallow depression in the ground. That low spot was his only chance to save the boy. Aaron tightened his muscles, ready to jump.

"I'm going to save you, Ezra. Don't worry. Just stay where you are."

Movement off to the side distracted him. The other men, racing from the house. The bull saw them, too, and bellowed. They wouldn't reach the pasture in time.

The big animal dug his hind feet into the turf, propelling himself forward, and Aaron leaped, running at full speed. He grabbed Ezra and rolled into that hole, covering the boy with his body.

The ground shook as the bull overran them. As it passed over the depression where Aaron pressed their bodies as close to the ground as he could, a blow hit Aaron on the back of the head as strong as the percussion explosion of artillery. He crouched over Ezra, using his body as a shield. The bull would turn at the end of his run and come back.

Aaron glanced up and saw the horns flash in the last light of the setting sun. Flashing like the fire from the Yankee artillery. A roaring bellow split the air just as he heard the explosion. It was the last he knew.

11

Elizabeth volunteered to sit with Aaron on Thursday. She had avoided the task all week, but Mamm and the others were making cheese in Anna's dairy at Samuel's house across the road. With Solomon's interest in her at the top of her mind, she wasn't sure she could keep from talking about him during the work frolic, and she wanted to keep these new feelings close to her heart for now.

She wrung out a cloth in the basin of cool water and replaced the warm one lying across Aaron's forehead. Her biggest job was to keep the stubborn man in bed when he was awake. The bull's hoof clipped the back of his head as he had crouched over Ezra, protecting him, and Mamm said the best way to recover from an injury like that was to rest for at least a week, perhaps more.

Whenever he was awake, Aaron insisted he was ready to work, but Mamm was firm, and Elizabeth trusted her judgment on injuries and illnesses. She resisted smoothing the vertical line between his eyebrows, evidence of the pain he was suffering.

In the weeks she had known Aaron, becoming acquainted with him and even becoming friends, Elizabeth had never taken the time to look closely at him. He didn't appear like the Amish men she knew. His face was lean, his cheeks hollow. His hair was as wiry as his beard and hard to tame. Mamm had cut it shorter than Aaron had been wearing it to make caring for him easier, and now it looked more like an Amishman's simple cut. But his beard and mustache were thick and long. And red. As red and hairy as Esau in the Bible.

She removed the cloth and replaced it with a new one, pushing his hair off his forehead. She stroked it again. It didn't feel as wiry as it looked. It felt soft, like a lamb's woolly coat. She paused. Was his beard that soft? Or was it coarse like Reuben's had been? Her fingers curled in anticipation. No one would know if she felt it. She was alone in the house with the sleeping man.

Letting her hand drift down to his chest, Elizabeth took the edge of his beard between her fingers. Not as soft as the hair on his head, but still—

A rough hand caught hers and she looked up to see Aaron's blue eyes watching her. She snatched her hand back and buried it in her lap.

"You're awake."

His mouth twitched in a smile. "I'm awake."

Elizabeth's face was burning. "How long have you been watching me?"

"Long enough. I was dreaming that Ma was waking me up in the morning, but when I opened my eyes, it was you."

A memory from long ago flashed through Elizabeth's mind: her mother stroking her hair to awaken her in the morning. She had forgotten that in the intervening years. How many mornings had Mamm gently woke her in that way? Yet she had turned her back on her loving family, thinking she knew best. She shook her head to dispel the memories.

"How are you feeling?"

"Like I'm tired of staying in this bed." Aaron glanced at her. "I'm sorry. It isn't your fault I'm here."

"How can I help you?"

"Tell me what's going on outside of this room. Is Ezra all right?"

"Ja, he's fine. The bull isn't, though. Datt says he won't have an animal on the farm that's a danger to anyone."

"He shot it, didn't he?"

"Just before it was going to run over you again." Elizabeth closed her eyes, but that didn't erase the image of the bull running down Aaron and Ezra. "I'm glad you weren't hurt any more than you are."

"What else? How is Jonas?"

"He had his meeting with the ministers. They're going to let him join the church."

"And that means he can marry Katie, right?"

Elizabeth grinned. "I'm so happy for them." She looked at the clock. It was almost noon. "Are you hungry?"

He stretched, his long arms reaching above his head. "Hungry and thirsty. I'll go down to the kitchen and get my dinner."

"You will not. Mamm says you're not well enough to go

downstairs yet." She straightened the light blanket covering him. "I'll slice some bread and cheese for you."

"Is there any of that summer sausage left?"

She smiled. His hunger was a good sign that he was improving. "I'll bring some of that too." She started toward the door. "Don't try to get out of bed. Mamm wants you to stay there."

"I have to get out of bed, but I won't leave the room. Just be sure to knock before you come back in."

By the time she had fixed a plate for each of them and took them back upstairs, he responded to her knock with a grunt. When she opened the door, he was sitting on the edge of the bed, wearing a clean shirt and loose trousers. Drops of water sparkling in his beard told her that he had washed up, but he leaned his head into his hand.

Elizabeth watched him for a moment. When he didn't move, she adjusted his pillows and helped him recline on them. The pillows were stacked so he could sit up enough to eat without choking, but he could rest his head back whenever he wanted. Then she lifted his good leg up onto the bed next to the stump of his other leg and covered him with the blanket up to his waist. His eyes remained closed.

"Aaron," she said, sitting on the chair next to his bed and picking up his plate, "eat something. It might make you feel better."

He opened his eyes and reached for a slice of bread. As he chewed, he leaned back and stared at the ceiling.

"Did you overestimate your strength?"

Aaron attempted to nod, then winced. "I was all right until I bent down to pull on my trousers. I've spent enough time being sick and crippled since I was wounded last year and I'm tired of it. All I can think is that if I just make myself get out of this bed, I'll work through the pain."

"If you try to work now, you'll only make the injury worse. You know that. Mamm says you need to rest until Saturday, then you can get out of bed. But no strenuous work for several days after that."

He took another bite of his bread. "You said Ezra is all right. He wasn't injured?"

"Not hurt at all, thanks to you. He has promised he will never go into a pasture without looking to see what animals are there first." She picked up her own slice of bread and laid a piece of cheese on it. "You were very brave. You could have been killed."

"I'm not brave. I just knew I couldn't stand by and watch that bull run the boy down without trying to do something."

"But you risked your life. Not many men would do that, especially men with . . ." She let her voice trail off.

"You mean because I'm only half a man?" His voice was bitter. Caustic.

"That isn't what I meant. Just because you're missing a leg doesn't mean you're not a man. You proved that when you saved Ezra. But your missing leg would have given you a good excuse to do nothing."

His eyes narrowed. "I only did what needed to be done."

Elizabeth broke a piece of her cheese in half. "I don't know many men who would have seen it that way, except perhaps Solomon." Surely, he would have leaped into the pasture to rescue a little boy.

"Do you believe Solomon would have tried to save Ezra?"

He stuffed the crust of his bread into his mouth. He spoke around the food, his words muffled. "Somehow, I don't think so."

Elizabeth took a small bite of her bread, chewing it slowly. Of course, Solomon would have, her mind protested. But she turned in her chair so Aaron couldn't see her thoughts as they flitted through her mind and across her face. She had to admit that she couldn't imagine Solomon running to intercept that bull the way Aaron had.

"I hope Solomon would have rescued Ezra. He's a good Amishman and would risk himself for those of the community."

Aaron set his plate aside, one slice of bread left uneaten. "Do you really know him, Elizabeth? Is he the kind of man you want to spend time with?"

She snapped her head in his direction. She had never spoken those ideas aloud, but they had played at the back of her mind.

"You've seen the kind of man he is," she said. She took a deep breath remembering the look in Solomon's eyes when she told him she hadn't found Reuben's papers yet. Was she trying to convince Aaron, or herself?

Aaron reached for her hand and she tried to pull it out of his grasp as she set her plate down.

"I have seen the kind of man he is." He tightened his grip on her hand and pulled her closer. "I've met him before. He denies it, but I know I saw him in Virginia during the war."

"That can't be true. He is from Pennsylvania."

"I couldn't forget his voice, his stance, and his veiled threats. He's a dangerous man." He dropped her hand and rubbed his head along his hairline like his headache had suddenly grown worse. "I hate to see you ruin your life with him."

Elizabeth pressed her lips together. Aaron Zook had no right to talk to her this way. She held her fist to her mouth as her chin started quivering. And what he didn't know was that her life was ruined anyway.

"You don't know what you're talking about. Solomon is . . . is a good man." She hiccupped. "He is Amish and—"

"And I'm not." Aaron's voice was bitter again. "He's a whole man and I'm not. He's a wealthy landowner and I'm not." He glared at her. "If you don't want to listen to me, then go away. I don't need your company. I promise I won't try to get out of bed."

He slumped down under the covers and turned his back to her.

Elizabeth picked up the plates and walked to the door. As she turned to close it behind her, she looked at that hard back again. He knew nothing about Solomon. She slammed the door and went down the stairs to the kitchen.

Aaron was feeling good the next Monday but still took Jonas's advice to hitch up the horse and wagon rather than walk to the Zooks' harness shop. He chuckled to himself as he tossed the harness up onto Rusty's back, remembering the first time he had tried to harness the horse alone. He had his strength back, he was steady on his feet. Or foot. And his headaches had dwindled to a reasonable level.

On Sunday afternoon, a week after the incident with the

bull, most of the community had stopped by the Weavers' farm to see how he was faring. He had sat on the back porch, Ezra close by his side. The little boy didn't seem to notice Aaron's missing leg as he listened to the adults talk about bulls and how dangerous they could be. Everyone seemed to have a story about a run-in with a bull, and every one of the men shook Aaron's hand, thanking him for his heroic action.

By the end of the afternoon he still didn't feel heroic, but he felt welcomed like he had never felt before. Except for Elizabeth—and he couldn't reckon why it bothered him so much when she ignored him. She hadn't come to visit him or her parents since Thursday when she had refused to listen to his advice about Solomon Mast.

Only that wasn't his name. Aaron had spent the hours through Thursday afternoon and evening searching through his memory, and that name wasn't one he recognized. He had even started doubting that he had the right man again, until the name slipped into his consciousness. The spy in the camp when Aaron was in the Shenandoah had been called Simon Miller. Rumors had been that he was a Mennonite farmer who helped both sides destroy the rich farms up and down the valley to prevent their enemies from living off the land.

A waste of resources, for sure, but the generals had all said it was the way to win a war. That might be so, but it still didn't change the fact that all the officers, even a captain like himself, knew that Simon Miller was a snake. A useful spy, but not a man to be trusted.

Then late on Thursday night while lying awake with that pounding headache, Aaron had remembered another rumor that had circulated around the camp when they were in the same area as Simon Miller. The rumor of a predator who attacked girls and young women among the Mennonite and Dunker farms and small towns in the southern Shenandoah Valley. Folks had speculated that the man could be one of the soldiers, but Aaron had been tempted to connect that rumor with the spy. The thought that Solomon Mast could be that man made his blood run cold, but he blamed his imagination. No girls or women had gone missing since Solomon had moved into the Weaver's Creek area. He had dismissed the thoughts and tried to sleep.

Solomon was still on his mind when he turned the horse into the Zooks' farm lane and pulled to a halt outside the harness shop. He had been here often since Casper and the rest of the family had moved to the area, and he knew Dan's boy Cap would be watching for him.

He was right. The ten-year-old had seen him coming and ran from the house to greet him.

"I thought you'd never get here."

Aaron used his cane to steady himself after climbing down from the wagon seat and tousled the boy's hair. "I'm here right when I told your grandpop I would be." He started toward the horse's head to tie him to the hitching rail. "What are you up to today?"

"I'm going to hoe the garden for Mamm. She says the weeds are about to overrun everything and steal all our food."

"Then you have an important job, all right."

Aaron started to tie the lead rope to the rail, but Cap took it from him.

"I'll put Rusty in the pasture for you. *Grossdawdi* says you're going to be here all day."

"Thank you." Aaron grinned at the exasperated look on the boy's face. "All right. In Deitsch. Denki, Cap."

Aaron walked into the harness shop. Just as he expected, Casper was already at the workbench, cutting the strips of leather needed for a set of harnesses from a tanned cowhide.

"Where can I start?" Aaron asked.

Casper finished the strip he was working on and pushed it off the worktable onto a pile of others.

"This harness has been ordered by an Englischer in Berlin. He wants it double strength for his driving carriage. I've already dyed the leather black, and next we'll need to measure the lengths of the straps and sew them together." He turned to a large paper tacked to the wall with the various parts of the harness listed, their measurements, and the number needed next to each one. "We'll work off this list. As you finish each piece, you can mark it off with the pencil there. Start wherever you have a mind to."

"Will Dan and Ephraim be working on it, too?"

"They're in the tanning shed, getting hides ready for the next project after this."

Aaron started sorting through the pile of straps for the sizes he needed. "What's that project?"

"A set of horse collars. Have you ever made one?"

"It will be something new for me. I hope I'm around long enough to learn how to make them."

Casper picked up his knife and rotated the cowhide to the side he wanted. "Why wouldn't you be here?"

"Ever since the war, I thought I might go west. There are a lot of opportunities out there for a man who needs a fresh start." Especially a fresh start away from Elizabeth Kaufman.

If she still thought Solomon Mast was a good choice, he would have to move on.

The older man worked silently for a few minutes while Aaron measured the straps and trimmed them to the right size.

"What do you think you will find out there that we don't have here?"

Aaron shaved a jagged spot on the edge of the leather until it was smooth. "For one thing . . ." He stopped, trying to think of what had drawn him to the West when he had heard the other southerners talking about it, other than a place to escape from the memories. "For one thing, a man won't be judged by which side he fought for in the war."

"Do you think we judge you?"

"Ne, but an Englischer might."

"What else?"

"I could establish my own business there, build a home, and start a family."

"It's hard to start a new business from the beginning." Casper finished with the hide he had been working on and slid another one from the big table where they were stored onto his work surface. "Why not work here with us?"

"I couldn't do that," Aaron said, turning away from Casper as he selected the right size awl from the rack above the bench. "The three of you have a family business. Tobias should be the next man you take on."

"Are you saying you can't be part of it because you aren't one of my sons?" Casper dropped his knife on the table and walked over to Aaron. "You are family. You're one of us."

Aaron turned the awl between his fingers, still not looking at the man who was Pa's cousin. He had been playing at belonging in this family. They had been gracious, going along with it. But now they were talking about a business, not a family reunion. As much as he would like to stay and be part of this community, he hadn't been born to it. Belonging wasn't something he could claim.

"I need to make a home for myself." He looked at Casper. "I don't really belong here, you know that. I'm an Englischer. An outsider."

Casper kept his gaze on Aaron's face, the wrinkles around his eyes softening into a look that was the same as one Aaron had seen on Grandpop's face many times. The look that was willing him to understand.

"A home. That's what you're looking for? A place to belong?"

The sweetness Aaron had felt as he stood in the doorway of Abraham's barn last week flooded his senses. A home.

He nodded.

"You won't find it out west. You won't find it anywhere you go looking for it. Home is right here. Now." He spread his arms to take in the workshop and everything beyond it. "Home is with these people and in this place." He poked his forefinger into Aaron's chest. "Where God is, that's your home. And he is where you are."

Aaron stared at his feet, thinking. If Casper was right, then . . . "I don't need to go anywhere?" Saying it felt good. "I'm already home?"

Casper nodded. "That's right. Because home isn't a building, or a farm, or a business. It's where you belong. The place where God has brought you to and with folks who love you." He took a step closer to Aaron. "Do you want my advice?"

Aaron nodded.

"Stay here. Join the church. Learn to know us better and be part of our family. We'll help you build your own house, your own place on Zook land. Then find the right woman to marry."

Casper's words described a dream that danced in the air just beyond his reach. "Did you forget that I'm not a whole man?"

Casper laid his hand on Aaron's arm. "No man is whole when he is by himself. All of us are broken on the inside until we find our place with God—broken, sore, and weary. Your brokenness is visible, but the solution is the same as it is for any other man. God will make you whole."

Aaron couldn't speak.

Casper patted his arm, then went back to his worktable. "Think about it, son. I would hate to see you leave us to chase a dream that you'll never catch."

Picking up the awl and a hammer, Aaron started the slow process of marking the stitches in the leather. As he worked, a song Ma used to sing formed itself in his mind.

> *Come, ye sinners, poor and needy,*
> *weak and wounded, sick and sore.*

That described him for certain and sure. He couldn't remember the next line, but it had something to do with Jesus curing all those ills, like Casper had described. A whole man.

He hummed the tune as he continued his work, and another line came into his memory.

> *If you tarry till you're better,*
> *you will never come at all.*

The awl wavered and he dropped the hammer onto the workbench. The last eight months he had been waiting until he was healthy again. Waiting until he was back to normal. Waiting until he was better. A better man than he was now. But too much had happened. He had seen too much. The brokenness would never heal itself.

> *If you tarry till you're better,*
> *you will never come at all.*

Elizabeth stood in the old cabin on Reuben's farm on Wednesday morning. With the beam lying on the floor, chinking pried out from between the logs, and dirt and debris everywhere, it was no longer a place anyone could live. The best thing that could happen to it was for lightning to strike and burn it down.

She turned in a circle, looking for any spot she might have missed. Aaron had taken a methodical approach the day he helped her, examining the walls inch by inch, while she had gone from place to place, searching everywhere she thought Reuben might have hidden the box. Behind the bed, inside the fireplace, in the kitchen cabinets. But it hadn't turned up for either of them.

Perhaps there was a place for the box higher up in the chimney than she could reach. Walking over to the fireplace again, her shoes thumped against the wooden floor. Then one footstep sounded different. Elizabeth tried the spot again, stomping her foot on it, then stomping on the floorboard next to it. The first spot sounded hollow. It had been underneath the bed until she had pulled it away from the wall.

As she knelt on the floor, trying to pry the board loose with her fingers, Elizabeth imagined the look on Solomon's face when she finally brought him the papers. He said he hadn't been successful in Millersburg. Either Reuben had never filed their marriage certificate, or it had never existed. More than anything, she wanted to prove to Solomon that she could be the kind of woman he thought she was. Honorable, truthful, faithful. A good Amish wife.

Before the floorboard gave way, Elizabeth had broken two fingernails. But no matter. When she lifted the board out of its place, she found a square hole dug into the dirt beneath the floor. And in the hole was a dull, rectangular metal box. She snatched it from its resting place and took it out into the morning sunlight. This was it. This was the box she had seen in Reuben's hands the night she lost her baby. Her hands shook and she whooshed out a breath along with the lingering threads of the painful memory. That was in the past. This box held the key to her future.

She pried it open. The box was full of paper. On the top was money. Elizabeth lifted the stack of bills out and counted it. Nearly one hundred dollars, all in Confederate money. Useless to anyone now.

Underneath the money were folded documents. As she opened the first one, she could tell it was the deed to Reuben's one hundred sixty acres, with an additional paper declaring that the mortgage had been paid in full. The second document was faded, but legible. A marriage certificate, stating when she and Reuben had been married. At the bottom was another paper, the letter Reuben had received after his father had passed away. She kept the marriage certificate and the deed but placed everything else back in the box. After she returned the box to its place under the floorboard, she started off for Solomon's house.

As she drove Pie up the hill, she dusted off her skirt as well as she could. Solomon wouldn't want to see her in such a state, but he was anxious to see these papers. She couldn't take the time to go home and change her clothes.

Solomon must have seen her coming. He stood on the top step of the porch watching her drive toward him. His face wore a frown, but that wouldn't last long once he saw what she had.

As she pulled Pie to a halt at the hitching rail, she waved the folded documents. "I found them!"

She had been right. His face opened into a wide smile as he bounded down the steps and gave her his hand to help her out of the buggy.

"I'm so glad, my dear. This is the deed?"

Elizabeth nodded as she brushed a cobweb off her sleeve. "And the marriage certificate. I came over as quickly as I could after finding them."

"Come in. I assume you have not had lunch yet?"

She shook her head and let him take her arm as they went into the house.

"I'll ask Dulcey to fix a meal for you. Perhaps the two of you could eat together in the kitchen and become better acquainted."

Dulcey stood at the kitchen door, smiling at Elizabeth.

"I would like that very much." She smiled back at the woman she hoped would be a good friend and companion.

"Take your time and visit all you want. After I look through the papers you brought, I have some work to do in the barn, so I won't disturb you."

Elizabeth followed Dulcey through the swinging door into the kitchen.

"It will just take a minute to fix your lunch, Miss Elizabeth."

"Just call me Elizabeth, please. And I'll call you Dulcey. If we're going to be friends, then we shouldn't let formalities stand in the way."

"No, Miss."

Elizabeth gave up. "I can fix my own lunch if you tell me where things are."

"Oh, no, Miss. I can't do that. You set yourself down and I'll do it." She hesitated. "And I'll fix enough for the two of us so we can eat together?"

"For sure we should eat together. How can we visit if we don't?"

Dulcey worked quickly, slicing some cold chicken and arranging it on two plates with a dish made from peas with a creamy sauce. She also put a plate of sliced bread on the table and two glasses of water. Then Elizabeth bowed her head for her usual silent prayer, but Dulcey prayed aloud.

"Dear Father, Lord of all of us. Hear our prayer of thanksgiving for this meal you done given us, and for the life you done given us, and all. In Jesus' name, Amen."

Then Dulcey started eating, not looking at Elizabeth once.

Solomon had said they should visit, but Dulcey looked so nervous that Elizabeth didn't know how to start.

Finally, she asked, "How did you come to start working for Solomon?"

Dulcey looked startled, then glanced at the door before she answered. "Masta Solomon found me working in . . . in Millersburg. I wasn't happy in that place, so he offered me this job."

"Do you enjoy working for him?"

"Oh, yes, Miss. Masta Solomon is a fine man. Always treats me well." Dulcey's hands shook as she took some of the peas on her fork. "And you? Masta Solomon says you is widowed?"

"Yes, I am. My husband was killed in the war."

Tears welled in Dulcey's eyes and she rose from the table. She walked over to the swinging door but didn't open it. She stood as if she was listening. When she came back, she took Elizabeth's hands in her own and leaned close to her.

"You are a nice woman, Elizabeth."

Dulcey's voice was a whisper so low that Elizabeth had to lean closer to hear her.

"So are you. I know we'll be good friends."

Dulcey shook her head emphatically. "No, Miss. No. You need to go away from here. Don't ever come back. Masta Solomon, he ain't the kind of man you think he is."

Elizabeth looked into the young woman's eyes. They were filled with tears.

"I trust Solomon. He's never given me any reason not to."

"You listen to me. I was married, but I lost my man during the war. He may be dead, he may have just run off. But after emancipation, I had nowhere to go. You understand? Nowhere. I had to eat. I went from place to place, following that North Star to the land of promise I heard tell of all my life, but when I got across the river, nothing was different than in the South. Freedom don't fill no stomachs. I found a job in a terrible place, but I didn't starve. I did what I had to in order to survive."

Pulling her lip between her teeth, Elizabeth stood on the brink of that whirlpool spiraling downward, leading to that dark pit. She knew. Oh, she knew what a woman would do when she had no other choice.

"I understand." She turned Dulcey's hands in her own and squeezed them gently. "I know exactly what you mean."

Dulcey's smile was grim. "Masta Solomon, he found me there. Said he had work for me if I would take it. He don't pay me like he said he would, and he beats me some, but I eat and I got a dry place to sleep." A tear escaped from one eye and rolled down her cheek. "But I can't do what he wants me to do now."

Elizabeth's stomach twisted. The Solomon Dulcey described couldn't be the man she knew . . . or thought she knew. He would never beat a woman, would he?

"What does he want you to do?"

"He wants me to find out things about you to use against you. He wants you to tell me things you wouldn't tell anyone else."

"Why?"

A thump sounded from beyond the kitchen wall. Dulcey jumped in her seat, her eyes wide.

"I daren't say, Miss. Just tell me something, please." Her

voice had dropped to a soft whisper again. "Just tell me something he don't know."

Elizabeth's mind raced. Dulcey was frightened of Solomon, that was clear, but Solomon wasn't as threatening as Dulcey seemed to think. Elizabeth knew him well enough to know that. Solomon was nothing like Reuben had been. The poor woman must have been badly mistreated by her master when she was a slave and expected that same treatment from Solomon, but what could she do to help?

Suddenly, the words of Gideon's sermon came into her mind. *"God has provided the way for you to be free of your sin."*

She smiled, thinking she finally knew what Gideon had meant.

"Dulcey, God will help you and me. He will set us free."

She would be free from the memory of those sins that beset her by exposing them. She wouldn't hide Reuben's sins from the world anymore. She swallowed, hesitating. What would the other church members think of her if they heard?

But if she never told the secret, how would she ever gain her freedom from Reuben's hold over her?

"Tell Solomon that my husband caused our child to die before it was born because he thought he couldn't be its father."

Dulcey gripped her hands even harder. "Oh, my Lord, oh no."

"Reuben was a cruel man and a drunkard." Elizabeth could no longer see Dulcey's face because of the tears in her eyes, but she clung to the other woman's hands. "I've never told anyone this, Dulcey. It's a secret I thought I would take to my grave, but Reuben doesn't deserve for me to protect him anymore. You can tell Solomon that. If he thinks he can use it against me somehow, then let him."

"That is a terrible thing to keep hidden. It's the kind of thing that eats at your soul."

Elizabeth shuddered. Dulcey had described it exactly. Her soul had been eaten away, but no more.

"Do you think the Lord will help you now?" Dulcey's tone was that of a woman clinging to a slim thread of hope. "After all you been through, do you think he'll help you find peace?"

Elizabeth blinked away the tears and looked into Dulcey's face. "I'm certain he will. And he will help you too." What had Gideon said? "Turn to Jesus, Dulcey. He's the only one who can help us."

12

After months—years—of trying to walk through hidden, muddy trails, Aaron finally felt like his life was back on course. Talking to Casper on Monday had shown him that the Zooks didn't think of him as an unwanted tagalong cousin but saw him as part of the family. As they had continued working day after day on the order for the harness, Casper had talked about where they could build Aaron's house, and where his forty acres would be. Dan and Ephraim had purchased a one-hundred-sixty-acre quarter section when they came to Ohio, but Casper didn't want to farm anymore. The harness making work was enough for him, so he was glad to pass on his forty acres to Aaron. Eating with the family during the noon meals, he felt a sense of belonging he had never experienced before.

In the days since then, his path had been clear. He grinned as he fed grain to the horses in Abraham's barn on Saturday morning. Nothing was better for a man than knowing what he wanted out of life and how to achieve it.

Suddenly a forkful of hay fell out of the haymow and onto his head.

"Watch what you're doing!" He pulled his hat off and brushed bits of hay from the brim, his shoulders, down his front. He looked up to see Jonas's head through the opening.

"I didn't know you were there." Another forkful of hay dropped into the manger. "You need to make some noise while you work."

Finished with the hay, Jonas came down the ladder.

"You knew I was graining the horses," Aaron said, tossing some chaff in his friend's direction.

"But you usually whistle or something. Why are you so quiet this morning?"

Aaron put his hat back on and rolled his shoulders to try to dislodge the hayseeds and chaff stuck to his back. All thought of horseplay had disappeared with Jonas's question.

"What would you say if I stayed around Weaver's Creek?"

Jonas leaned his pitchfork against the horse stall. "You mean you've changed your mind? You don't want to go west anymore?"

He paused, sifting through the empty promises his plans had held. "I'm not sure if I ever really wanted to. During the war, it seemed to be the only way I could start my life over."

"I think that is wonderful." Jonas's grin was sincere. "We'd love to have you stay here. There's plenty of room."

Aaron looked at the floor. "That isn't the plan. The Zooks have offered me a place on their farm and as a harness maker. I'm learning a lot from Casper."

"A home?"

A sweet thrill ran through him at those words. He hoped

it would never feel too familiar. "A home. A house, a trade, a family." His throat squeezed at that last word. He had lost the only family he knew and now God was healing that broken place.

Jonas laughed with delight and slapped Aaron's back. "The next thing you'll tell me is that you're going to become Amish."

Grinning, Aaron returned Jonas's gesture. "I start meeting with Gideon for membership instruction next week."

Jonas turned serious. "Do you mean it?" He gazed into Aaron's face. "You do mean it! We'll become members at the same time, then. The ministers said I can start my membership instruction as soon as it can be arranged." He returned the pitchfork to its place on the wall and took down the mucking rake. "The only thing left for you is to find a wife."

As Jonas went into the back of the barn to start cleaning the cow's pen, Aaron walked to the doorway of the barn, the same place he had stood on the day Ezra wandered into the bull's pasture. The same feeling overwhelmed him, but this time coupled with a certainty that he would find his dream. Somewhere, there would be a woman who could overlook his missing leg.

He ran his hand under his shirt collar, brushing out particles of hay. None of the women he had known before he was wounded would have done that, though. The thought of one of those—he shook his head at the man he had been—one of those saloon girls living here in this peaceful setting was impossible. No, whoever he married would have to be a special woman. One who could see beyond the man he used to be, beyond his wounded exterior, to the man he was becoming.

Movement on the road caught his attention. It was Elizabeth, walking across the bridge toward the house. On her way to see her family. He watched her sure gait, her slim figure looking barely larger than a child's at this distance. He didn't have to be close to see the warmth in her eyes and the way those crinkles appeared around them when she laughed. But she was vulnerable. If only she would listen to him. If only she would let him . . . An ache started in his chest and spread to his shoulders, his arms, down to his fingers, causing him to clench his fists. He wanted to protect her, but she had turned her back on him, setting her cap for Solomon Mast. He couldn't think of marrying a woman whose dreams were so different from his. Just like the other women he had known, what a man appeared to be on the outside was the only thing that mattered to her.

He grabbed the other mucking fork from the wall and entered the nearest box stall. He couldn't change her and couldn't change the past. But—

Pausing, his load of soiled straw midway to the wheelbarrow, the truth hit him with the sifting thoroughness of a forkful of hay, filling every pore of his being. He loved her. He loved Elizabeth. He loved that exasperating, stubborn, willful, beautiful woman. Dumping the load into the wheelbarrow, Aaron let that knowledge take hold.

But what could he do? He couldn't force Elizabeth to love him. She had her sights set on someone else. With gritted teeth, he thrust the fork in the horse's bedding once more and tossed a load into the wheelbarrow.

Her love would be a precious thing to earn, but Solomon— Simon Miller—would only use her and throw her away.

Somehow, he had to find evidence to prove what he knew was true and convince her to trust him.

And if Simon Miller acted first, before Aaron could prove who he really was?

Aaron leaned on the fork and wiped his sweating brow. He would need to stick close to Elizabeth so he would be there to protect her. She might resent him. She might even refuse to let him near her. But at least she would be safe.

⁓

By Saturday, Elizabeth no longer cared who knew about the terrible secret she had held close for so long. As she walked to Mamm's house, an elusive breath of joy blew through her. She wasn't looking for pity, although that would be the reaction of some of the women. She refused to speculate what Salome's opinion would be. The most important thing was to tell Mamm before any hint of a rumor reached her. Then, if Solomon decided to use her secret against her, at least he wouldn't take Mamm by surprise.

Mamm was in the kitchen pulling fresh loaves of bread from the oven. Elizabeth took in a deep breath of the homey aroma. She had known Mamm would be baking this morning, just as she did every Saturday.

"I need to put the pies in the oven next," Mamm said as Elizabeth came in the kitchen door, "and then we'll sit down together for a chat."

Elizabeth pumped water into the big cast-iron teakettle and set it on the hottest part of the stove. While it was heating up, she took the jar of tea from the cupboard.

"What brings you by this morning?" Mamm put the last pie in the oven and sat at the table.

"I have something to tell you." Elizabeth got two mugs from the cupboard and set them on the table with the teapot.

Mamm smiled. "It must be good news. I haven't seen you look this content for a long time."

"It isn't good news. It's something I should have told you a long time ago."

Elizabeth joined Mamm at the table. It would be several minutes before the water was hot enough to brew the tea.

"So, it isn't something about Solomon?"

"It's about Reuben."

Now that the time had come, Elizabeth wasn't certain how to begin. Mamm sighed as if she was preparing herself.

Elizabeth put her hands on the table, lacing her fingers together. She concentrated on the way each finger curved around the one next to it. "Several years ago, I found out I was expecting a baby."

"Ach, Elizabeth. You never told me."

"I . . . I couldn't. I knew Reuben should be the first to know." She looked at her mother. "Isn't that right?"

Mamm nodded. "For sure. Your husband should have been the one to hear the news before anyone else."

"But when I told him—" Elizabeth bit her lip as tears welled in her eyes. "When I told him, he didn't believe me. And then he accused me—" She took a deep breath, willing her voice to remain steady until she had told the whole story. "He believed that he couldn't be the child's father. That someone else must have . . ."

She swallowed. No more words would come. The teakettle

started grumbling and Mamm rose to pour the hot water into the teapot to brew.

"So, Reuben didn't believe he was the father of your baby?" Mamm took Elizabeth's hands as she sat at the table again.

"He caused my baby to miscarry." The words rushed out. "I couldn't tell you. I was too ashamed and too scared."

"When you were married to him, I was afraid that he might have mistreated you. I felt like we had lost you and we didn't know what to do. How to reach out to you. But it sounds like your life was much harder than we imagined."

"It wasn't your fault. I could have come to you at any time . . . but I told myself that you wouldn't want me since I had turned my back on you and the family." Mamm started shaking her head and Elizabeth went on. "I know that isn't true. I should have come home as soon as I knew the terrible mistake I had made. But I didn't, and my baby paid for it with his life."

Mamm was silent as the clock in the front room ticked away the minutes. Finally, she spoke. "You can't blame yourself for what Reuben did. If he were still alive, I would have a hard time forgiving him for how he treated you and your child. But why are you telling me this now?"

"Because someone else knows about it." Elizabeth drew a deep breath. "I decided that I wasn't protecting anyone but Reuben by keeping that secret, but by burying it, I was reliving that horrible time over and over again. I wanted to be free."

"The truth shall set you free," Mamm said, a faint smile on her trembling lips.

Uneven footsteps on the back porch told Elizabeth that

Aaron was on his way in. She wiped any remaining tears with the edge of her apron and Mamm rose quickly and opened the oven to check on the pies. Aaron paused in the doorway.

"I didn't mean to interrupt anything," he said as he stood with one hand on the doorknob. "I just came in for the pail of slops for the pigs."

Elizabeth forced a smile as he went to the sink and lifted the pail from its spot underneath. He turned to go out again, then paused, looking at her.

"Is everything all right?"

"For sure it is." Elizabeth fought to keep her smile steady. "Why wouldn't it be?"

He glanced at Mamm, standing at the stove with her back to them, then at the still-empty mugs, then at Elizabeth again.

"No reason." He shifted the pail in his hand. "But if there is something wrong, I listen pretty well."

No man had ever wanted to listen to her problems, not since she was a little girl and Datt would take her on his lap. Aaron's offer tapped gently on a closed place in her heart.

"I'll remember that," she said.

After Aaron was on his way to the barn, Mamm came back to the table, a plate of piecrust cookies in her hand.

"I made these for your datt, but he won't miss a few."

Elizabeth picked up one of the diamond-shaped cookies dusted with cinnamon. For as long as she could remember, Mamm had made these cookies from the leftover scraps of piecrust dough on baking day. As she took a bite, the taste of the flaky pastry took her back to her childhood.

"Have I ever told you how sorry I am that I ever looked twice at Reuben?"

Mamm patted her hand. "I always knew the Good Lord would help you find your way through."

Elizabeth took another bite of her cookie. What would Mamm say if she knew about Solomon's intentions? He would be a man her parents would approve of, but Dulcey's warnings rang in her ears. Solomon couldn't be the man his servant had described, but only Dulcey knew what he was like behind closed doors. She reached for another cookie.

Solomon seemed to be the man who could make her dreams come true. He wanted children and was a good Amishman. He was friendly and helpful to everyone in the community. She wouldn't risk losing her chance at a good life just because Dulcey didn't like him.

"I can't get over how Aaron has changed," Mamm said, breaking into her thoughts. "When Jonas first brought him home, I didn't know what to think. He knew nothing about our ways and appeared to be so sickly. But he has learned our language and willingly goes to church with us, and it turns out that he's related to our Zook families."

"But he isn't Amish."

Mamm's eyebrows rose. "Does he need to be Amish?"

Elizabeth shook her head. "I thought you were getting ready to say he would make a good husband."

Laughing, Mamm squeezed her hand. "I don't know who would be a good husband for you, but if Aaron was Amish—if he joined the church—would you consider him for a husband? The two of you get along well."

"I made a promise to myself that I would never marry a man who wasn't Amish. I made that mistake once. Aaron isn't Amish, and I don't think he'll ever join the church. He wants to go west, not stay around here."

"You never know what might happen," Mamm said as she went to the oven to check on the pies.

Elizabeth finished her cup of tea. Solomon might not be perfect, but she could trust him to treat her well. He was the man to help her dream of having a family come true.

She reached for another cookie, ignoring the unsettled thoughts in the back of her mind.

~~~~~

One bothersome thing about Elizabeth Kaufman, Solomon thought as he fought boredom during the first sermon on Sunday morning, was that she was cautious. Too cautious.

He forced his knee to stop bouncing and glanced at the man sitting beside him. Amos Beiler sat with a straight back on his bench, gaze forward, as he watched Gideon Fischer preach, his eyes widening or narrowing, depending on whether he agreed with the point Gideon was making or not. In front of him, Abraham Weaver's head nodded.

Looking across the aisle to the women's side, he let a brief smile twitch his lips as he watched Salome. She had proven to be a better source of information than he had first thought. Thanks to her, there was little he didn't know about the members of the community.

The Beilers' home was too small for Sunday meeting, but they took their turn at hosting twice a year like everyone else. At least the place had plenty of windows on all sides of the house, and they were all open to the warm late-June air.

Solomon stifled a sigh. By the end of the morning, these backless benches would be torturous. But it was the price he needed to pay. A landholding the size he had his eyes on didn't come easy. He watched Abraham's snowy hair rub against the man's neck as his head bobbed. What had Weaver done to acquire his farm? No one achieved the success that he enjoyed without destroying a few lives to get there. Two sections of land, if he included Elizabeth's quarter section. One thousand two hundred eighty acres of prime farmland, and parts of it were still uncut timber. He flexed his fingers.

Old Abraham would die soon, and the Weaver land would be divided. Before then, he had to have Elizabeth's land firmly in his grasp. She was the key to everything.

The chatter he had heard this morning before the services started was unfortunate. He thought he had the information he needed to keep her in line, but for some reason, she had told everyone she knew about it, not only Dulcey.

"A secret," Dulcey had said.

But it wasn't a secret anymore.

He let his eyes drift to the side without moving his head. Elizabeth sat one row in front of him next to some of those tiresome brats. She was lovely, at least. Living with her wouldn't be as painful as it had been with his last wife. The cow. It had been a chore to just sit across the table from her during the few meals they ate together. But when she had started complaining, well, he knew how to put an end to that. It had been quick, and the fact that there had been a child involved made him the object of sympathy for months afterward.

Elizabeth was a better prize. The curve of her neck looked

soft, with fine hairs curling against her tanned skin. The future was a ripe plum ready to fall into his hand, except for her skittishness. He had worked too hard for the privilege of taking her hand, but she had never let him go any further than that. He wouldn't be able to compromise her that way, but he would find another way.

After the meal, Solomon looked for an opportunity to steer Elizabeth away from her friends. Soon, he would have to start weaning her away from them for good. A confidant was a threat to his plans. Finally, she left the kitchen to join the group of women sitting together in the yard. He intercepted her just before she reached the door of the farmhouse.

"I haven't had the opportunity to visit with you this morning." He stood close to her, bending his head toward hers.

"I've been busy."

She backed against the wall and glanced toward the door, but Solomon had made sure to place himself between her and her view of her family and friends.

"I thought perhaps we could go for a drive this afternoon. We need to talk about our future plans."

Then she looked at him, her expression calm. Where was the eagerness most girls showed at this stage?

"We do need to talk. Was the deed in order? And does the marriage certificate prove that I am Reuben's heir?"

Solomon was all too aware of the possibility of others listening to their conversation. "We can't talk here." He gave her his most seductive look, but she didn't respond.

"Let's take a walk, then. We can walk down the road as far as your house, and then back again." She bit her lower lip and glanced toward the door again. "I'll meet you at the end of the farm lane in a few minutes."

Ten minutes later, Solomon paced in the road, waiting. Finally, she appeared and fell into step beside him as they walked down the road. She had taken control of the afternoon, leaving him to catch up. That wasn't how things were going to be, and he needed to show her that now. But how to do that without scaring her off was the problem.

"I wondered if you were ready to set a date for our wedding." He caught her hand in his. "I can't wait until we are man and wife."

He stopped walking and pulled her closer to him, bending his head toward her, ready to catch those soft lips in a kiss. To his surprise, she let him place a quick kiss on her lips before she turned away and continued walking, her arms crossed.

"I'm not convinced we should get married. I've made the mistake of marrying the wrong man once, and I don't want to do it again." She looked at him, her expression hopeful. That was his opening.

"Have I ever done anything to make you think we weren't meant to be together? Just think of the home we will build together." He counted. *One, two, three.* "And our family. The children that will fill our home."

She stopped, then turned to face him, her eyes searching his. "Is that what you really want, Solomon?"

He took both of her hands in his. "A home. A family. You by my side."

Her expression hardened. "I thought you might only want to marry me because I own the quarter section of land next to yours."

She was too smart for her own good. He smiled. "I have to admit, that was one reason why I was attracted to you at first. But now that I know you—"

"If I hadn't found those papers, the deed and my marriage certificate, would it have made a difference?"

Solomon worked to keep the irritation off his face. It was time to use his ace. "There was no marriage certificate."

That surprised her. Her face turned white and her mouth dropped open. "I saw it. I read it. It was in the papers I gave to you."

Solomon shook his head, steadying his sorrowful expression.

"You were mistaken. There is no proof that you were ever married to that Reuben character. Obviously, the man was a reprobate and took advantage of a young girl."

Her face was still white. He led her to a fallen log at the crossroads where she could sit and have a view of the roof of his house. He sat next to her and placed one arm around her shoulders.

"Without the certificate, how will I prove that I own Reuben's land?"

"I've already taken care of that."

Solomon smiled to reassure her. The wheels were in motion. He would own her land as soon as they were married.

"The problem," he said, keeping his voice calm and reassuring, "is that the Amish community thinks you are a moral woman. Foolish, perhaps, but moral. They believe you were in an unfortunate situation, having no idea of the truth."

She shook her head. "The truth is that I was married to Reuben."

"The truth is that there is no proof. I'll give you the benefit of the doubt. Perhaps he lied to you and you believed you were married for all those years."

Elizabeth's eyes blinked several times, her fingers were cold and trembling. Solomon could have laughed. He had her right where he wanted her.

"But I thought that even if a person isn't legally married, that they are considered married after a time?"

"You mean common-law marriage?" When she nodded, he adopted his most condescending tone. "Oh, my dear, do you think the church would consider that to be a true marriage?"

She dabbed at her eyes with the hem of her apron. "What can I do?"

Solomon rubbed her shoulder, then brought her closer to his side. "There is only one solution. We must get married before people start asking questions. You know how damaging rumors can be. All it would take would be for someone to mention something to the wrong person . . ." He let his voice trail off, letting Elizabeth draw her own conclusions.

"I . . . I need to think about this."

Elizabeth stood. Solomon took her arm to walk her back to the Beilers' farm, but she pulled away.

"I'm going to walk home." She took a step back. "Please tell the others I'm all right. Only a bit tired."

Solomon weighed the risk of letting her go against forcing her immediate agreement to their wedding. Elizabeth was cautious. He decided to give her time.

"When can I expect an answer to my proposal?"

She gave him a quizzical look, then shook her head as if

clearing cobwebs from her mind. "I'll let you know in a day or two."

"Until then." He bent to give her another kiss, but she pulled back and walked away from him, down the road toward her home.

Solomon watched her go. He could pursue her. Force her. But his first thought had been correct. Let the rumors about her past start circulating, and she would come to him of her own free will. Chuckling, he turned to walk back to the Beilers' farm and the willing ears of Salome.

13

Aaron had watched Solomon and Elizabeth as they walked down the road. Elizabeth had gone willingly, he could see that, but he still paced between the house, the barn, and the end of the farm lane.

Jonas and Levi were near the barn in the shade, talking with Dan and a few of the other men. He stood with them, not listening to the conversation, then decided to go and look down the road again. Perhaps Solomon and Elizabeth were coming back. But Jonas followed him and caught his sleeve.

"What's wrong with you? I've never seen you this jumpy."

Aaron wiped the perspiration off his nose. "It's probably nothing. Just my imagination."

"Your imagination doesn't make you act like this."

"Solomon and Elizabeth went down the road together a little while ago."

Jonas shrugged. "It's common enough for couples who are courting to go off together during the afternoon. They'll be back."

Aaron glared at his friend. "Who says they're courting?"

"I only assumed they were, if they walked off alone. I know Elizabeth has been interested in him, and it makes sense. They're both widowed, both alone. They're neighbors. Why wouldn't they try to find out if marriage is a good idea?"

Aaron stared at his foot, leaning on his cane. "I don't think Solomon Mast is the man he says he is, but I don't have proof."

Jonas watched him, his arms crossed. "How certain are you?"

"I know what I know. I'm sure."

"Except that your imagination could be making you think things that aren't true."

Jonas could be right, but Aaron was sure he remembered Simon Miller correctly . . . or did he?

Touching Aaron's shoulder, Jonas nodded toward the road. "There's Solomon now."

"But where is Elizabeth?"

Aaron made his way toward Solomon. The other man had stopped near a group of the women who were sitting together in a circle near the house. As he drew close, Katie left the group, heading toward the house.

Aaron stopped her. "Did Solomon say where Elizabeth is? She didn't come back from her walk with him."

Katie fanned herself with her hand, her face flushed. "She told him she was tired and not feeling well, so he walked her home."

She went on past him and Aaron tapped his cane on the ground, watching Solomon. It didn't add up. Solomon hadn't taken his buggy, and he hadn't been gone long enough to go all the way to Elizabeth's house and back.

Heading down the farm lane, he started off after Elizabeth. Solomon could be telling the truth, but the only way to find out was to find Elizabeth.

By the time he reached the cabin that Katie and Elizabeth shared, Aaron was walking slowly, nursing his bad leg. When he saw Elizabeth sitting on the front porch, he was relieved, then disgusted with himself for being so suspicious. He stopped in the shade, resting, until she saw him and waved.

"Aaron, what are you doing here? Come on up and sit down."

He felt each step up to the porch and sat heavily in the chair closest to the door. Elizabeth sat with her feet under her, a glass of water in her hand.

"That looks good," Aaron said, nodding toward her glass. "Could I trouble you for some?"

When she brought it, he took a long drink. The water was cool and sweet.

"Did you walk all the way here from the Beilers'?" Elizabeth asked when he finished. "It's such a hot afternoon. You should have waited until evening."

Aaron turned the cup in his hands. Now that he was here and she was safe, it did seem a bit silly.

"I was worried about you. When Solomon came back from your walk without you, I wasn't sure what happened."

"He didn't tell you I came home?"

"He did."

"But you didn't believe him."

Aaron ignored the frown on her face. "I worry about you."

"There is nothing to worry about. Solomon and I are getting along fine. I know you think he's this man that you met in Virginia, but I haven't seen anything that tells me he's anyone except who he says he is."

"Then why don't you seem happy?"

She shot a look at him. "I'm happy."

Then why the tears in her eyes on Saturday when he saw her in Lydia's kitchen? "I think you're mistaken." He turned his cup in his hands again, watching the droplets of water threatening to fall from its sweating surface. "I think you're telling me what you hope is true, and you're trying to believe it yourself."

Minutes passed. A cardinal called from the tops of the pines. Elizabeth sniffed as if she was trying to keep from crying.

"You don't know anything, Aaron. You're only guessing. Solomon has asked me to marry him, and I'm thinking of saying I will. He can give me everything I've ever wanted."

"If he's a respectable Amishman, solid, secure, and faithful, like you claim, then why do you always look a bit frightened when you're around him?"

She snorted. "You're imagining things."

"You look like you're afraid you'll do something that will displease him. You've seen him when he's angry, haven't you?"

Silence. The cardinal called again.

Aaron steepled his fingers, looking through them to the porch floor. "Do you love him?"

More silence.

"Does he love you?"

"Of course, he loves me. That's why he wants to marry me."

He turned his head, catching her gaze in his own. "It isn't love if you feel like you need to earn it. How many times do you do what he wants just to appease him?"

"You don't know what you're talking about, Aaron Zook." She stood, her fists clenched. "It isn't any of your concern if I marry Solomon or not, and you have no right to question what I'm doing. You aren't my father or . . . or my brother."

She stomped past him to the door, her bare feet thudding on the wooden porch floor. She paused with her hand on the door as if she wanted to say more but went inside, letting the wooden screen door slap closed on its spring.

Aaron rose and started the walk back to Abraham and Lydia's house. She was right. He had been too harsh. But he couldn't stand by and watch her make the biggest mistake of her life.

What would he do if she married Solomon?

He thumped along the dusty lane down to the road.

He would have to watch them on church Sundays. Watch their family grow. Watch her face for signs that she was unhappy. But he wouldn't be able to do anything about it, not once the wedding was over. Until then he had hope she would come to her senses.

But if she didn't . . . If she didn't, he would have to leave. She would be another memory he would leave behind.

Aaron stopped at the trail that led across a log bridge to the house Jonas was building for Katie. The rafters rose above the little willows that lined the creek, and he knew the siding was almost complete. Soon Jonas and Katie would be getting married and he would bring his bride home to this house he had built for her.

How would he explain his leaving to Casper? The man had taken him into his family. They had talked about his future and started drawing up plans for his house. He shook his head, still unable to believe it was true. His house.

Would Casper resent him for running away and leaving behind the family he had so recently found? Would they mourn for him as Casper's father had mourned for Grandpop?

Being part of a family meant making the commitment to stick together through good times and bad. Aaron ground the end of his cane into the soft gravel on the roadside. A real man would face up to the bad and go through it, not run away from it.

He would stay, even though he was helpless to change the course of the disaster he saw ahead for the woman he loved.

Elizabeth didn't sleep well that night. It seemed that every time she sank into slumber, she would hear Solomon's voice again, telling her there was no marriage certificate.

Finally, as the approaching dawn turned the sky outside her window from black to a slightly lighter shade of gray, she gave up. As she got ready for the day, she went through finding the metal box again in her mind. Step by step, she followed her actions in her memory. The Confederate money, the deed to the farm, the letter from Reuben's father. And the marriage certificate. She was certain she had seen it. The writing had been faint. Feathery. Had she put it back in the box instead of taking it to Solomon?

205

In the kitchen, she built up a small fire in the stove and started the coffee. There was a chill in the air this morning as the weather was changing. Clouds covered the sky she could see between the pine trees, low-hanging and dark. Thunder rumbled in the distance.

She needed to talk to Ruby. Once the thought passed through her mind, it took on an urgency. Her mind was foggy with trying to remember where the marriage certificate could be. Solomon's words swirled in her consciousness, confusing her. He seemed to say one thing and mean another. Did she feel this way only because she hadn't slept well?

Thunder rumbled again, still far away. If she hurried, she could reach Ruby's before the rain started. Her sister wouldn't mind company, even this early in the morning.

Elizabeth scribbled a note to Katie, apologizing for leaving her with the morning chores, and hitched up Pie. The pony sensed her hurry and trotted through the gray morning. The thunder was closer now and Pie put his ears back. He didn't like the rain.

"Keep going," Elizabeth said. "You'll stay dry in Gideon's barn."

Pie swiveled his ears and trotted faster. In only a few minutes they had reached Ruby's house. She drove Pie through the open barn doors where Gideon was bringing the cows in from the pasture for their milking.

He called to her from the back of the barn. "Elizabeth? What brings you here so early this morning?"

"I wanted to talk to Ruby, so I came to help with her Monday chores."

Gideon let himself out of the cows' pen and took Pie's

halter. "You go on in before the rain starts while I take care of Pie. Ruby will appreciate your company. Rainy days always make her a bit gloomy."

Big drops were beginning to fall as Elizabeth ran from the barn to the house. By the time she reached the cover of the back porch, the rain was falling in sheets. Ruby had seen her and opened the door.

"Welcome, Elizabeth! I didn't expect to see you today."

Elizabeth gave her sister a hug, then went around the table to hug each of her nephews and nieces, avoiding their sticky oatmeal mouths. "I hoped you might like some company today. I know how you hate rainy Mondays."

"For sure, I do." Ruby turned back to the stove where a pan of bacon was frying. "I'll have to hang the laundry in the loft, but I can't complain too much about a summer rain. We know the crops need it."

Elizabeth ate breakfast with Ruby and Gideon and their family, enjoying the lively company. Ten-year-old Roseanna took charge of little Lovinia after the meal was over, taking her into the front room to play until her nap time. Eight-year-old Sophia and the boys, Ezra and Daniel, cleared the table, piling the dishes in the dishpan. Gideon stood at the door, watching the steady rain.

"It's eased some," he said, reaching for his hat. "I have plenty to do in the barn, and the boys can help." He lifted Daniel in his arms and handed Ezra's hat to him. "We'll be back in time for dinner."

As they left, Sophia joined her sisters in the front room, leaving Ruby and Elizabeth alone.

"Now," Ruby said as she poured hot water from her

teakettle into the dishpan, "tell me what this is all about. You didn't just come all this way to help me with my chores."

Elizabeth took the bar of soap off the shelf above the sink and started paring shavings into the hot water.

"You're right. I thought we could talk."

"About you and Solomon?"

Elizabeth replaced the soap in its dish. "Are we that obvious?"

"You left the fellowship time after church yesterday and went off together. Then Solomon came back alone. When he said you weren't feeling well, Mamm almost went after you, but Solomon said it was only the heat and you would be all right."

"That's almost true."

"Almost?" Ruby tested the temperature of the dishwater, then pumped some cool water in. "Were you feeling ill?"

Elizabeth opened the cupboard to get a clean dish towel. "I wasn't ill. I just wanted to think over what Solomon and I had discussed."

Ruby began washing the plates. She rinsed each one in the pan of clean hot water and handed them to Elizabeth.

"Are you going to tell me what the two of you talked about, or do I need to pry for the details?" Ruby made a face and Elizabeth laughed.

"I'll tell you because I need your advice."

"All right. I'll try." Ruby finished the plates and reached for the bowls.

"Solomon asked me to marry him."

Her sister grinned and gave her a hug, wet hands and all. "I thought he might get around to that sooner or later."

Then Ruby grasped her shoulders and held her at arm's length. "You don't seem as happy about this as I thought you would."

"I'm just not sure why he wants to marry me."

"Who wouldn't want to marry you?"

"I mean, he is such a . . . well . . . handsome and desirable man. He could have his choice of any woman around. Why would he choose me?"

"Because he loves you?"

Elizabeth dried the rest of the plates while she thought about Ruby's words. He had never spoken of love, only about their future together. "He says he wants a family. You have seen his house. He wants to fill it with children."

Ruby took her hands from the dishwater. "Isn't that what you want, too?"

"Did Mamm tell you?"

"About your baby? She did. I'm so sorry, Elizabeth. I wish I had known."

"I wish you had too. But I didn't tell Mamm what I found out yesterday." She pointed to the bowls still soaking in the water and Ruby started scrubbing them again. "It appears that Reuben and I were never legally married."

Ruby didn't say anything, and Elizabeth waited. She dried the first bowl, and then the second.

"I always thought you were. You said you and Reuben were married in Millersburg."

"I always thought I was too. I'm sure I saw the marriage certificate, but Solomon says it doesn't exist. He said if he and I get married quickly, then no one will worry about whether Reuben and I were really married or not."

"So, you think you might marry him because of that?"

"That's why I wanted to talk to you. Is that enough of a reason to get married?"

Ruby finished washing the dishes and swirled her dishcloth through the rinse water. "Do you love him?"

"Aaron asked me that same question."

"Aaron?" Ruby's brows went up. "You talked to Aaron about Solomon?"

Elizabeth shrugged her shoulders, not sure what to say. "He asked, and I told him about Solomon's proposal."

"What did he say?"

"He doesn't like Solomon and doesn't think I should even talk to him."

"That is interesting." Ruby wrung out her dishcloth and hung it on a bar under the shelf that held the soap. "But what did you tell Aaron? Do you love Solomon?"

"I didn't tell him anything." Elizabeth hung her dish towel on the same bar. "How can you tell if you love someone? I was married to Reuben for thirteen years, and I still don't know if I ever loved him."

"That man killed whatever love you might have had for him."

"If I married for love when I married Reuben, then why should I take that chance again? Don't you think I should marry for a good reason and let love happen later if it will?"

"It depends on the reason. Why would you marry Solomon?"

Elizabeth pulled her lower lip between her teeth. Ruby would understand. She had a good home now, with a loving husband and children, but a few years ago all she had were dreams, just like Elizabeth.

"He could be my last chance for happiness. With him, I could have everything I've dreamed of—a home with a loving husband, and children." Tears filled her eyes. "I can see the fulfillment of that dream in front of me, waiting for me to reach out and take it. All I have to do is tell Solomon I will marry him, and it would be mine."

"But what good is that dream if you don't have love?"

From the front room, baby Lovinia started crying.

"It's time for her nap." Ruby turned to go to her daughter, then hesitated. "Think carefully, Elizabeth. You know what it's like to be married to a man who doesn't love you. Don't make that same mistake again."

As Ruby left, Elizabeth turned to the pile of laundry in the corner of the kitchen and started sorting it. Was Ruby right? Or could she make Solomon love her?

Elizabeth held up a small dress, one of the baby's. She held the little scrap of fabric to her chest. If she could give Solomon a baby—a son—then he would have to love her.

On Thursday, Solomon hitched his black horse to the buggy for his weekly trip into Millersburg. Dulcey had brushed the horse and washed the buggy early in the morning, but Solomon still inspected his rig from all sides, rubbing off bits of dust with a rag before he was satisfied. Then he went into the house to dress for the trip.

Dulcey had laid out his town clothes while he was in the barn. Solomon dressed himself in the linen shirt and wool suit. It was a warm day for such attire, but he hadn't been able to purchase a linen suit yet. Patterson had divulged the location of his money, but it wasn't as much as Solomon had hoped, and he was close to the end of it. Soon, though, if his business dealings in the South panned out, he wouldn't have to worry about cash again. That, added to his land-holdings here in Ohio, would provide well for him for the rest of his days.

He put the finishing touches on his attire and combed his hair back. He picked up his bowler hat and gloves and went downstairs. Using the mirror in the hall, he adjusted his cravat and settled the hat on his head.

"Dulcey!"

The young woman came from the kitchen and stood next to him, her head bowed as he had taught her.

"While I'm in town today, I don't want you to let anyone come into the house."

"Yessir."

"Not even Elizabeth. If she comes, tell her you're too busy to visit. I don't want you talking to her unless I'm in the house."

"Yessir."

"What am I having for supper tonight?"

"Cold roast, sliced fine, with pickled beets and cottage cheese."

He turned to glare at her. "Do I look like one of these Amish farmers?"

"No, Masta."

"Then will you come up with an appropriate menu for me?"

"I can roast a ham, but it will make the kitchen awful hot."

The stroke with the back of his hand was swift and hard, knocking Dulcey off her feet.

"I don't care if the kitchen is hot. That isn't my problem. I want the ham, with mashed potatoes and green beans. Cook them with bacon. And I want fresh bread. The toast you gave me this morning was stale."

Dulcey cowered on the floor.

"I'll be back at my usual time, and I expect my supper to be on the table, hot and waiting for me." He nudged her with his foot. "Do you understand?"

She nodded. "Yessir."

As he drove toward Millersburg, he considered the state of his household. He needed another servant. Perhaps a man to be a likely husband for Dulcey. The two could work for him as cheaply as one, and then the farm work would get done without having to soil his own hands. Then as Dulcey's children grew, they could also work in his growing household. The vision pleased him. He would make inquiries in town.

The livery stable he normally used was full, so he drove to the new establishment down the street and made arrangements with the boy for his horse, requesting that the animal be fed, rested, and ready to go by two o'clock. The next stop was the post office. The rest of the Weaver's Creek community used the post office in Farmerstown, but he didn't want his business passing through the hands of the shopkeepers there. He called for his mail and took it to his favorite bench in the shade of the bank on the south side of Main Street. The limestone walls were cool, even in the middle of the afternoon, and it made a pleasant place to observe the business of the town as he read his letters.

Sifting through the envelopes, he saw one from that lawyer who had contacted Elizabeth. His last missive should have been enough to dissuade them from trying to contact her again.

Solomon slit open the envelope and scanned the letter, then shoved it back into its cover. Keeping a pleasant look on his face as he nodded to the businessmen who passed by on the sidewalk, he went over the letter in his mind.

The woman in Mississippi was desperate, the letter had said. She had been cast out of her family when she married Reuben Kaufman and could not return to them with her son. The only resource she had was the property Reuben had mentioned that he owned in Ohio. She needed possession of that property to support herself and her son, and it was owed to her son as his only legacy from his father.

Solomon slit open the next envelope in the pile. Stupid woman. She should have known better than to marry a reprobate like Kaufman. He dismissed her from his mind as he read through the letter in his hands and fingered the check that had been included. The sale of the property he had invested in had gone through, and he and the rest of the syndicate had realized a tidy sum. The next three letters yielded similar results, and Solomon rose from his seat. He would deposit the checks in the bank before he left town. With results like this, he would consider expanding his business ventures in the South. The postwar years might be even more profitable than the last four years had been.

When he returned to the livery stable, the large black man

that had been there before was hitching his horse to the buggy. He turned to greet Solomon when he came in.

"The horse is all ready for you, just as promised."

"Very good." Solomon tossed a dollar coin to the man, then looked at him a second time. Young, strong, and polite. "Are you looking for a job, boy?"

The man's eyes narrowed. "No sir, I'm not."

"Well, if you're ever unhappy with your employment here, I can offer you a job on my farm. I'm looking for a strong young man like yourself. You'd be overseeing the whole place, if you're fit for that kind of work."

The man threaded the reins through the guides on the buggy. "No, thank you. I'm not interested."

"I have a girl working for me. She doesn't have a husband, and I'd like to find a man who would . . ." The man's expression had grown hard. Solomon frowned at him. "I can see you wouldn't suit me at all."

He climbed into the buggy seat and picked up the reins, but the man laid his arm over the horse's back.

"Mister, my name is Elijah Wilson, and I own this livery stable."

He pointed to the sign above the door, inviting customers to come back to Wilson's Livery as they drove out onto the street.

The man continued. "You are welcome to use the services of my establishment as long as you remember that I am a free man. I don't have to listen to any customer of mine talk the way you have to me this afternoon. If you can't respect me and my property, sir, you are not welcome back here."

"You don't need to worry about that." Solomon sat

straight in his seat, looking down on Elijah Wilson. "You will not see my buggy in any establishment owned by a—"

Before Solomon could finish his sentence, Wilson stepped aside and slapped the horse on the rump. Solomon lost the reins and clung to the dashboard of the buggy as the horse jumped, then galloped out of the livery stable and down the road. By the time Solomon regained his grip on the reins and was sitting in his seat again, he had decided that Elijah Wilson was definitely not the man he wanted to hire to work on his farm.

14

Elizabeth woke on Sunday morning feeling stiff and sore. Her head throbbed. Every time she had tried to sleep during the night, the same dream pursued her—the dream of Reuben chasing her, catching her, overpowering her, smothering her. And every time she had woken with a start, sitting up in bed, breathing hard.

Swinging her feet to the floor, she gathered her blanket around her and headed downstairs, following the smell of coffee.

"You're finally awake," Katie said as she pushed a chair away from the table for Elizabeth with her foot. "The coffee has been ready for an hour and you look like you need it. Didn't you sleep well?"

Elizabeth took the pot from the back of the stove where it had been keeping warm and poured a cup. As she sat down, she said, "I'm glad today isn't a church Sunday."

Katie leaned forward. "I heard you dreaming during the night. Was it that same dream about Reuben?"

"I don't know how I can stop them, and they're getting more frequent. Ever since . . ."

Elizabeth's mind went in a direction it had never gone before.

"Are you all right? Elizabeth?"

"I'm all right." She forced a smile and took a swallow of her coffee. "I just remembered something I have to do this morning."

"On a Sunday?" Katie turned to watch her as she took a final swallow of coffee and poured the remainder of the cup into the slop bucket. "You won't miss our picnic lunch today, will you?"

The picnic. Elizabeth had forgotten all about it. Jonas and Katie had invited her to come along with Levi and Elise. She had been looking forward to it so she could get to know the new girl better.

"You'll have to start without me. You're going to that spot on the Beilers' farm, aren't you? The one by the little stream? I'll join you later if I can."

Elizabeth headed back upstairs to get dressed. Those dreams of Reuben had come more frequently ever since Solomon had come into her life, and in last night's dreams, she didn't know if the man attacking her had been Reuben or Solomon. Somewhere in her mind, the two men had become one. Why hadn't she seen it before? Aaron had been right—Solomon was not a man to be trusted. She had to find that marriage certificate. If she found that, then Solomon would have no hold over her.

When Jonas came to pick up Katie, Elizabeth stood on the porch, watching them walk down the lane together under the pine trees. Bitterness welled up, but she shoved it down. Katie and Jonas deserved their happiness. Perhaps someday, her dreams would come true, too, but not with Solomon.

The morning was pleasant for early July. Elizabeth hurried down the road, staying behind Jonas and Katie until they passed out of sight up the hill, going toward the Beilers' farm. As soon as she reached the turnoff to Reuben's cabin, she quickened her pace.

Pulling the door open to let the morning light in, Elizabeth went straight to the loose floorboard and pried it up. The box was still there. She opened it, dumped the papers onto the floor, and sifted through them. The letter from Reuben's father's lawyer, more Confederate money . . . but no marriage certificate.

After she gathered the papers into a loose pile, Elizabeth sat on the floor, leaning against the bedstead. There was no question in her mind that she had seen the marriage certificate. She remembered the faint writing. Her name and Reuben's. The official seal from the notary public. She hadn't imagined it. But where was it?

As she retraced her movements in her mind, a seething restlessness filled her breast. Her feelings might have been muddled by Solomon's handsome face, but now her mind was clear. She had found the certificate in the box along with the deed to the farm. One quarter section of land in Reuben's name, or his heir's. She was Reuben's heir. The land was hers.

The deed and the certificate had both been in her hand when she had driven to Solomon's house. He had taken the papers from her, then she had gone into the kitchen to have dinner with Dulcey.

Where had Solomon gone? Into his study. With the papers.

He had lied to her last week. He had the certificate. Solomon lied only to gain power over her, to force her to marry him quickly.

But why would he do that? Because of the land?

Elizabeth put her fist to her mouth. What about the letter from Mississippi? There was someone else who could claim the land. If the marriage certificate existed, then Elizabeth's ownership of the land was without question. If she married Solomon, then the land would belong to him. So why would Solomon say the certificate didn't exist?

A cloud passed over the sun and a gust of wind blew the door shut, making Elizabeth jump. With last night's dreams fresh in her mind, the shadowy corners of the cabin seethed with memories. She jumped to her feet.

"Never again, Reuben Kaufman!" She shouted the words into the air. "I'm not going to be any man's victim again!"

Elizabeth felt for the matches she had always kept above the kitchen cabinet. There was one match left. She went back to the pile of useless papers she had left on the floor. Her mouth dry, she struck the match and held the faltering flame close to a Confederate bill. The dry paper caught, the flame gaining strength, full of color from the ink. She fed the little fire with more bills, then the letter, then some dried leaves she found on the floor.

Backing away from the growing flame, Elizabeth found more fuel. Old kindling in the box by the fireplace. Pieces of the beam that had fallen. The kitchen cabinet door that pulled easily off its hinges.

The fire took on a life of its own, jumping up to lick the

leg of the bed, spreading across the wooden floor, curling around the beam. Elizabeth backed toward the door. The flames no longer needed her to feed them.

They leaped to the wardrobe where Reuben had kept the belt he had used on her. The stand where he had inverted his boots to dry. The box where he had kept his liquor . . . all burning. All consumed by the fire that had started from the single flame of her match.

Elizabeth pushed against the door, making her way outside, and air rushed in. The inside of the cabin grew into a ball of flame. Elizabeth fled to her garden and stood, watching the fire. Flames licked the logs through the places where Aaron had pulled out the chinking. The orange and yellow fingers crawled up the dry logs to the roof, completely consuming the cabin. Soon it would be reduced to a pile of ashes.

Tears streamed down Elizabeth's cheeks as she watched the fire devour years of nightmarish memories . . . destroying them forever.

"*Look to Christ*," Gideon had said, "*and he will set you free.*"

"Why don't I feel free?" Elizabeth sank to her knees. "Dear Lord, why don't I feel free?"

Aaron sat by the stream that ran through the corner of the Beilers' farm, plucking blades of grass and throwing them into the water. The place was pleasant in the shade with the sound of the water trickling through. The picnic lunch that Katie and Elise had brought was delicious, including the blackberry cobbler Katie had made for dessert. She had even brought a small jar of cream that she set in the running water until it was time to pour the cool rich liquid over the treat at the end of their meal. Aaron hadn't tasted anything that good since he was a young boy.

But now the sun was past the noon hour and the two couples had gone for a walk, Katie and Jonas in one direction and Levi and Elise in another.

"It's no problem," he told the chipmunk that peered at him around a tree trunk. "They want to be alone together, I understand that."

But . . .

He threw another blade of grass into the water and watched it float away. Katie had said Elizabeth might come. She had told her she might be late, but she would try to come.

Aaron yanked a dandelion from the grassy bank and threw the yellow flower into the stream after the grass.

She was with Solomon. Of course, she was with Solomon.

He plucked another dandelion blossom and spun the stem between his fingers.

Most likely making plans for their wedding.

The stem dissolved into a mess of pulp and he threw that flower into the water too.

He didn't blame the others for leaving him behind with the excuse that someone needed to be in the agreed-upon spot when Elizabeth showed up. He wasn't good company today.

A cloud passed over the sun and he looked up. It wasn't alone. Other clouds in the west were following on its tail on a gust of wind. It might rain tonight.

Then, on the next breeze, he smelled smoke. A brush fire? Aaron got to his feet and climbed to the top of the rise above the stream. Another whiff of smoke. Not grass or brush. This was a wood fire.

"Jonas!" He turned, looking for his friends. "Levi! Where are you?"

The smoke smell grew heavier.

The two couples came running toward him.

"Where is that smoke from?" Jonas said when he came closer.

Aaron pointed south, toward the Weaver's Creek valley. "In that direction. It's wood smoke. Could be a house or a barn. We should see if there's trouble."

"I knew I should have brought the wagon. It would be quicker." Jonas went to help Katie put the blanket in the picnic basket.

"You go on," Aaron said. "You can move faster without me. Leave the basket and we'll pick it up later. I'll come behind you."

Jonas and Levi left with the girls, running across the field to the road. Aaron followed, using his cane for balance on the rough surface. The others would arrive at the fire long before he did. They would find out if it was someone's house, or if it was just someone cooking dinner.

Smoke rolled toward him on the south wind, strong and deadly. It wasn't someone cooking dinner.

Step by step, Aaron made his way to the road. He couldn't move any faster, not in the long grass of the pasture, but the possibility of someone being in danger made him careless. He stepped wrong with his wooden leg and stumbled, falling headlong in the soft grass.

He felt the self-pity start closing in and shoved it away. He got back on his feet and started again. He might not get to the fire in time to help, but he would get there, and then all he could do was try his hardest.

No. The thought came to him with sudden surety. No, that wasn't all he could do. He could pray. Ma had taught him long ago, and he had listened to the ministers pray in church. Gideon had prayed for him, and Casper. He wasn't as powerless as he thought.

Each step that brought him closer to his goal was accompanied by a word of prayer. For the safety of his friends, for the well-being of the people whose house or barn was burning, for his own careful steps. He glanced up at the sky and prayed for rain.

By the time he reached the road, he could see the column of smoke above the trees and increased his speed. He had been afraid it might be at Gideon's farm, but now he could see it was at Elizabeth's old cabin. Had she been there? He hobbled faster. Had she been trapped inside? That cabin was old and dry as tinder. It wouldn't take much to destroy it.

When he reached the fire, he let out a breath he didn't know he was holding when he saw Elizabeth sitting away from the cabin, surrounded by Katie, Elise, and Ruby. She was safe. The others who had gathered from the neighboring farms were hauling buckets of water out of the old well and running with them to the cabin, trying to keep the fire from spreading. One cabin wall had collapsed, and the roof was gone, but the fire still burned in pulses of searing heat.

Aaron placed himself at the well and took the rope from Samuel Weaver.

"I'll do this part. I can't carry water back and forth, but I can haul it out of the well."

Hand over hand, he brought up the wet rope and poured the water from his bucket into a waiting pail. Again. And again. He lost count of how many times he hauled that bucket up. His hands bled from the rope burns and everyone's faces were dirty with smoke and soot. Finally, the wind died down and Gideon motioned for him to stop.

"I think we're all right for now."

At that moment, a light rain started, growing heavier, the drops hissing as they hit the still-burning logs of the cabin, now lying in a heap. The whole crowd, at least a dozen people who had been helping with the fire, raised their faces and hands up, welcoming the cool water from heaven.

Aaron dragged the cover over the well and lay on the ground next to it. He couldn't remember being so exhausted since he was in his last battle. He held his hands up. Blisters had formed, then popped, then the skin had turned raw across both palms. He sat up as folks started going home. Jonas found him.

"I'm going to walk Katie home. Levi and Elise have already left. Do you want to come with us?"

Aaron looked around for Elizabeth. She was still standing by Katie and shaking her head.

"I'll stay with Elizabeth, then walk home with her. It doesn't look like she's ready to leave yet."

Jonas gave him a hand to help him up, then walked over to Katie. As the couple walked toward the road, Elizabeth looked at Aaron, then back at the smoldering timbers. The rain had stopped, and the wind was still.

He made his way over to her. "Are you all right?"

Someone had thrown a blanket over her shoulders and she held the edges together in front of her. "I'm fine. How are you?"

He closed his hands, ignoring the pain of the broken blisters. "I'm all right. A little tired."

She gave him a small smile. "Ja, a little tired."

Everyone else had gone home, and the area around the smoking and steaming logs was empty, but from the road, Aaron heard a horse and buggy. Solomon drove into the yard, pulled his horse to a stop, and jumped down from the buggy.

He stared at the ruined cabin. "What happened here?"

Elizabeth lifted her head, her voice steady as she faced him. "I burned down Reuben's cabin."

Solomon turned on her, one hand half raised, until he saw Aaron standing near. He let his hand drop.

"What do you mean, you burned down the cabin? That was my cabin on my land. You had no right to do that."

Elizabeth's answer was calm. "It is not your land and not your cabin."

Solomon's gaze shifted from Elizabeth to Aaron and back again. He cleared his throat. "I meant, as soon as we marry, the land will be mine. You shouldn't have acted without consulting me first."

"I'm not going to marry you, Solomon." She walked toward the fire, her back to both of them.

Solomon shot a deadly look in Aaron's direction, but his eyes narrowed as he watched Elizabeth's back. He grunted as he seemed to come to some conclusion.

"You've proven to be more trouble than you're worth,

anyway." He turned to climb back into his buggy. "You'll be sorry you refused me, Elizabeth."

He turned the horse around and was gone, back up the road toward his house.

The sun had sunk toward the horizon as the rain clouds scudded east, and the evening star shone just above the trees. When Aaron looked back at Elizabeth standing huddled in her blanket next to the glowing coals, his mind went back to a thousand or more campfires glowing in the dusk, with the sound of taps being played softly on a distant bugle.

Someone else might shrug off Solomon's threat, but Aaron wouldn't. He walked up behind Elizabeth and put one hand on her shoulder. She leaned against him as if she had no strength left.

"Do you really think Solomon is dangerous, Aaron?"

"I do. But don't worry. I'll be watching both him and you."

She turned around in his arms and clung to him.

"I'll protect you, Elizabeth," he whispered into her hair. "I won't let anything happen to you."

Elise shivered as they left the scene of the fire, but Levi resisted putting his arm around her.

"Are you cold? I could let you wear my coat."

"Ne, not cold. I just can't get over how our peaceful afternoon almost turned to tragedy." She walked closer to his side. "The fire was so frightening. Didn't you think so? I'm thankful that no one was injured."

Levi stole a glance at the woman beside him. Not the first

time to enjoy her lovely profile this afternoon, with the walk they took after their picnic.

She ducked her head. "I hope you will come to our house sometime. My parents would like to learn to know you better."

"Do you want me to visit?"

"I would like that very much."

Continuing to walk, they passed Levi's house. Mother had lit the lamp in the living room, and he could see her sitting in her rocking chair. They were almost to Elise's house. The Zooks lived on the next farm past his own.

He ran a finger around the collar of his shirt. He should say something, but what could he say that would interest a girl like Elise?

"My brothers say you could be the next minister in the church." Elise stopped in the road and turned to him. "They said that even though you appear to be very shy, you are a scholar, and have read many books."

"Um . . ." What could he say to that? "I enjoy learning about theology." He glanced at her. "That's the study of God."

She nodded. "I know. My father, who passed away, was the bishop in our district. He also loved to study the Bible and read the writings of Menno Simons and other Mennonite and Amish leaders. He would often read aloud to us during winter evenings."

The tips of Levi's ears started to burn. She described a home life he could only imagine. "Did you enjoy that?"

She smiled at him. "I did. I know not many people enjoy learning as much as I do, but I can't get enough of reading."

"Which is your favorite writer?"

"Menno Simons. I particularly enjoyed his rules for the Christian life." She started walking again. "Do you think a Christian can follow those rules exactly, or are they guidelines for us to aim for?"

Levi caught up with her. By the time they reached her house, they had discussed five of the rules, plus debated whether the *Christenpflicht* was a collection of prayers that they should pray or examples of prayers. That led to a discussion of the Lord's Prayer as it was given in the book of Matthew. Levi was about to compare Matthew's version of the Lord's Prayer with Mark's when Casper opened the front door of their house. Suddenly, Levi realized they had been standing on the porch for at least an hour.

"Are you going to stand out here talking all night?" Casper asked, his eyebrows bristling.

Levi took a step backward. "I didn't realize it was so late. We got started talking . . ."

Elise slipped past Casper and into the house, but before she disappeared, she gave him a smile. "Denki, Levi. I enjoyed our talk."

"I did too."

Levi craned his neck to watch her as she continued into the house, but Casper stepped into his line of sight.

"I hear you're a fine young man," Casper said. "A scholar." He came out onto the porch and closed the door behind him. "Do you have something you want to ask me?"

Did he have . . . ? Levi swallowed. "Elise and I are just getting to know each other, but . . . I don't know how to say this." He looked at Casper. "I think she is the woman I'm going to marry."

Casper chuckled. "That wasn't a question, and it wasn't the question I had in mind. I thought you'd want to ask if you could spend time with our family some evening."

"Ja, for sure."

The older man squeezed his shoulder. "There is nothing like spending time together to know if two young people are right for each other."

Levi nodded.

"Why don't you come over tomorrow night after supper. Spend some time with Elise's brother Tobias and her mother. Let them get to know you."

Levi nodded again.

Casper opened the door and stepped halfway in. "Good night, Levi."

"Good night." He smiled, but his feet didn't move.

"Your house is that way, son." Casper pointed toward the road.

"Ja." Levi's mind started to work again. "Ja, for sure. I'll see you tomorrow, after supper."

"We'll see you then."

Levi walked down the farm lane, past the harness shop, and down the road toward home. The moon hung in the western sky, just past the last quarter and on its way to full. He went over every detail of his conversation with Elise.

"I should have told her," he said aloud, kicking at the step as he climbed the porch steps at home.

"Told her what?" Mother asked.

He hadn't seen her sitting on the porch in the dark. He sat on the chair next to hers and watched the moon.

"I walked Elise Beachy home."

Mother started tapping her toe on the wooden porch floor. "She seems like a nice girl."

"I'm going to marry her, Mother."

"Perhaps someday, after we have learned to know her parents better. The family has just recently moved into our district, and Casper Zook is only her stepfather. We must find out what her real father was like."

"No, Mother, we don't need to do anything. And I'm not going to marry her someday. I'm going to marry her soon."

The toe tapping increased. He had never contradicted Mother before.

"Please understand. I have been looking for the right girl to marry for a long time. Elise is the one."

"You thought Katie Stuckey was the one."

"I was young and foolish."

"And what are you now?" Mother's voice had taken on that waspish tone he hated.

"I am older and wiser now. And if I am making a foolish mistake, then it's mine to make. You need to trust my judgment."

The tapping stopped and Levi looked at her. The moonlight shone on her face as a tear traced its way down her cheek. He grasped her hand.

"What is wrong?"

"First Millie goes off and marries that boy. And now you want to leave me too."

"Millie lives in our district and has given you twin grandbabies. And I'm not leaving. I'll live somewhere close by. I don't know where yet, but I'll be in our district."

Mother's voice turned wheedling. "You could live here

with us. Married children often share a house with their parents."

Levi stood. "That is not going to happen." He bent down and kissed her forehead. "I love you, but I am not bringing my wife home to live with you."

Mother sighed.

"I'm going upstairs to bed. I'll see you in the morning."

Mother sighed again. "I suppose I could ask Elise if she would like to live here."

Levi stopped partway into the house. "No, Mother, you won't. You're not going to do anything to interfere in our lives or we will move to . . . to Indiana." He let the screen door slam closed behind him.

15

By Thursday, Elizabeth knew what she had to do.

Solomon had her marriage certificate, the only proof that she had been legally married to Reuben and was his heir. She had to get it back or she would never be free of Reuben or Solomon.

She tossed a forkful of soiled straw from Pie's stall out the door and thrust the fork into the bedding for another load. If only she could throw all men out of her life as easily as mucking out the barn.

Well, maybe not all men. Warring with the memory of Solomon's sneering face was the prickling warmth on her skin where Aaron had held her so lightly, so gently.

She shook her head and threw another forkful of straw out the door.

Why did she ever consider marrying Solomon? Tears gathered in her eyes as the answer echoed in her mind. To achieve her dream. Solomon's lies had led her to believe that he held the same dream, but his only goal was his own greedy lust for land. All he wanted was the farm.

And her dream of a home and family would never come true. She didn't deserve for it to happen. No Amishman would consider marrying her with the stain of her marriage to Reuben in her past. And without the certificate stating that it was a legal marriage? No one would marry her. Perhaps another Englischer might take the chance, but she would never make the mistake of marrying outside the church again.

The only thing she could do to keep her dream alive was to find that certificate.

She tossed another forkful of soiled straw.

To find that certificate, she would have to go to Solomon's house.

Trading the fork for the broom, she swept the last of the chaff and dirt out of the stall and onto the manure pile outside.

But if she confronted Solomon, she would lose. She would have to appeal to his better nature to hand it over to her, but after listening to him berate her on Sunday evening at the fire, she didn't think he had a better nature.

As she scattered fresh straw throughout Pie's stall, she remembered that Solomon often went to Millersburg on Thursdays. Perhaps he would be going today, also.

Changing her plans to spend the afternoon helping Margaret with her wedding quilt, she told Katie she would be going to visit Ruby, then hitched Pie to the pony cart. The drive to the burned-out cabin was quick, and she left Pie tied in the shade of the tree by the garden. She hauled a pail of water from the old well and made sure he could reach the grass. Elizabeth stopped at the end of the farm lane and glanced down the road toward Ruby's place. She would have to remember to stop for a quick visit on the way home.

Setting out on foot, she watched for any sign that Solomon was at home as she approached the house. His big black horse wasn't in the pasture. She kept walking until she could see into the open doors of the barn—no buggy.

Elizabeth stepped off the road and into the woods opposite Solomon's house and barn. Smoke trickled from the kitchen chimney. Dulcey came out the back door and hung some dish towels on the clothesline. Before she went back into the house, she stood by the clothesline, her arms crossed at her waist, looking toward the south, across the road and Reuben's woodlot. Would she indulge in those few minutes if Solomon was at home?

After Dulcey disappeared back into the house, Elizabeth took another look at the house and barn. No sign of Solomon anywhere. She crossed the road, hurried around the side of the house and up the back steps. Dulcey was at the stove, stirring something. Elizabeth rapped on the screen door.

"Is that you, Miss Elizabeth?" Dulcey moved the pot to the side of the stove and pushed the door open. "You shouldn't be here. Masta Solomon, he told me specially that you aren't to be here when he isn't."

Elizabeth closed her eyes and breathed a silent prayer of thanks. Solomon wasn't in the house.

"When do you expect him home?"

"He usually comes home on Thursday in time for supper, around six o'clock."

"Then we have plenty of time. I need to look in his study."

Dulcey shook her head. "If he catches you in there, you'd sure to be getting a whipping, and me too."

"He won't be home for several hours. I just need to find a paper that he stole from me. It has to be somewhere in his study."

"I don't want us to get in trouble." Dulcey turned back to the stove.

"If you're not going to help me, at least keep watch for me and let me know if he comes home early."

"That room is locked. Masta Solomon don't let anyone in there without him being there."

Elizabeth bit her lip to keep from screaming in frustration. Of course, Solomon would lock the door. But . . .

"You know where he keeps the key, don't you?"

Dulcey opened the oven door, letting a blast of heat into the already sweltering kitchen. "I know where he keeps the key." She poured gravy from the pan on the stove over a beef roast, then slid the roast back into the oven. "You got to promise me he won't find out I let you in there."

"He will never learn it from me, and I won't tell anyone else." Elizabeth's heart beat fast and she gulped for air as if she had been running for miles.

"All right, I trust you." Dulcey went to the kitchen door and beckoned for Elizabeth to follow her. "And I think Masta Solomon is the kind of man no woman should marry." She looked at her as she stretched as tall as she could to reach above the doorframe over the study door. "You've gotten that idea out of your head, I hope?"

"I was blinded by my dreams for a little while, but I know better than to marry a man like him."

"I need your help getting the key." Dulcey stopped in front of the study door. "Can you give me a boost?"

Elizabeth laced her fingers together and Dulcey stepped into her hands to reach the top of the doorframe. When she hopped back down, the key was in her hand.

Dulcey unlocked the door and peered into the dusky room. Elizabeth walked to the desk, then turned in a circle. A fireplace dominated one wall and a closed and curtained window was opposite the door. In the center of the room was the desk with a large leather-covered chair facing her. Papers were stacked in neat piles on the desk.

As she started looking through the piles of papers, Dulcey took a step into the room. "Careful you don't muss up them papers. He's particular about how they lay on his desk."

"I'll be careful." Elizabeth straightened the letters she had browsed through and went to another pile on the opposite side of the desk.

The top letter was from a bank in Charleston, Virginia. Underneath that was a familiar-looking envelope. It was from the same lawyer that had written to her, but the envelope was addressed to Solomon. She lifted the flap. The letter inside looked very similar to the one she had received, written in the fancy script she couldn't read. She put the letter back in the envelope. Then directly below that was another letter, this one from Solomon and addressed to Harlan Hoben, the lawyer in Vicksburg. She was about to put it aside with the others when she saw her name. Picking up the letter, she sank into the leather chair to read it.

"You find it?" Dulcey asked in a hoarse whisper.

"Not yet, but this is a copy of a letter that he sent to the lawyer in Vicksburg. It says that I am no longer considered to be Reuben's heir, so the land passes on to Reuben's next of kin, which is his son. It appears that Reuben's wife in Mississippi has passed away." Elizabeth read through the letter again. "Solomon has asked to be named the guardian of the child. He said the lawyer should bring the boy here as soon as he can."

She leaned back in the chair. What did it all mean? Why would Solomon want the child to come here?

A terrible idea passed through her mind. "Dulcey, you don't think he would hurt a child, would he?"

Dulcey sniffed as if an unpleasant odor had just entered the room. "If that boy has something he wants, and he could get it, ain't nothing would stop him."

"Then I have to find that marriage certificate. If I can prove I'm the owner of the land, then there will be no reason for Solomon to hurt the boy."

She riffled through that pile of letters and found nothing. Then she opened the center drawer of the desk, then the left-hand drawers, then the right-hand drawers. No certificate.

Dulcey looked into the fireplace. "You think he burned it?"

"I hope not."

Then Elizabeth remembered what she and Ruby used to do when they left notes for each other. They would stick the note under one of their dresser drawers. She pulled out the top right drawer and felt underneath. Pulling out the paper she found there, she unfolded it. It was the marriage certificate. Solomon had hidden it where he thought no one would ever find it.

She held it up for Dulcey to see. "Now Solomon doesn't have a chance to get that land."

"He won't be happy about that." Dulcey shook her head.

Elizabeth scanned the copy of Solomon's letter again, then noticed the date. "He has probably already mailed this letter, which means the lawyer could be on his way here with Reuben's son."

Dulcey motioned for her to hurry. Elizabeth straightened the piles of papers she had looked through and made sure the desk drawer was closed tightly. Then she followed Dulcey out of the room.

"Help me put the key away," Dulcey said.

Elizabeth laced her fingers together again and Dulcey slipped the key back onto the doorframe.

Gideon examined the harness Aaron had just delivered.

"What do you think? If there's something that isn't right, I can take it back to the harness shop and fix it right away."

His friend grinned. "This is good work. It should last for years with care."

Satisfaction in a job well done. Aaron could get used to this feeling. He grinned back at Gideon. "I'm happy you like it. I'll pass on the word to Casper."

Gideon hung the harness on the pegs set for it on the barn wall. The sound of a cart entering the barnyard drew their attention outside. Elizabeth pulled her pony to a stop and climbed out of the cart.

"Ruby will be glad of your company," Gideon said as he went to take the pony's lead rope. "I hope you'll be able to stay for a while."

Her face was flushed, her eyes bright as she glanced at Aaron.

"I can stay for an hour or so. Could you keep Pie in a shady place? It's a hot day again."

"For sure. I'll take good care of him."

"And can I talk to you before I go in, Gideon? I have something to tell you."

Aaron could take a hint. "I'll be getting back to the shop, then. Let me know if you run across anything you need done on that harness, Gideon, and I'll make it right."

"Don't go, Aaron." Elizabeth held out her hand to stop him. "I want you to hear this too." She took a breath, glancing at each of them. "I found out that Aaron was right to warn me about Solomon."

A cold, sinking feeling ran to Aaron's toes.

"Solomon Mast?" Gideon asked. "What about him?"

"Aaron told me that Solomon might not be who he was trying to appear to be. I know he is a liar and can be cruel. I think he might not be Amish, like he claims he is."

"This is a serious accusation. Do you know this for a fact? You didn't hear it from someone else?"

She pulled a paper out of her waistband. "Solomon told me he had never seen this paper, yet he lied to me. I found it at his house."

Gideon took the paper and unfolded it. "It's your marriage certificate from when you married Reuben." He folded the paper again and paced to the back of the barn, then returned. "I had heard that you were never legally married to Reuben. Was that just a rumor started by Solomon? Why would he do that?"

"I think I have figured it out." She glanced at Aaron and he nodded, hoping to reassure her. "Solomon asked me to marry him, although I couldn't understand why. But I think it's because he wants Reuben's farm for himself."

"He isn't happy with the Patterson place?" Gideon asked.

"He . . . he gets a look in his eye when he talks about land. A greedy look. I don't think he would stop at anything to get his hands on more land."

Gideon tapped the folded certificate against his pursed lips. Aaron's mind raced to an unsavory possibility.

"By marrying you, he would be part of the Weaver family. If things happened in the right way, he could eventually own all of Abraham's land."

"But to do that, he would have to swindle his way through legalities," Gideon said.

"Or position himself correctly and wait."

"For what?"

"For Datt to pass away," Elizabeth said, breaking into their speculations. "He could write a new will, forge Datt's signature, then just wait for the end."

"Or make sure the end happened sooner than anyone would expect." As soon as the words were out of his mouth, Aaron realized what he had said.

"You're talking about murder." Gideon's face grew hard.

Aaron pulled his hat from his head and ran a hand through his hair. "If Solomon is the man I think he is, that could be exactly what he has planned."

Gideon turned to Elizabeth. "But now that you've found your marriage certificate, he can't do that, can he?"

She shook her head. "I don't see how he could. But there's something else. Reuben had a son, a little boy who is now an orphan. I saw a copy of a letter Solomon wrote to a lawyer in Mississippi, requesting that he be made the boy's guardian. If he went to court, he could find a judge who would say that Reuben's son actually owns the land instead of me, couldn't he?"

"Do you think he would steal the land from you, using this child?" Gideon's eyebrows were raised.

"I do. I can't see how he could gain control of Datt's land after that, but he might have some scheme brewing."

Aaron stepped closer to Elizabeth. "He knows how much you love children. What would you do if he threatened the boy's life? Would you marry Solomon to save him?"

As Elizabeth nodded, her face crumpled, and a tear slid down her cheek. "I would do anything to save a child from Solomon's control."

"This is something I need to talk over with the other ministers," Gideon said. "Solomon has established himself in our community, and we need to decide how to handle this situation." He grasped Elizabeth's hand. "Denki. I'm glad you came to me. We'll do everything we can to protect you."

He gave Aaron's shoulder a pat and then left.

"I suppose you want to go in and talk to Ruby now," Aaron said.

He should follow Gideon and go back to the Zooks' harness shop, but Elizabeth's tears had multiplied. Her shoulders shook as she covered her face. Aaron put an arm around her shoulders and steered her toward the bench near the barn door. He sat next to her, his arm still around her shoulders. She sniffed, then took a deep breath and wiped her eyes on her sleeve.

"You must think I'm such a fool."

Aaron pulled her closer. "Not at all."

"I was taken in by Solomon's charm and his looks, but I should have listened to you. You tried to warn me about him."

"I wasn't certain it was the same man."

Another sob bubbled out. "I thought he was the one I had been waiting for. The one who could fulfill my dreams."

Aaron let her cry. He didn't know what to do when a woman cried. His mind went back to his last membership class with Gideon, when the minister was discussing *Gelassenheit*, surrendering to God's will and plan.

"Maybe you're dreaming the wrong dreams."

Her shoulders tensed and she pulled away from him. "The wrong dreams? My dreams . . . they're mine. Who is to say if they're wrong or not?"

Aaron stretched his good leg out, letting the muscles relax. "Gideon told me that one of the first things the Amish teach their children is to give up their own will and surrender to God's. He teaches them to put Jesus first, others second, and themselves last. Perhaps your dreams have turned that around."

Elizabeth didn't answer, but she didn't walk away, either. Finally, she leaned closer to him again, under the arm that was still stretched out along the back of the bench. "Don't you have dreams? What about going west?"

He fingered a lock of hair that had escaped from her kapp and rested on her shoulder. "I think I was wrong about those plans. If I went west, then I would only be living for myself."

"Isn't that what you wanted?"

Aaron rubbed his stump, the leg that was closest to Elizabeth. In fact, since they were sitting so close together, it rested against her skirt. She hadn't seemed to notice. "Not anymore. Since I've been here, things have changed."

She turned toward him and rested her hand on top of his, the hand that had been rubbing his leg. Her fingers brushed his trouser as she laid her hand on his leg, near the edge of his stump. She didn't cringe. Didn't shy away. Didn't give him a look full of pity. She only took his hand again, allowing him to curl his fingers around her small, soft one.

~~~

As Aaron's hand grasped hers, Elizabeth relaxed into his gentle touch.

"I know things have changed a lot. With your new leg you're able to get around much better."

"I'm not talking about my leg." His soft voice tugged at her heart. "I've found my true dream right here in Weaver's Creek."

"Your family." She smiled. "I always knew you needed a family."

He nodded. "The Zooks are part of that. But it's much bigger than that. The one thing I missed since the beginning of the war was my home. I had seen it destroyed and Grandpop killed in front of my eyes." His gaze took on a faraway

244

look, as if he were seeing the past recreated in Gideon's barn. "But what I've found is my true home."

"Do you mean Weaver's Creek?"

Aaron smiled. "This place is just the beginning. But now I understand that my dreams are nothing without the Lord. He's the one who gives us our heart's desire."

Elizabeth's eyes grew moist again. She would never have her heart's desire. God had already shown her that.

"Do you understand what I mean?"

"You mean that you've given up making your own dream come true and now you're waiting for God to give it to you."

Aaron sighed. "Not exactly. I stopped thinking about what I want. Now I'm watching while God gives me what he wants me to have. Once I set my sights on pleasing him and obeying him, then I could see how he is working to give me what I want most, after him."

"You're talking in circles."

Elizabeth started to draw her hand away. Ruby would make more sense than Aaron. But he grasped her hand harder until she looked into his eyes.

"Let me say it plain, then. And in Englisch." He ran his thumb along the back of her hand. "My dream is to have my own home. A place to belong. A family . . ." His gaze dropped to her hand. "And a wife. A woman like—" He stopped. "No, not a woman like you." He looked into her eyes again. "You. No one else. I want you to be part of my dream."

"But—"

He stopped her with a kiss, quick and gentle, on her lips. She pulled back to see his face turn scarlet, his blue eyes boring into hers. He let go of her hand and touched her lips with one finger.

"Don't say anything. Not yet." He took her hand again, as if by holding it she could never leave him. "I love you, Elizabeth, and it has been painful to watch you over the past few weeks as you've grown closer to Solomon. But at the same time, I've discovered that I had the wrong dream. I needed to put God first in my life and accept what he had planned for me."

Aaron lifted her hand and kissed it. Her thoughts swirled.

He continued. "I hope what he has planned for me is you, but only if you want me. I will do almost anything for you."

A bubble of hope turned inside her breast and she smiled. "Almost?"

He nodded, serious. "I won't turn away from God for you, but I would do anything else."

Elizabeth chewed the inside of her lip. His dream sounded so much like hers, except for one thing.

"You aren't Amish, though."

"Not yet."

She shot her gaze up to his eyes. He wasn't teasing, but he was smiling.

"What do you mean? Ever since you came here you said you weren't Amish."

"I went to the ministers and asked about joining the church. I want to become part of this community. To set down roots here. To embrace the Amish faith and life my grandfather ran away from."

"You can't just decide you're Amish and then you are."

"I know. I'm not Solomon. But I didn't just decide to become Amish. I thought about it for a long time." He chuckled. "All right. I didn't think about it as much as I argued with God. But nobody can argue with him and win."

How often did she spend her prayer time arguing with God? Bargaining with him? "So, you want to join the church?"

"Is that such a surprise?" His smile was sure. "Of course, I'll have to finish my classes with Gideon and Jonas—"

"Jonas?"

Aaron grinned. "Now I've really surprised you. Jonas and I are taking the class together."

Elizabeth slumped against the back of the bench. She had been wrapped up in her own problems . . . Katie probably even told her about Jonas taking the membership class, but she hadn't noticed.

When Aaron squeezed her hand again, she looked at him. "I've told you what I want, and I'm willing to accept whatever God provides for me. If that is for you and me to hitch our lives together, then that would make me very happy."

Elizabeth closed her eyes. It seemed that his dream danced with hers in a swirling whirlwind of leaves on a fall day. But she had been so wrong about Solomon, and so wrong about Reuben. She couldn't trust her feelings or her ears when it came to Aaron. She couldn't risk making another mistake.

"I can't give you an answer."

She opened her eyes, expecting to see a frown on his lean face, but instead he was grinning.

"I hope you won't until you're certain. If that takes a long time, then I can wait. It seems like I've waited my whole life, so why not wait a little longer?" He ducked his head. "I'm sorry I kissed you earlier. I couldn't help myself."

Elizabeth put her fingers over her lips. His kiss had been so gentle, demanding nothing from her. She had never been kissed like that before, but suddenly she longed for another one. If she did marry him, would Aaron always be so gentle and thoughtful with her?

"I enjoyed the kiss." He turned bright red again and she smiled. "I will think about what you've said, but I don't know if I'll ever marry again."

He leaned over and brushed a kiss on her cheek. "Think about it and pray about it."

"I will." A sunbeam of clarity pierced her cloudy thoughts. "I'm going in to see Ruby now."

"And I need to get back to work. Casper is probably wondering where I am."

They walked out of the barn together, then Aaron winked at her as he turned to go toward the road and back to the Zooks'. Elizabeth went to the kitchen door, knocked softly, then opened the door. Ruby called from the front room.

"Come on in, Elizabeth." Ruby sat in her chair, a needle in one hand and a pair of boy's trousers in the other. "I saw you drive in. Have you been out in the barn this whole time?"

Briefly, she told Ruby what she had found at Solomon's house. "Gideon left to talk to the other ministers about the situation."

"They'll spend all afternoon discussing it, I'm sure. But Gideon left quite a while ago. You've been alone with Aaron since then?"

"Aaron and I were talking." She sat on a chair opposite Ruby's. "Where are the children?"

"Roseanna and Sophia took the boys down to Mamm's house, and Lovinia is taking her nap."

"And how are you feeling?" Elizabeth remembered how sick she had been for those few months when a little one was growing inside her.

"The worst of the illness is over and I'm feeling good. I do get tired in the afternoon. Sometimes I lie down and nap with Lovinia. Roseanna is such a help at those times." Ruby cut off the end of her thread and folded the small trousers. "I think of you often, since you told us about the baby you lost. I can't imagine how you must still grieve at times."

Elizabeth picked at a piece of chaff sticking to her skirt. "I wonder about that child often, if it had been a boy or a girl. If its eyes were brown like mine, or green like Reuben's. But it has been a long time since then . . ."

"Only a few years."

Six. It had been six years and three months. She would never forget.

Ruby picked up another pair of trousers, frowning at the hole in the knee. "I don't know how these boys can be so rough on their clothes."

Elizabeth grinned, forcing the sad memory to the background. "They're boys. They're supposed to be active."

"But do they always need to crawl on their knees when they play?"

They both laughed, and Ruby looked at Elizabeth.

"It is good to hear you laugh. I was afraid with what you told me about Solomon that you would not be happy. So, tell me. What is going on with Aaron?"

"Aaron?"

"He's the one who put that smile on your face, isn't he?"

Elizabeth found another piece of dust on her skirt. "It is nice to know a man who is gentle and kind."

"You know a lot of men like that. There's Gideon, and Jonas, and Datt."

"But they're all related to me. That's different."

Ruby threaded her needle and took a stitch. "Aaron comes by here every Friday evening."

"For his membership class."

"He told you about that?"

Elizabeth nodded. "I think it's wonderful that he's thinking of joining the church, but it will be hard for him, won't it?"

"From what Gideon said, he has his heart set on it. He's very dedicated and shows up early every Friday. His enthusiasm is wearing off on Jonas too. I was afraid Jonas was only going through the motions of joining the church so he and Katie could be married."

A warm feeling started in Elizabeth's middle. "So, you think Aaron is serious?"

Ruby smiled at her. "Very serious. He wants to become Amish."

The warm feeling expanded. He was becoming Amish because he wanted to, not because he wanted to impress her. He didn't give her an ultimatum and he didn't try to wheedle his way into her affections. He didn't even try to threaten her by saying he wouldn't continue the classes if she didn't marry him.

Whether there was any future between them or not, Aaron would still be Amish by his own choice.

16

The town of Millersburg was festooned with banners, bunting, and flags even today, two days after Independence Day. Solomon hunched his shoulders as he drove through the crowded street to the livery, keeping his gaze down. With this many people around, he couldn't keep track of them all. It was best to lie low and get his business done.

The livery stable was full again.

"You could try at Wilson's around the corner," a thin man with one eye said, jerking his thumb in that direction. "He usually has room since so many folks around here won't do business with one of his kind."

"No, thank you. I've patronized that establishment once, but I won't go back."

The one-eyed man grinned, then spat a stream of tobacco juice toward the corner. "Then I can put your horse up in the corral. There's water for him in there. Two bits for the afternoon."

Solomon peered into the corral that was already crowded

with a dozen horses or more and shook his head. The horse would have to make do with whatever he could find on the street.

He guided the horse to a watering trough on the side of the courthouse, and when the beast was finished, he found a spot along the hitching rail near the post office to tie him.

As he stood in line inside the building, Solomon pulled out the letters he had ready to mail. The most important was the one requesting to take over guardianship of Kaufman's son. He smiled at the thought of owning Kaufman's property free and clear without having to deal with Elizabeth. She had proved more bothersome than she was worth. Although, if he needed to, he could still manipulate her. She was foolish to trust him with such important papers as the deed to the land and her marriage certificate.

"Good afternoon, Mr. Mast," the clerk said when he reached the window. "I think I have a telegram for you today."

He went to the boxes lining the wall behind them and retrieved a folded paper. When Solomon saw that it was from the lawyer, he shoved the letter he had written to Hoben in his coat pocket and mailed the rest of his missives. Walking out of the post office, he fingered the telegram. It could be good news that would make his letter to the man obsolete. He sought out an open bench and sat down.

The message was short.

Court in Vicksburg awarded custody to aunt Elizabeth Kaufman. Will accompany boy to Ohio on first train.

Solomon checked the date on the note, then crumpled the paper in his fist. He was too late. Much too late. The court had already given the boy to Elizabeth and he was on his way here. Might even be here as soon as Saturday. He should have straightened out that misunderstanding about her relationship to Reuben early on rather than waiting to see if he could use it to his advantage, but instead the opportunity had slipped through his fingers.

He barely noticed the bank draft contained in the other letter, more proceeds from his investments in the South. He deposited the draft in the bank, then gathered his horse and set out for home.

All the way to his farm, he sifted through the possibilities of how to use the changed situation to his advantage, then discarded them one by one. The only way he could see to maintain his control of the situation was to marry Elizabeth. While at one time he had looked forward to having her close to him, available to him any time he wanted her, now the thought was a bit distasteful. He liked his women compliant and naive, and Elizabeth had turned out to be neither of those things. But since she had been named the guardian of the boy, she held the key to Reuben's property. Once they were safely married, then he would decide when and how to dispose of both of them.

He noticed Dulcey's guilty expression as soon as he entered the house. He watched her as she took his hat from him and hung it on the hall tree, followed by his jacket.

"Has anyone been here, Dulcey?"

She kept her gaze down. "Miss Elizabeth stopped by, but I told her you weren't at home."

Solomon's eyes narrowed. "Elizabeth? What did she want?"

"I don't know. She didn't say."

Dulcey cringed, her left shoulder rising, giving her a crab-like appearance. She was lying, but Solomon let it slide for now. He had plans to make.

"When will my supper be ready?"

"I can have it on the table in ten minutes."

Solomon checked his watch. Nearly six o'clock.

"I'll be in my study. Call me when it's ready."

Dulcey scuttled toward the kitchen as he strode across the hall to the study and reached for the key he kept above the doorframe. His fingers touched nothing. He groped to the left, and then to the right until his fingers touched the key. As he took it down, he glanced toward the kitchen door just as it swung closed. Suspicion filled his mind. Dulcey wouldn't go into his study when he wasn't in there. He had trained her better than that. But Elizabeth might have convinced Dulcey to show her where the key was.

Turning the key in the lock, he swung the door open and strode in. Everything looked just as it should. The desk was orderly, the piles seemed untouched. Why would Elizabeth come in here? Shuffling through the papers, a thought came to him. He had told her that marriage certificate didn't exist, and she had believed him. But what if . . .

He pulled the right-hand drawer open and felt underneath. The certificate was gone.

Solomon burst out of his study and grabbed the buggy whip from its holder.

"Dulcey!" He let his voice carry all of his rage as he thrust the kitchen door open. "Dulcey!"

He found her in the pantry, cowering behind a barrel of

flour. Grabbing her hair, he pulled her out into the open and shook her.

"You traitor. You helped Elizabeth betray me. No one crosses me, Dulcey. No one."

He threw her to the floor and raised his whip. The beating only fed his rage rather than satisfy his appetite. He struck the woman at his feet until the whip broke, then resorted to kicking, but nothing gave him the release he needed. Not even her sobs as she curled on the floor, begging him to stop.

He finally turned away from her, exhausted but not sated. He staggered up the stairs and fell onto his bed, cradling his pillow to his stomach. If she survived, Dulcey would never cross him again. But she wouldn't have done so today if she hadn't been coerced by Elizabeth.

Gripping the pillow in his fingers, he imagined Elizabeth's slim arms in his hands. The pain in her eyes as he gripped harder, his fingers sinking deep into her flesh, then he ripped his hands down and out, tearing the pillow in two. He lay back on the bed as feathers drifted around him. Someday he would have Elizabeth in his hands, and she would know the power of his wrath.

Aaron finished his work at the harness shop just before supper. He declined Casper's invitation to stay for the meal and started the walk home.

Home? He chuckled as he got into the rhythm of his stride. The Weavers' farm had become home for now, with Lydia mothering him as well as Jonas, and Abraham willing to give fatherly advice. Aaron watched Abraham's interactions with Jonas carefully. His own father had lost touch with his family and with reality when Aaron's mother died in childbirth, disappearing into the woods for days and weeks at a time while Grandpop had raised Aaron. As wonderful as Grandpop had been, he wasn't Aaron's father. Witnessing Abraham and Jonas together gave him an idea of what he had lost, but also gave him hope that someday he could be that kind of father with his own children.

Supper was ready when he arrived at the Weavers', but Lydia wasn't there.

"She went to help Susanna Lehman with her lying in," Abraham said as he flipped hotcakes on the stove. "She'll likely be there all night, so the three of us will be bachelors for supper."

"Datt always makes hotcakes when Mamm is gone at suppertime," Jonas said as he took a bottle of maple syrup from one of the cupboards and put it on the table.

"That's right." Abraham moved six hotcakes from the griddle to a covered plate inside the oven. "Easy to fix and easy to clean up."

Abraham had made enough hotcakes to feed the entire church, Aaron thought, but somehow the three of them managed to eat half of them.

"Don't worry about the leftovers," Jonas said as Aaron patted his full stomach. "We'll have them for breakfast, warmed up and rolled around sausage links. There's nothing like it."

After they finished eating, Abraham asked, "You're working at the Zooks' every day now, aren't you?"

Aaron leaned back in his chair. "Casper has me doing

small jobs to help out, but I'm learning as I go. Every week there's something new to work on."

"Have you heard what Elizabeth is going to do now that that old cabin is destroyed?" Jonas asked.

"She hasn't said anything to me about it. I'm just glad we were able to keep the fire from spreading."

Abraham stood and started clearing the table. "I've worried about that old well, sitting so close to the house. Reuben never repaired the cover, but so far it has held up. Now that no one is living there, we'll need to either fill it in or make the cover safe before one of the children falls in."

"I hadn't thought of that," said Jonas. "I'll work on that tomorrow morning. We don't have any farm work pending, do we, Datt?"

"The oats are cut and shocked, and the hay is cut. It needs another day or two to cure, and then we'll be able to start hauling it to the barn. So, tomorrow would be a good day for that project. I'll help you with it."

Aaron hadn't thought about the dangers of that old well. As he had been hauling buckets of water up out of it, he hadn't been able to see the bottom. But he had to drop the bucket down at least twenty feet before it hit water, and he had no idea how far the bottom might be.

"Are there many wells like that one around the area?"

Abraham sat at the table again and ran his fingers through his beard as he thought. "The original landholders in the last century didn't always build homes on their land grants, so there are only a few. I think I remember there being an old log house on Abel Patterson's place, about the same age as the one on Reuben Kaufman's farm. Abel never lived in that old place though, so I don't know if it's still there. But there's always a possibility that a well existed there at one time. The other farm from that time is where Gideon and Ruby live now. The house was rebuilt, and they updated the place when they got married a few years ago. They still use that old well, although they've cleaned it out and built a new cover for it with a windlass. Old root cellars and springhouses hold the same dangers, though. No telling how many of those are around the old homesteads."

Jonas and Aaron washed the dishes and straightened the kitchen for the morning.

"I'm going over to see Katie before it gets dark," Jonas said.

"I'll walk with you as far as the road." Aaron grabbed his cane. "I haven't heard Elizabeth's pony cart go past yet."

"Didn't you say she was at Ruby's this afternoon? She probably stayed and had supper with them."

"You're right, but still, I'm uneasy about it. She should have gone home by now. The sun is going down."

Jonas grinned as they left the house and walked toward the stone bridge. "It sounds like you're putting your claim on her, worrying like that."

"Would you mind?" Aaron grinned back. "I don't think she would."

"I think it would be wonderful if you became part of the family. I'm looking forward to it."

"Don't give out congratulations yet," Aaron said. "She hasn't said she would marry me."

"She will." Jonas stopped on the bridge. "She wouldn't dare turn you down, or she would have to answer to me."

"I think the woman knows her own mind."

Aaron chuckled as his friend continued onto the road and turned toward Katie's house. But even with the bantering, his unease continued until he finally saw Elizabeth's pony cart coming down the road. She saw him and turned into the farm lane.

"You look like you're waiting for someone." Her smile was calm.

"Did you have a good time with Ruby?"

She nodded. "It's always good to spend time with her. Even if I'm feeling sad, she never fails to lift my spirits."

Aaron stepped to the side so he could see the road more clearly. Up the hill, someone was coming, staggering with an uneven gait. Elizabeth turned to see what he was watching.

"It's Dulcey." She moved over in her seat. "Get in the cart, Aaron. It looks like she needs help."

Elizabeth turned the cart around and urged her pony into a quick trot. By the time they reached Dulcey, she had fallen in the middle of the road. Elizabeth handed the reins to Aaron and ran to her.

"Dulcey! Are you all right? What happened?" Elizabeth, as small as she was, pulled the other woman up off the ground, cradling her shoulders in her arms.

Aaron drove the pony closer to the two women, then eased out of the cart. "Is she badly hurt?"

"I don't know. She has blood all over and she has lost consciousness. Can you help me get her into the cart? We need to take her to Mamm."

Aaron braced his legs and lifted the young woman's shoulders while Elizabeth carried her legs. They laid her carefully in the back of the pony cart. Elizabeth climbed in with her and held her head on her lap.

"Hurry, Aaron. We have to get her home."

"Lydia isn't there," he said as he climbed onto the seat of the cart. "She's gone to be with someone during their lying in."

"We'll still take Dulcey there. We can clean her up and help her the best we can until Mamm gets home."

Aaron drove slowly to keep the cart steady until they reached the hitching rail at the kitchen door of the Weavers' house. Abraham came out to meet them.

"What is wrong?"

"It's Dulcey. She's hurt, badly. We have to help her."

Abraham lifted the slight woman out of the back of the cart and carried her in while Aaron held the door open. Elizabeth went into the front room and lit the lamp.

"Aaron, if you bring a sheet to cover the couch, we can lay her there."

She hovered nearby while Aaron got a sheet from the cabinet under the stairs and spread it on the couch. Abraham laid Dulcey down.

"I'll fetch Lydia's clean nightdress," he said, then looked at Aaron. "We'll need hot water, a basin, and some clean cloths."

Aaron nodded and headed for the kitchen, but before he left the room, he looked back. Elizabeth bent over her friend, wiping her face with the edge of her skirt. Where he came from, white women didn't treat the black women like that, but he could see the love in Elizabeth's expression. Nothing would keep her from helping Dulcey the best she could.

He smiled as he went to the stove and lit the fire laid for the morning. Maybe that was one reason why his love for Elizabeth was growing stronger every day. She was always surprising him.

~~~~~~~

By the time Aaron brought a basin of hot water and Datt found Mamm's clean nightdress, Dulcey had woken up.

She groaned and tried to sit up.

"Shh," Elizabeth said, holding on to her friend's shoulders. "You stay right there. We need to get you cleaned up and bandaged."

Aaron and Datt left the house, leaving the two women alone.

"He knows." Dulcey grasped Elizabeth's arm. "Masta Solomon, he knows you was in the study."

Ice water froze Elizabeth's veins. "Did he do this to you?"

Dulcey nodded and took a washcloth from Elizabeth's hands. She tried washing her face with it, but Elizabeth took it back and carefully dabbed at the drying blood.

"He's a hard man. I tried to warn you," Dulcey said.

Elizabeth nodded, tears filling her eyes. "It's my fault, Dulcey. I talked you into helping me." She rinsed the cloth and started washing the cuts on Dulcey's legs.

Her friend shook her head. "There's no one to blame but Masta Solomon. You didn't hold no whip, did you? He did this himself."

"I need to wash your clothes, there is blood all over them. You can wear Mamm's nightdress until your clothes are clean and dry."

Dulcey's eyes widened. "I can't. Your mama's nightdress? I daren't. It ain't right."

"But Mamm would want you to. What else will you do while you wait? I don't have any clothes here for you to wear."

"I'll wrap myself up in this sheet. I can't wear no fine lady's nightdress."

Since Dulcey was adamant, Elizabeth gave up. She held the sheet ready while Dulcey undressed, biting back a gasp of horror when she saw layers of scars on her friend's shoulders and legs. Finally, Dulcey's outer clothes were in a pile on the floor and she held the sheet around her.

"Will you be all right while I take your clothes into the kitchen?"

"I'll be fine." Dulcey lifted the washcloth from the basin and tried to wring it out, but her hands were trembling.

Elizabeth took the cloth from her and helped her lie back on the couch. "You're hurt and you're exhausted. Let me take care of you for once."

Dulcey's eyes grew moist. "I ain't never known a white woman who would do for one like me."

Elizabeth smoothed Dulcey's curly hair. "I don't know about that. We're equal in the Lord's eyes."

She waited until Dulcey closed her eyes, then took the clothes into the kitchen to wash. She took a pail of cold water that sat on the side of the dry sink and plunged Dulcey's dress into it to soak. Then she went to the back porch where Datt and Aaron were talking. The moon was rising in the east, nearly full.

"How is she?" Datt asked.

"She is bruised and bloody, but other than that and being

tired, she seems to be fine." Elizabeth clasped her hands together to keep them from trembling. "This isn't the first time Dulcey has been beaten. She has a lot of scars on her back and legs, old scars, as if she has endured these beatings most of her life."

Datt moved over on the bench to give her a place to sit. "I've never seen her before, but you know her. Who is she?"

"She works for Solomon. She's his cook and housekeeper, but before he hired her, she had been a slave somewhere in the south until the war ended."

Aaron frowned. "Did she say who beat her so badly?"

"She claims it was Solomon. But even though I've seen that he has a cruel streak, it's so hard to believe he would beat her like that."

Datt leaned forward, his elbows propped on his knees. "That is a serious charge, but I was at the Beilers' house when Gideon called for a meeting of the ministers this afternoon. From what he said, Solomon is never going to be part of the community in spite of his assumption that he will be."

"What can we do about Dulcey?" Elizabeth asked.

"She shouldn't go back to Solomon, no matter what she says." Aaron held Elizabeth's gaze with his own. "We'll need to be firm about that."

"Why do you think she would want to go back?" Datt asked.

"Because she hasn't left before now, even though I'm sure he has treated her badly ever since she started working for him." Aaron turned his cane slowly between his fingers, the end resting on the porch floor. "Someone in Dulcey's situation might not be willing to hope that another place could be any better than where they are. I've seen it happen. I used to go hunting with a slave that lived on a farm near ours. In spite of the freedom his master gave him to wander the hills, hunting and whatnot, Sam would never consider running away. Even though he was a slave, he had a better life than Dulcey found working for Solomon. He was safe, fed, and had a job to do. He wasn't willing to exchange that for the unknown he might encounter if he tried to escape." He clenched the end of the cane in his fist. "I wonder what happened to him. The last I knew, his master was burned out by the same Yankee patrol that destroyed our place."

The three of them sat in silence for a few minutes. Elizabeth understood Dulcey better than either Aaron or Datt could imagine. She had had many opportunities to leave Reuben, but she hadn't. Shame had held her back. Shame and fear. If she had left Reuben, he might have come after her, and then her situation would have been much worse.

The moon rose higher and Elizabeth stood up. "I'm going to finish washing out Dulcey's dress, then sit up with her tonight."

"Do you want me to sit with you?" Aaron asked.

His offer was tempting, as Elizabeth imagined them talking quietly in the moonlit room while Dulcey slept, but she couldn't ask him to stay only to keep her company. "I'll be fine. I'll call you if I need you."

Datt and Aaron went to bed, Datt to his room on the main floor off the kitchen, and Aaron upstairs to one of the bedrooms there. Elizabeth lit the kitchen lamp and worked to remove the stains from Dulcey's dress. Once it was clean, she hung it on the clothesline. The night was fresh after the hot day, and nearly as bright as daytime with the moon so large. If Datt had pressing farm work to do, he could work by the light of this moon.

She walked back into the front room, taking the lamp. Dulcey woke up as she came in.

"I didn't mean to wake you. Did you have a good rest?"

"I slept hard, 'til a dream woke me up. An old alligator was chasing me across the swamp and briars clung to my legs. Jus' like Old Scratch grabbin' at me 'til blood ran like a river."

Elizabeth smiled. "No alligator will get you here, whatever that is."

Dulcey didn't return her smile. "But Masta Solomon, he might. He might guess where I went to when he wakes up. I need to get back there."

"You'll do no such thing."

"But if he wakes up and finds I'm gone—"

"You have to stay here where it's safe. If you go back, you know he'll beat you again." Elizabeth took Dulcey's hand. "You never have to go back there again. You'll stay with us. Make your home here. Or we'll help you go wherever you want."

Dulcey looked at their hands. Elizabeth grasped tighter, her light fingers entwined with Dulcey's dark ones as she waited for Dulcey's decision.

"I won't go back if you'll help me. I daren't go back to the saloon either. That was an evil place."

"We'll look for a place to live. A nice place where you only need to work for yourself. We can build a lovely little cabin for you, and you could have a garden and chickens."

A tear dropped onto their hands. "That sounds like

heaven, sure enough. But it's just a dream. Masta Solomon, he's gonna be lookin' for me, and for you. We got to run and live however we can."

"Don't worry about that right now. You need to get some sleep. Things will look better in the morning."

"Only with Jesus's help. No matter what men do, Jesus is more powerful."

Elizabeth didn't answer. Even though she had done everything she could to be free of the memories of Reuben, she had no freedom at all. And now Solomon . . . would she ever be free from him?

Dulcey squeezed her fingers. "Elizabeth, you reckon that's right, don't you?"

"I believe Jesus can save people, but I don't know if he'll save me. I try to pull myself out of Reuben's clutches, but I'm still there. I don't know how to get free. I don't think I deserve to be helped by Jesus."

"Oh, Elizabeth! Hush now. None of us deserves Jesus's love. None of us deserves his saving." Dulcey rose up on her elbow, still grasping her hand. "And you said you tried to pull yourself free of Reuben? Honey, we can't never save ourselves. Only Jesus can. Pray for him to give you the faith you need to look to him and him alone."

"Faith? Not help to be safe from men like Solomon?"

"God never done promised to keep us safe on this here earth. But he promised he would never leave us or forsake us, just like it says in the Good Book. Our bodies may be beaten, and we may even be killed. But our Jesus suffered worse an' he always promises to be right here by our side. And when the time comes, he done promised to take us safely to heaven.

He has a home there waiting for us." Dulcey settled back on the couch. "Think about that. Turn to Jesus."

Elizabeth was full of questions, but Dulcey's eyes were closing with exhaustion. "I will think about it."

Elizabeth blew out the light, then waited until Dulcey's hand relaxed in hers and her friend's deep breathing told her she slept.

Dulcey's dress might be dry by now, so she went out to the clothesline. In the gentle breeze, the dress had dried quickly. She reached up to pull the pins off the line, but then a hand clapped over her mouth and an arm grabbed her waist and pulled her against someone large and strong.

"You did just what I wanted you to, Elizabeth, my dear. I was waiting for you to come outside."

Solomon. Elizabeth struggled against his hold. She had to call for help, to warn Dulcey.

His grip over her mouth shifted to cover her nose. As gray clouds swirled, she fought to get free. To get one breath of air.

A chuckle sounded in her ear. "You'll do what I want, I guarantee it."

Her lungs demanded air, but the blackness overtook her

17

Aaron woke suddenly with the morning light. The weather had changed during the night with the wind swinging to the north and banging the shutter on his open window, then he had heard Jonas come home sometime after midnight. His sleep after that had been fitful, full of dreams. Now, trying to come fully awake, he sat on the edge of the bed, rubbing his face and scratching his beard. He couldn't shake the feeling of his dreams. The feeling that something wasn't right.

He dressed and went downstairs, careful to keep his wooden leg quiet so he wouldn't wake the rest of the house. He peered into the front room. Elizabeth had said she would sit up all night, but she wasn't there. Dulcey slept on the couch, one hand curled on her stomach. Perhaps Elizabeth had gone home once Dulcey had gone to sleep, but that hadn't been her plan last night.

Starting a fire for breakfast was the first chore. He didn't know when Lydia would be home, so he went ahead with the morning kitchen chores. Abraham had laid the kindling last night, so he struck a match and started it burning. Then he took the coffeepot from the back of the stove and filled it with the last of the water in the pail on the dry sink. Measuring the coffee grounds, he set it on the stove, then fed the fire with larger sticks.

Next, he went out to the wood box on the porch to bring in more split firewood. He stopped. Something hung on the clothesline, dark against the light fog that covered the fields. He took a step closer to the edge of the porch. It turned, swinging from one pin, like a crow, dead and hanging by one foot. Now he recognized what it was. Dulcey's dress, hung by a clothespin on one side, the other shoulder sagging toward the ground.

Footsteps sounded behind him in the house and Jonas stepped out onto the porch. "What is that?" he asked as he walked up beside Aaron.

"I think it's Dulcey's dress hanging on the clothesline. It spooked me, too, when I first saw it."

"Who is Dulcey, and why is it there?"

Aaron described how he and Elizabeth had found Dulcey on the road the night before.

Jonas shook his head. "But Elizabeth wouldn't leave clothes out on the line in this damp weather. And why hang it with only one clothespin?"

The unsettled feeling he had woken with now pushed Aaron off the porch and toward the clothesline, Jonas right behind him. The dress was clean, but damp from hanging in the morning mist. The second clothespin was on the ground.

Aaron swallowed. "Have you seen Elizabeth?"

"She hadn't come home when I left Katie last night. I

figured she decided to spend the night at Ruby's." Jonas turned to him. "Elizabeth and her friend were both here when you went to bed last night?"

"She was going to wash out Dulcey's dress, then sit up all night in case Dulcey needed something."

"And she's not in the house?"

Aaron shook his head. "Not in anyplace I looked." The house was large, but there weren't many rooms.

"We have to look for her. We'll go to every house in the area and ask if they've seen her, and we'll recruit helpers at the same time."

Jonas went into the house to wake Abraham and tell him about Elizabeth's disappearance while Aaron fingered the dropped clothespin. He would take Jonas's spring wagon and retrace Elizabeth's steps from last night. Maybe she had gone back to Gideon and Ruby's place. Or perhaps Solomon's house. She wouldn't have gone to confront him, would she? She had to know that he'd want to hurt her the way he had hurt Dulcey. A chill ran through him at the thought.

He finished unpinning the dress and took it inside the house.

By the time Aaron had the horse hitched up, Dulcey was awake and dressed. She came out on the porch along with Jonas and Abraham.

"We'll go in different directions to cover more ground," Abraham said. "I'll go to the Stuckeys'. Jonas, you head toward the Lehmans' and stop at every house in that direction."

"I'll start with Solomon Mast." Aaron's insides squeezed together as he remembered the veiled threat Solomon had made after Reuben's cabin had burned. "Someone needs to go there first. If she isn't there, I'll go to Gideon's, then head north to the Beilers' and the Zooks'," Aaron said. "Dulcey should come with one of us. If Solomon is out looking for her, she shouldn't be alone."

"I'll ride with you," Dulcey said. "I got to help you find Elizabeth."

Aaron moved over on the wagon seat and Dulcey climbed up.

"Are you feeling better this morning?" he asked as he clucked to Rusty and they headed for the road.

"A mite stiff and sore, but I slept better than I had done for a long time." Dulcey didn't meet his eyes. "We got to find Elizabeth. Do you think Masta Solomon done taken her away?"

"I don't know, but I don't think she left by herself. She wouldn't have left you alone, for one thing."

She nodded. "I know that. We just need to pray for Jesus to watch over her."

Dulcey closed her eyes, her lips moving. Aaron tried to pray with her but couldn't think of what words to say. The prayer from the *Christenpflicht* he was memorizing for membership class didn't seem to express the panic that threatened to overtake him.

As they drew near the top of the hill, Dulcey laid a hand on his arm. "Don't take me when you talk to Solomon, please. Let me out somewhere and I'll meet you again when you're done."

"All right." He pulled the horse to a halt at the drive leading to the burned-out cabin. "This is where Elizabeth used to live."

"With her husband? The one called Reuben?"

"That's right. There's a possibility she might have come here, but it's also a good place to hide. I'll meet you here after I get done talking to Solomon."

After Dulcey climbed down from the wagon, Aaron drove Rusty up the hill and turned on the Millersburg Road, heading toward the red brick house on the rise. The place was quiet, but Solomon, or Miller, as Aaron now knew he was, must have seen him coming. He stepped out onto the porch in fancy clothes, the kind a businessman would wear in town. It appeared that Simon Miller was ready to show his true colors instead of pretending to be Amish.

"What can I do for you?"

"Elizabeth is missing. I was wondering if you had seen her last night or this morning."

"So, she has run off? I was afraid something like this might happen."

"Why?"

"She refused to marry. The woman has no sense of morality at all. I wouldn't be surprised if she has gone off where no one will ever find her. You know what women like that are like. She'll find a place with others like her."

Aaron's fists clenched around the reins. For once, he was glad for his wooden leg, otherwise he would have launched himself off the wagon seat to plant a fist in Miller's smug face. Instead, he lifted the reins to drive off, but the other man took a step closer.

"In fact, she was quite dismayed at the news I gave her." His smile broadened to show his white teeth. "I have found Reuben Kaufman's true heir, his son. I will be acting as guardian for the boy until he comes of age. When she found out she would be left penniless, she became quite unhinged, even though I offered to marry her. Perhaps she'll come to her senses eventually."

"When did you talk to her?"

A slight hesitation. "Why, it was yesterday afternoon, I think. Sometime in the late afternoon, if I remember right."

Aaron let a smile lift the corners of his mouth. "I caught you in another lie, Simon Miller. I know for a fact that Elizabeth was at her sister Ruby's house then. I saw here there."

The other man's eyes narrowed. "Simon Miller? I haven't heard that name since the war and no one will hear it again."

Before Aaron knew what was happening, a gun was in Miller's hand, pointed at his chest. A very familiar braided lanyard dangled from the pistol's handle, Simon Miller's trademark. Aaron ducked to the side, throwing himself off the wagon seat, just as a shot rang out and Rusty jumped, taking off running with the wagon behind him.

A burning sensation in his side told Aaron he had been hit, but before he could check to see how serious it was, Miller planted a black boot on his head. Aaron's eyes closed as his enemy lifted Aaron's cane and it descended toward his head.

⌐───────

The first thing Elizabeth noticed was the sickening odor. She opened her eyes, but the only light came from a few narrow sunbeams swirling with dust motes. She was lying on a cold floor with her hands tied behind her and a gag in her mouth.

Struggling, she pushed herself to a sitting position and

leaned against a wall behind her. The faint light showed walls built of stone and a rock floor. Somewhere to her left, water trickled in a dark expanse. To her right, the rock wall continued in a circle. The light came from cracks in a wooden door at least seven feet above her.

She drew her knees up and huddled against the wall, trying to remember what happened.

Solomon. Her mind cleared and it came back to her. She had woken up on the seat of his buggy after she lost consciousness when he seized her at the clothesline. He had been talking. Whether it was to her or to himself, she couldn't tell. But from his mutterings, she understood that he was focused on one thing, owning Reuben's farm. When he saw that she was awake, he laughed.

"You will marry me, my dear, because you are the key to more than just Kaufman's quarter section. After I marry you, your father's farm will be next. You are an important part of my plan."

"Why?" Elizabeth's throat was raw as she spoke. "Why does the land mean so much to you?"

"Land is wealth. You understand that, don't you? When I own enough land, everyone will know how important I am."

"I will never marry you. You can't make me marry you against my will."

The darkness hid his expression, but the moon was still bright, and his teeth flashed in its light.

"That's the beauty of my plan, Elizabeth. Kaufman's son will arrive on Saturday from Mississippi, and that lawyer Hoben has instructions to deliver him to me as your representative."

She tried to twist her arm out of his grip, but he only tightened his fingers.

"We will marry as soon as the ministers admit me into the church. We will be the perfect Amish family, and little Jefferson Davis Kaufman will be our son." He chuckled.

"I won't do it."

Then he turned her arm around so far that she was afraid he would break it.

"You will, because if you refuse, that little boy will meet with a terrible accident. And I know you wouldn't want to live with his death on your conscience. Your family will be devastated when they hear that you took your own life."

At that, she launched herself toward the side of the buggy and the safety of the dark woods, but Solomon pulled her back so forcefully that her head hit the edge of the buggy seat and everything had gone black.

She shivered in the damp chill and her head ached. She must get out of this pit and warn the community. Thanks to Gideon's warning, the ministers would be watchful, but Solomon had fooled all of them. All spring and summer they had welcomed him into their midst and worshiped with him. Even considered him for membership. Only Aaron had been suspicious of the man all along. She felt the burn of shame as she remembered how close she had been to agreeing to marry him.

And now she was trapped. Helpless. How was she going to escape? With her hands tied, she couldn't hope to climb out, and with the gag she couldn't call for help. She pushed herself to her feet and walked around her prison, looking for a way out. The passage where the trickling sound came from was also where the worst of the odor was. With no light coming from that direction, she couldn't see how she would be able to get out that way.

She sank down to the floor again and laid her forehead on her knees. Was there no way out? Was there no hope? Solomon was right. She would marry him and go along with his charade for the sake of Reuben's son. A little boy she had never met. She would spend the rest of her life protecting that boy . . . Solomon knew her so well.

But Aaron would never understand her change of heart. Her chance at happiness with a man she could trust was gone.

Dulcey's words from last night echoed in her head. *"Turn to Jesus,"* she had said.

Full of doubt, Elizabeth closed her eyes.

I don't deserve anything from you, Lord God. But have mercy on me. Save me from this pit I've gotten myself into.

Suddenly, noise came from above her and dirt sifted from the ceiling. The wooden door opened with a bang and light streamed in, blinding her.

"Here's some more company for you, my dear."

A body dropped down and landed in the center of the floor. Elizabeth squinted as Solomon leaned over the opening.

"No, he isn't dead yet, but he soon will be. Enjoy your last moments together."

The door slammed closed again and Elizabeth heard Solomon driving away. She crawled forward on her knees and saw that the body Solomon had tossed into the pit with her had red hair. She pushed with her elbow until she was able to roll him over on his back. Blood soaked his shirt.

"Aaron." His name echoed in her mind but was muffled from the gag in her mouth. Was he dying as Solomon had said?

His head moved to one side. "Elizabeth?" He raised a hand to his head. "Is Solomon gone?"

She shook her head to show him she couldn't speak, then he reached for her gag and untied it.

"Solomon isn't here." She coughed. "He said you were dying."

"I don't feel like I'm dying, but he shot me and then hit me over the head. I hoped he thought he had taken care of me for good." He sat up. "Turn around and I'll untie your hands."

"You've been shot? And the fall down here was enough to kill a man."

"I came to while Solomon was driving me here but pretended to be out. He was talking about you and I had to find out where you were." Aaron stopped and cupped her cheek in his hand. "His talk didn't make much sense, but I heard enough to know that his mind isn't right. Perhaps it never has been."

After he finished untying Elizabeth's hands, he tapped his wooden leg. It was in two pieces, broken in his fall.

"I'm glad this is the only leg that broke." He unstrapped the leg and pushed it to the side. "We will have to work together. I need your help to get out of here."

"But you're bleeding."

Aaron pressed a hand to his side. "It's just a crease. I've had much worse than this."

Elizabeth helped him stand.

"It sure smells bad down here." Aaron looked around.

"Have you been able to explore much?" He pointed toward the dark passageway. "What is that way?"

"That's where the odor is coming from. I didn't see any light down there, so I didn't try going in that direction."

Aaron looked up at the door in the wooden ceiling. "If I had two good legs, I could boost you up there, but we have to work with what we have." He nodded toward the darkness. "Let's see where this goes."

Leaning on Elizabeth, he used her for a crutch. They went three steps into the darkness, then four. The sound of the trickling water grew stronger and so did the stench.

"Let's stop here for a minute and let our eyes get used to the darkness."

Elizabeth's arm encircled his waist. She could feel the strong muscles under his shirt and his confidence as he peered into the darkness. A sense of wonder broke over her.

"I prayed, and you came."

"What do you mean?"

"I prayed for the Good Lord to save me from this pit, and he sent you."

Aaron laughed. "Solomon sent me down here."

Elizabeth had no doubts. "Then the Lord used Solomon. Just like in the Bible story about Joseph and his brothers. Solomon meant it for evil, but God meant it for good."

After a moment, she felt him nod. "You're right. I used to think God wasn't interested in me, but the more I learn, the more I realize how good he is."

Elizabeth peered into the dark space in front of them. "I can see a little. It looks like it isn't a passageway at all. It's just more of the same wall all the way around." She couldn't see the source of the water, but the faint light gleamed off wet walls. She looked down. "But what is that on the floor?"

Aaron looked down at the heap at his feet and stiffened. "That's what is causing the putrid odor. Turn around and we'll go back."

They made their way to the light again, and Aaron lowered himself to the floor.

Elizabeth looked back. "Do you know what that is?"

"I thought I recognized the smell. It's a body, and it's been here for a while."

"A while? How long do you think?"

"A couple months, at least."

"Who do you think it is?"

"Is there anyone from the area who is missing? Anyone who has disappeared?"

"No one from the community." Elizabeth thought about it. "The only one who has left is Abel Patterson, but Solomon told us he had gone back east to live with his son."

"And sold him his farm and everything with it." Aaron put an arm around Elizabeth's shoulders and drew her close. "I don't think Abel moved back east. I think he's been here the whole time."

The thought of Abel in this pit, unable to get out . . .

"Do you think Solomon killed him before throwing him in here?"

Aaron's voice was grim. "I hope so, for Abel's sake." Then he drew her closer to him. "Remember, Solomon intends to come back here for you. He needs you for his plans, so he won't leave you in here for more than a day or two."

Elizabeth leaned her head on his chest, closing her eyes. "But even if he comes back for me, he'll never let you out of here alive."

His heart beat faster under her ear. "We'll pray for someone to rescue us. Both of us."

⁓

As Elizabeth slept, Aaron watched the beams of sunlight move across the floor. By now, the folks searching for Elizabeth would realize that he was missing, too. Did Dulcey go to find the others when he didn't meet her like he had promised? Did she tell them where he had gone?

But even if she had, did anyone know about this place? It was on the Patterson farm, but part of the old homestead, not the new and modern buildings near the road.

The sunbeams were slanted toward the wall when he heard a wagon coming.

"Elizabeth." He kept his voice to a whisper as he jiggled her shoulder. "Someone is coming."

She raised her head, instantly alert. "Is it Solomon?"

"I don't know, but we should be ready. Help me over to the shadowed part there, where he won't see us right away when he opens the trapdoor. Maybe he'll come down here to look for you."

"How will he get down?"

"There's a ladder outside. That was probably how he got you down here earlier."

They waited in the shadows, watching the trapdoor. At the sound of voices, Aaron drew a hopeful breath. Miller would come alone.

The door opened, silhouetting a man's head against the afternoon sky.

"Aaron?" It was Gideon. "Are you down here?"

"Ja," Elizabeth said. "We're both here."

"Watch out. We're going to send the ladder down."

As the ladder descended, Aaron held Elizabeth against the wall, then let her go once it was in place. She grasped the ladder, looking up at the familiar faces, then turned back to him.

"I'll be able to climb up, but you'll need help. You go first and I'll help you balance."

He hopped over to the ladder, grabbing it to steady himself, then reached for her. "Climb up there. I want to see you safe before another minute goes by. Then Gideon can help me out."

By the time Aaron emerged from the pit, Elizabeth was in the arms of Lydia, Katie, and Dulcey. Abraham and Jonas were also there, along with Levi and the Zooks.

"Has anyone seen Miller? I mean Solomon?"

"We saw him driving toward Millersburg a couple hours ago," Abraham said.

Aaron met Elizabeth's gaze. "We need to go there too. We have something to report to the sheriff."

As the group listened, Aaron told them what had happened, with Elizabeth interrupting with her version as needed.

"I never met Abel Patterson," Aaron said, "but if someone wants to go down there with a light, we could identify him for the police."

Gideon volunteered, his face grim. He lit one of the candles they had brought for the search and went down the ladder. He was back up within minutes, shaking his head.

"It's tragic. Ja, it's Abel Patterson. I recognized his clothes. He must have ended up in here soon after I last spoke with him." He passed a hand over his eyes. "We don't have any evidence to show that Solomon is the one who murdered him, but I think the circumstances might be enough for the sheriff to arrest him."

"One question I have is, how did you find us?" Aaron asked, looking around. "Who knew where to look?"

"It was Dulcey," Jonas said. "She said she saw Solomon come this way often, and one time she followed him. She thought he hid money somewhere around here. And when Rusty came home pulling the wagon behind him, but without you or Dulcey, we knew something was wrong."

"Then Dulcey told us that you had gone to talk to Solomon, and we thought we knew where to start looking," Casper added.

Dan and Ephraim helped Aaron into the back of Abraham's wagon where he could sit with his foot hanging over the edge. Elizabeth and Dulcey joined him, and the group started for home.

The Zooks headed north to their homes when they reached the Berlin Road, Dan and Ephraim shaking Aaron's hand. Before Casper followed his sons, he grasped Aaron's hand.

"Thank the Good Lord we found you. If it hadn't been for Dulcey, we would never have known where to look."

"He was watching over us, I think."

"He knows how much we need you." Casper's eyes were wet as he turned and followed his sons home.

Gideon went to his own home while the rest of the silent

group rode to the Weavers' farm. When they arrived, Abraham climbed down from the wagon, his face grim.

"Everyone come in. We'll have a quick supper and make our plans," Abraham said.

Aaron hopped off the back of the wagon while Lydia went to get his crutches. He patted them like old friends. He would make another wooden leg, but until then he was thankful to be able to get around.

Lydia tended to Aaron's wound while Elizabeth and Dulcey fixed a light supper. Aaron couldn't shake his exhaustion and ate less than he thought he might. Elizabeth, sitting next to him, took only one slice of bread and buttered it, but didn't finish even that morsel.

He took her hand under the table and squeezed it. "Are you all right?"

She nodded. "But I feel like we aren't done yet. Solomon is still out there somewhere, and tomorrow morning a little boy will be arriving on the train from Mississippi. If we don't do something, he will be in Solomon's clutches and under his influence."

Abraham leaned forward. "We need to decide what we're going to do. First, we need to meet that train."

"Elizabeth and I will do that," Aaron said. "The lawyer thinks she is the boy's aunt and is intending to give him into her care."

"The lawyer's name is Harlan Hoben," Elizabeth said. "We have to tell him who I really am."

Abraham nodded. "He needs to know the truth of the matter. We also need to go to the sheriff and tell them what we suspect about Solomon."

"His name is Simon Miller." Aaron looked around the table. "At least, that was the name I knew him by in the Shenandoah Valley. I couldn't be sure I had the right man until today. When I saw his pistol, I knew it had to be him. He kept it on a red-and-gold-braided leather lanyard. I've never seen another one like it."

"I'll go to the sheriff." Jonas looked at Abraham. "Will you come with me?"

Abraham nodded. "Is there anything else?"

Lydia spoke up. "What about Dulcey and me? Do we just wait for word of what happened in Millersburg?"

Abraham smiled at his wife. "I think you should both come with us. The sheriff might need another witness, and Dulcey can tell them what she knows."

"The law won't listen to me," Dulcey said.

"You're not in the South anymore," Jonas said. "If you are willing to make an accusation, the sheriff will take your statement. It could make a difference in whether they decide to arrest him or not."

Abraham stood up. "It's going to be a hard day tomorrow, and we will have to leave early in the morning to get there in time." He glanced at Elizabeth and Dulcey. "Until then, I don't think either of you should leave the house. We aren't certain that Solomon, or Simon Miller, went into Millersburg. He could still be looking for Dulcey, thinking he has Elizabeth safely imprisoned."

As Aaron attempted to settle down to sleep that night on a pallet on the floor of Jonas's room, the day's events ran through his mind. He tried to relax, but he still felt the jitters of facing down the barrel of Miller's pistol. At least he had found Elizabeth, safe and alive. He turned his head toward the door. Beyond that piece of wood, across the landing at the top of the stairs, in the bedroom he had been using since he came to the Weavers' farm, Elizabeth was sleeping in the company of her friends, Katie and Dulcey.

He prayed that they would all be even more secure by this time tomorrow.

18

Elizabeth was up before dawn. Datt had already milked the cow and hitched the horses to the wagon for the trip to Millersburg. Mamm and Dulcey had worked together to make biscuits and bacon, food that would provide both breakfast and dinner for them and could be eaten while they traveled, while the rest of them inserted board seats into the wagon bed. Seven of them would be driving to town, and it would be a long ride.

They were off before the sun had cleared the horizon. The morning mist lay on the fields but would soon burn off in the sunshine.

"It would be a good day for raking hay," Datt said.

Jonas sat on the wagon seat beside him. "The weather should hold until Monday. We'll have time to do the work then."

Elizabeth sat with Dulcey in the front of the wagon bed, on a seat facing the rear so they could chat with Mamm and Katie as they rode. Aaron rode alone in the last seat, his gaze never resting in one spot for long. He was as nervous as she was. Every once in a while, he caught her watching him and gave her a reassuring smile.

The morning was still early when they drove into town, but people were moving about and the stores were open. Datt walked the horses down the street.

"We'll put the team up in a livery stable," he said over his shoulder. "I rushed them to get here in time, so they deserve a good rest before we head home."

As they drew close to the livery nearest the courthouse, Jonas said, "That black horse in the corral looks like Solomon's."

Datt drove by slowly. Elizabeth sucked in her breath when she saw Solomon's gelding.

The horses turned the corner a block past the courthouse, and Datt pulled up at Elijah Wilson's livery. The place was quiet, unlike the stable they had just passed.

"Is anyone here?" Datt called.

A black man came from the back of the stable, wiping his hands on a rag as he came toward them.

"What can I do for you?"

"We need to stable our horses for a few hours. They need a good rubdown and some good feed. They've worked hard already this morning."

The man smiled. "I can sure take care of that for you."

While they were talking, Jonas helped the rest of their group out of the wagon. Elizabeth's arm was locked with Dulcey's. Her friend had been shaking with nerves ever since they had reached town.

"I'm Elijah Wilson," the man said, nodding toward the group but with his gaze on Dulcey. "You folks in town just for the day?"

"That's right. We have some business to take care of, but we don't know how long we'll be."

Elijah chuckled. "Well, as you can see, I have plenty of room for the horses. You can bring your wagon inside, too, if you want to keep it off the street."

While Datt and Jonas helped Elijah with the horses, Aaron gathered Elizabeth and the other women around him.

"Elizabeth will come with me to the train station while Jonas and Abraham go to the sheriff's office." He looked from Mamm to Katie to Dulcey. "What will you three do while you wait for us?"

Mamm looked at Katie and Dulcey. "I think we would like to stay in one place rather than walk through town visiting the shops."

Aaron nodded his agreement. "There might be a hotel near the train station where you could wait. They often have separate waiting rooms for ladies."

Dulcey shook her head. "You go on. I can't go there."

"Why not?" Elizabeth said.

Aaron frowned. "Dulcey's right. She would have to wait outside, and that won't do."

"That isn't right." Elizabeth felt her cheeks grow hot. "Why couldn't she come in?"

Dulcey squeezed her arm. "They got a sign there. I can't read, but I know what it says."

Datt, Jonas, and Elijah walked up to them. Elijah's face was stormy. "I can read that sign. It says, 'No colored allowed.' The lady is right, she would have to wait outside."

"Then we'll have to find somewhere else," Mamm said. "We can't leave Dulcey alone with Solomon in town."

"Y'all are welcome to stay here," Elijah said. "I don't have fancy chairs like at the hotel, but there's a bench in the back room and I can offer you some cool, clean water."

Datt smiled for the first time all morning. "Thank you. I have been worried about Dulcey, knowing who she might run into here in town."

"Are y'all in danger from something?"

"A man named Solomon Mast."

Elijah snorted in disgust. "I know the man. I won't serve him here, but I know what he looks like. I'll protect these women for you."

A train whistle sounded in the distance.

"We need to get to the train station," Aaron said. "How far is it from here?"

"Just two blocks," Elijah said. "One down and one over."

"We'll meet you there with the sheriff," Datt said.

Aaron could go quickly on his crutches when he needed to. Elizabeth hurried to keep up with him until they got to the crowded platform outside the passenger station. The train hadn't arrived yet, but the whistle blew again, closer than before.

Turning to Elizabeth, Aaron said, "It's the train from the south, so it should be the one with the lawyer. We need to keep an eye out for Miller. He is probably on the platform somewhere, and we don't want him to know we're here until the sheriff arrives."

They moved to a spot along the wall of the station and waited. Elizabeth watched the people, trying to calm her nerves. Reuben's son was likely on that train. When she rescued him from Solomon, then what would happen? She would keep him safe, warm, and protected, but could she ever learn to love this boy? Or would he grow up to be just like his father? She shuddered, suddenly afraid of what the future might bring.

"Are you all right?" Aaron grabbed her hand and pulled her closer to him.

"I'm nervous, I suppose." She looked into his eyes. "What if . . . what if I don't like the child?"

He smiled. "The Good Lord will give you a love for him and calm your fears."

Elizabeth smiled back. He was right. She could feel the assurance radiating from Aaron.

Then the whistle blew again, and the train was in sight. The noise grew too loud for any more talking, so Elizabeth just watched. As the train pulled to a stop alongside the platform, the crowd surged forward. In the middle, Elizabeth spied a familiar tall figure.

"There he is," she said, leaning close to Aaron so he could hear her.

At the same time, the doors to the passenger car opened and people spilled out onto the platform. Which door would the lawyer come out of? Would she know who he was?

"Follow me and stay close," Aaron said.

They wormed their way through the throng, Solomon's hat always floating above the thinning crowd ahead of them. Some people coming out of the car moved away quickly while others gathered in groups, visiting with the family or friends who had come to meet them. Finally, they were right behind Solomon as he made his way toward the passenger car.

Elizabeth saw movement on her left. Datt and Jonas were coming their way along with a heavyset man wearing a badge.

Then an older gentleman appeared in the doorway to the train car in front of them. In his arms was a sleeping child, no more than two years old. Aaron and Solomon started toward the man simultaneously. Solomon reached the lawyer and stretched out his hand.

"Welcome to Millersburg, Mr. Hoben," he said.

Aaron came up on his right. "Not so fast, Miller."

Solomon turned to him, his face blanching when he saw Aaron with Elizabeth behind him.

"No. You're . . . you're dead." He looked at the lawyer, then at the sheriff who had come up on his left side.

"Simon Miller? I'd like you to come with me. I have a few questions to ask you."

Elizabeth cringed as Solomon turned toward her, his face full of terror that turned in an instant to hatred. But as the sheriff put a hand on Solomon's arm, he tore away and ran down the platform toward the caboose at the end of the train. The sheriff ran after him as the crowd watched. Solomon launched off the end of the platform, stumbling as he landed, then limped around the caboose and out of sight.

"Stop!" the sheriff shouted. He followed Solomon off the platform and around the caboose. "Stop!"

Elizabeth heard a gunshot, then the sheriff lifted his pistol and fired. The sheriff went out of sight behind the caboose. In a few minutes, he came back into view and looked toward the crowd. He shook his head, and Elizabeth pressed her fist to her mouth. Solomon was dead.

At the sheriff's signal that Miller hadn't survived, Aaron looked at Elizabeth, then back at the lawyer. Mr. Hoben held the sleeping boy as if he were a sack of potatoes and fished in his vest pocket for his watch. He snapped it open, then looked toward the sheriff with distaste.

"It looks like my trip has been for nothing."

Aaron stepped forward. "Mr. Hoben? Harlan Hoben? My name is Aaron Zook, and this is Elizabeth Kaufman."

As he motioned for Elizabeth to come up beside him, the look on Mr. Hoben's face turned to relief.

"Thank goodness," he said, his voice rich with a familiar honey-smoothness that Aaron had missed since he had been in the North. "I have been corresponding with Mr. Mast, and he led me to believe that you were indisposed in some way, Miss Kaufman."

Elizabeth shook her head. "I think we have a few things to clear up—"

"But we should find somewhere quiet where we can talk," Aaron said.

"Very good," Mr. Hoben said. He shifted the boy in his arms, then finally handed the sleepy toddler to Elizabeth. "Is there an office somewhere in town where we can discuss these matters?"

"We'll try at the hotel," Aaron said. "It's over here next to the station."

The hotel was happy to rent them a room for a fee, which Mr. Hoben paid. "Send in a lunch for us also, if you will be so kind." He pulled out his pocket watch again.

"And can you tell me when the next train leaves for Cincinnati?"

Once they had settled themselves in a large room on the ground floor of the hotel and their lunch was brought in, Harlan Hoben picked up his knife and fork and glanced at them.

"Don't worry about me. I can talk while we dine. I only have an hour before my train leaves." He took a bite, then gestured to their plates. "Eat, please."

Aaron glanced at Elizabeth, then took the boy from her and set him on his lap. He was a handsome boy who looked nothing like Reuben. As he came fully awake, he started to fuss, so Aaron cut a bite of ham and gave it to him.

"One thing that needs to be cleared up," said Elizabeth, "is that I am not Reuben's sister as you assumed. I am his widow."

Mr. Hoben stopped chewing, then swallowed. "His widow? According to Mrs. Kaufman, that is, the woman I had assumed to be Mrs. Kaufman, he had said he was never married. She found your name and location in a pocket after Mr. Kaufman's demise, and came to the conclusion that you must be his sister."

"I understand that." Elizabeth pulled a folded paper from the reticule hanging from her wrist. "This is the marriage certificate from when I married Reuben."

Wiping his mouth with a napkin, Mr. Hoben took the paper and held it at an angle to get the best light.

"Yes. Yes, everything seems to be in order." He looked at Elizabeth. "But had he abandoned you or dissolved the marriage in any way before he married the other Mrs. Kaufman?"

Elizabeth shook her head. "He left to go to war, but I always assumed he would return, until I got word about his marriage and his . . ." She glanced at the boy sitting in Aaron's lap. "His son."

Mr. Hoben gave the child a look that told Aaron he didn't like children, especially two-year-old boys.

"I suppose I'll have to take him back to Mississippi, then. Unless there is an orphan home here?" He looked from Aaron to Elizabeth with a hopeful expression. "Not that I want to leave the boy," he added quickly, "but he is an orphan. His mother's people don't want him, considering how she had shamed them when she . . . well, that is a story that has no bearing here. Except that now that Mr. Mast is no longer with us, and you are not directly related to the boy, there is no other place for him."

The boy. Aaron felt the weight of the child on his lap and saw the bright curiosity in his eyes as he tried to capture a pea from Aaron's plate. He knew what it was like to grow up alone, without a father and mother. He had had Grandpop, but an old man's gruff companionship was a poor substitute for a mother's love.

"We'll take him." The words sounded before he thought. He glanced at Elizabeth's surprised face. "I mean, I'll take him. You don't need to find another place for him. I'll provide for him and raise him like my own."

Mr. Hoben finished the food on his plate and pushed it off to the side. He picked up a case and took some papers from inside. He read through them while Aaron and Elizabeth waited.

"These papers say that I am authorized to give the boy,

Jefferson Davis Kaufman, to Elizabeth Kaufman, or her representative, Solomon Mast." He looked at Aaron. "Are you related to Elizabeth Kaufman?"

Aaron couldn't look at her. He had spoken too soon. "No, I'm not."

Elizabeth leaned forward. "The papers only have my name on them, correct? There is nothing that states the relationship I'm supposed to have to the boy?"

He looked through the papers again. "That is correct."

"Then you can give the boy to me after all."

Mr. Hoben smiled. "Young lady, if you were a man, you would make a fine lawyer. If you're willing to take him, I can give the boy to you."

Aaron put one hand on her arm. "Elizabeth, are you sure?"

"More than anything in my life." The smile she gave him was clear and open, without any fear.

"Then that is settled." Mr. Hoben slid the paper across the table to Elizabeth and handed her a pen. "If you will sign here, my work is done."

She dipped the pen in Mr. Hoben's inkwell and signed her name without hesitation.

Mr. Hoben took another paper from the case. "Here is the boy's birth certificate. I must warn you, though. Do not try to contact his grandparents. Other than financing this trip to bring the child here, they want nothing to do with him. They have already paid a retainer fee to my partners and myself to react quickly if that ever happens."

"You don't need to worry about that," Aaron said. "When we said we would take him, we meant it."

"That is that, then." Mr. Hoben snapped his case closed

and stood up. "Please, feel free to stay and finish your meals. I have to arrange for my passage home."

The lawyer walked out, leaving Aaron alone with Elizabeth and the boy. She reached for him and took him on her lap.

"I'm not sure Jefferson is a good name for a child this young."

"He was named after the president of the Confederacy." Aaron gave the boy another bite of ham. "So, what should we call him?"

"We?" Elizabeth smiled as she brushed the boy's fine blond curls out of his eyes. "You heard the lawyer. I'm the one who was just awarded custody of him."

Aaron leaned closer, ignoring the teasing tone in her voice. "I meant we. A boy needs parents, not only a mother. I've told you before that I wanted you to be my wife. Over the last few days I've become even more certain. I can't go through my life without you. Will you marry me, Elizabeth? Will you be my wife?"

She rested her cheek on the boy's head. "How do you feel about children?"

"I love children." He grinned at her. "And I pray that we will be blessed with many of them, starting with little JD here."

"JD? What kind of name is that?"

"Then you come up with a better one." He scooted his chair closer to hers. "But first, I want your answer. Will you?"

Elizabeth's eyes grew moist. "You once told me that perhaps my dreams were the wrong dreams. That if I gave my will over to the Lord, he would show me the right way. The right dreams." She held JD closer. "I think that you were part of my dream all along. I still don't feel like I deserve this, but I will take it as a gift from my Father's hand."

"Does that mean that you will marry me?"

She nodded. "As soon as you join the church. And build your house."

Aaron stood and leaned over JD to kiss her, and the boy squirmed when his beard brushed his face. Aaron pulled back, just enough to look into Elizabeth's eyes.

"Will we always have children coming between us when I want to kiss you?"

She laughed. "I hope so, Aaron. I do hope so."

Epilogue

APRIL 1866

"Now you take care of yourself," Elizabeth said, hugging Dulcey. "I'm going to miss you."

Dulcey hugged her back. "God did a good thing when he brought us together, didn't he?"

Elizabeth held on to her friend with a tight grip. Letting her go meant that she would be leaving for Michigan and Elizabeth might never see her again.

"Are you going to write to me?"

Dulcey smiled, pulling away so she could see Elizabeth's face. "Don't you worry. Now that you and your mama taught me to read and write, I will send you letters regular. Just you see. And you got to write to me too. I want to hear all about how that boy of yours does when he grows up. You've got to tell me all about any others that the Lord blesses you with."

"You, too." Elizabeth shared a secret smile with Dulcey.

She was the only one Dulcey had told that she was expecting a child in the autumn.

A deep voice growled from the wagon seat. "We won't get any letter writing done if we don't get going."

Elizabeth and Dulcey laughed.

"That man of mine, he can sure try a woman's patience." Elizabeth looked over Dulcey's shoulder at Elijah. The two had gotten married in December and had made their home in the Weaver's Creek community after the businessmen in Millersburg had forced him to close his livery stable and move out of town. Elizabeth still didn't understand why a freedman wasn't welcome in Ohio. But then Elijah had heard about a job possibility up north.

"You won't stay?" Elizabeth knew when she asked what the answer would be.

"You know there ain't no place for us here. Elijah has got to have a job." She gave Elizabeth a final hug and climbed into the wagon seat next to her husband.

Elijah started the wagon down the road, waving goodbye to Aaron while Dulcey waved her handkerchief at Elizabeth until they turned the corner at the Berlin Road and were out of sight.

Elizabeth sighed. "I'm going to miss her so much."

Aaron put an arm around her shoulders. "I know you will. It's too bad they couldn't stay for the wedding, but Elijah has to get to Grand Rapids to get that job and he couldn't waste any time."

"Mamm, Mamm, look!"

As Elizabeth turned to walk back to the house with Aaron, JD came running out of the barn with Dan's son Cap close behind. The three-year-old held a ball of fluff in his hands.

"JD," Cap called. "Bring that kitten back here. You know it isn't big enough to leave its mother."

Her son stopped as Elizabeth walked up to him. He was always collecting something to bring to her. This time it was a little gray kitten, its eyes not even open.

"Listen to Cap, JD. The kitten needs its mamm."

"But look!"

"I see it. Now obey."

JD gave the kitten back to Cap, who took it into the barn.

"You know he'll bring home a bobcat next," Aaron said as he held out his hand for their son to hold.

"I hope not." Elizabeth took JD's other hand so he could walk between them.

"Are you ready to see your new house?" Aaron asked.

"Is it finished?"

"Nearly." Aaron opened the front door. "We've been working almost every day on it so it's ready in time for the wedding next week."

Elizabeth stepped into the spacious front room. The movable walls weren't installed yet, so the ground floor was open, large enough to seat the entire community when it was their turn to host the church meeting.

"The kitchen is done. The stove was delivered last Friday."

"It's beautiful." She ran her hand across the smooth top of the big table. Large enough for several children to sit around it.

JD tried to pull his hand out of hers. "I want to run."

"Not inside the house."

Elizabeth smiled. Aaron's response had been automatic. A father's response.

"I'm not sure I can wait a whole week," Elizabeth said.

Aaron's eyes crinkled as he grinned at her. "You're the one who decided on the date."

"I know. And I do want Katie to be able to attend. Her baby is still so young."

"Jonas won't let her leave the house, you know."

"I know. We'll wait."

"Come upstairs," Aaron said. "The bedrooms are finished."

They climbed the narrow stairway from the kitchen to the second floor. Casper had said they would appreciate having a full upstairs instead of just a loft and Elizabeth agreed. There were four bedrooms, one in each corner of the house, with two windows in each room to catch the summer breezes.

"Which one will be ours?"

"Ah, that's the surprise I've been saving for you. Let's go back downstairs."

Aaron led them to a room Elizabeth hadn't seen before, next to the kitchen and behind the stairway. He opened the door and Elizabeth walked in. It was already furnished with a bed and a wardrobe.

Aaron grinned at her. "This is our room. It's handy to the kitchen, and I won't have to climb the stairs so much."

Elizabeth gave Aaron a hug that quickly turned into a kiss that took her breath away. It would have lasted longer, but JD pulled on Elizabeth's skirts.

"Outside? I want to play."

"We'll go sit on the front porch."

JD led the way this time. The porch had a special swing just for him, and he knew right where it was. Elizabeth and

Aaron sat in the comfortable willow chair for two that Rosina and Casper had made for them and watched JD play.

Aaron grasped Elizabeth's hand. "I don't know about you, but I know my dream has come true."

She smiled at him. "A home."

"A family."

"And you." She squeezed his hand.

He pulled her closer and cupped her cheek in his hand. "And you."

Then he kissed her, sealing their promises to each other once more.

After the kiss, Elizabeth sighed as he held her in his arms. "Next week can't come soon enough."

Read on for an excerpt from
BOOK 1
in the Journey to Pleasant Prairie series.

"A compelling story of family and place. A great read."
—ANN H. GABHART, bestselling author of The Innocent

A NOVEL

HANNAH'S CHOICE

Jan Drexler

JOURNEY TO PLEASANT PRAIRIE

Available wherever books and ebooks are sold.

1

CONESTOGA CREEK, LANCASTER COUNTY
OCTOBER 1842

Hannah Yoder stamped her feet against the October evening chill seeping through her shoes. Darkness already reigned under the towering trees along Conestoga Creek, although the evening sky had shone pale blue as she walked along the path at the edge of the oat field minutes ago. The north wind gusted, sweeping bare fingers of branches back and forth against scudding clouds.

Where was Adam? She had been surprised to see his signal after supper, when *Mamm* had asked her to check on the meat in the smokehouse. She had been surprised to see the bit of cloth hanging on the blackberry bushes so late in the day. They had used the signal since they were children, ever since Adam had discovered that they both liked spying birds' nests in the woods.

She shivered a little. The cloth on the brambles had been blue instead of the yellow Adam always used. It could be a mistake. Perhaps one of her brothers had caught his shirt on the brambles instead.

A breeze fluttered dry leaves still clinging to the underbrush around her. She would wait a few minutes more, and then go back into the house. When a branch cracked behind her at the edge of the grove, Hannah lifted the edge of her shawl over her head, tucking a loose tendril of hair under her *kapp*, and slipped behind a tree. Let him think she was late. It would serve him right to worry about her for a change. He had been so serious lately. What was it about turning twenty that made him forget the fun they had always had? Would she be the same in two years?

Like a hunting owl, a figure flitted through the trees to her right. Hannah stilled her shivering body, waiting for Adam's appearance, but the figure halted behind the clump of young swamp willows at the edge of the clearing. So, he was waiting to frighten her when she arrived. Hannah smiled. She'd circle around behind and surprise him instead.

As she gathered the edges of her cloak to pick her way through the underbrush, she heard a giggle from her left. Liesbet? Hannah waited. She didn't want her younger sister spying on her conversation with Adam.

The wind tore fitful clouds away from the harvest moon, illuminating the clearing as Liesbet stepped into the light.

"Where are you?" Liesbet peered into the dark underbrush. "Come now, I know you're here."

Hannah clenched her hands. Liesbet was like a pesky gnat at times, always following her when she wanted to be alone. She was ready to step out from behind the tree to confront her when Liesbet spoke again, in English instead of *Deitsch*.

"George, stop playing games with me. You're going to scare me."

Hannah froze. Who was George?

Suddenly a man leaped from the trees behind Liesbet and caught her around the waist. She turned with a little shriek and fell into his arms.

"George, you did it again. I know you're going to be the death of me one day."

Hannah covered her mouth to keep a gasp from escaping. The man who had been hiding among the willows wasn't Adam.

"Ah, lass, you're so much fun to scare, but you know 'tis only me, not some ghoulie prowling around the woods here."

Liesbet giggled and snuggled closer to George. As he turned into the moonlight, Hannah could see him clearly, from his blue corded trousers to the snug-fitting cap perched on top of his head. His cocky grin reminded her of a fox carrying off a chicken from the henhouse. Certainly not an Amish man, or even Mennonite or Dunkard. She had never seen him before, but Liesbet had, for sure. She ducked farther behind her tree before either one of them could spot her.

"Give us a kiss, lass. The boys and I are only here for the one night. We're heading on to Philadelphia tomorrow."

Hannah could hear the pout in Liesbet's voice. "You're going away again? You never spend any time with me."

"Aye, and my sweet Lizzie, whenever I ask you to come along, you always play the little girlie who stays at home."

"It wouldn't be proper for me to tag along with you and your friends."

George's low laugh sent chills through Hannah. "No, lass, not proper at all." Then his voice took on its teasing tone again. "Admit it, you're just too young."

"I'm nearly sixteen!"

"Aye, like I said, you're just too young."

They grew quiet, and then Hannah heard a groan from George. She risked a glimpse around the tree. Liesbet was pressed up to him, her hands clinging to his shoulders while she kissed him. As Hannah watched, the man pulled Liesbet closer, one hand reaching up to pull off her kapp and letting her blond curls tumble to her shoulders. He buried his fingers in her hair, continuing the kiss until she struggled to pull out of his grasp. She stepped just beyond his reach and gave him a coy look.

Liesbet, what are you doing?

"Do you still think I'm too young?"

"Lizzie, you're enough to drive a man to distraction."

Hannah heard a warning in George's voice, but Liesbet turned her back on him and walked to the edge of the clearing. She was playing games with the man, but the look on his face in the moonlight was hungry. Predatory. Hannah shivered again.

"When will you get back?"

"In a week or so, you can bet on that, and then I'll be around for another of your kisses."

Liesbet turned to look at him, her face a careful pout. "Why can't you stay here? I don't like it when you're gone so much."

"I have to go, Lizzie, but you know I can't stay away from you too long."

There was another pause as Liesbet turned her back on the man. Hannah would have smiled if Liesbet's game wasn't so dangerous. It wasn't often she didn't get her way.

George snaked out a hand to catch her elbow and pull her close. "Lizzie, lass, give me another kiss. The lads are waiting for me."

After another lingering kiss, George released Liesbet and turned her around, giving her a solid swat on the behind before he took off along the creek bank, whistling as he went. Hannah watched Liesbet as she stood in the clearing, bouncing on her toes, humming the same tune George had been whistling, her pretend pout gone.

Stepping out from behind her tree, Hannah tugged her shawl off her head. "Liesbet, what are you doing?"

Liesbet jumped, and then turned on her sister. "You were spying on me?"

"It's a good thing I saw you. Who is that man and what are you doing with him?"

Liesbet hugged herself and smiled at Hannah. "He's my beau."

"Your beau? You mean he's courting you?"

"Of course he is. You were the one spying on us. Didn't you see him kiss me?"

"Just because a man takes a kiss doesn't mean he has courting on his mind."

Liesbet waved her hand in the air to brush Hannah's concerns away. "You're just jealous because you're not the only one with a secret beau. I know how you and Adam meet out here in the woods and your silly signal flag on the bushes." Her voice gloated.

Hannah felt the blood drain from her face. "Adam's not so secret, and he's not my beau. We've known each other all our lives."

"*Ne*, Adam's not secret, but *Daed* doesn't know he's asked you to marry him."

Hannah caught her lower lip between her teeth to keep herself from retorting to Liesbet's accusation. *Ja*, Adam had spoken of marriage, but it was just a game they played. He wasn't serious.

Liesbet's smile set Hannah's teeth on edge. "And I know I saw him kiss you the other day."

Hannah felt her face heat up. Adam had stolen a kiss, one that had made her heart pound, but one kiss didn't mean anything, did it?

"Surely you can't compare that to what I just saw between you and that . . ."

"His name is George McIvey, and I'm going to marry him."

"Liesbet, you can't!"

"I am, and you can't stop me. If you say anything to Daed, I'll tell him all about how you and Adam have been sneaking around." Liesbet lifted her chin as she faced Hannah. "I'll tell Mamm too."

"Liesbet, not Mamm. You'll set her off on one of her spells," Hannah protested, but Liesbet had won the argument. There was nothing she could do to stop her sister except give in to her demands, the way she had for the last nine years. Liesbet still played the delicate invalid, even though Hannah suspected she had outgrown the effects of the diphtheria long ago.

And she couldn't have Liesbet spreading tales about their neighbor. It didn't matter that Hannah was eighteen and well into courting age. Adam wasn't Amish.

"Then you keep my secret, and I'll keep yours," Liesbet said.

Hannah hesitated. Liesbet smiled the way she always did when she knew she was getting her way, and her eyes glinted in the moonlight.

"But what if that man is dangerous? Can he be trusted? How long have you known him?"

A frown crossed Liesbet's face, and then the moon disappeared behind another cloud and the clearing was shadowed once more. Hannah could barely see her sister's silhouette against the darker trees behind her.

When Liesbet spoke, her voice was unsure. "I've known him long enough, and he's never been anything but kind to me."

"He isn't one of us. He isn't Amish."

"He isn't a backward Dutchman, you mean." Liesbet's voice was bitter, her uncertainty vanishing as quickly as it came.

Hannah gasped. "You better not let Daed hear you talk like that."

"Don't worry, I won't. But you can bet I won't be marrying any stick-in-the-mud farmer, either."

Hannah took a step toward her sister. "But, Liesbet, you'll break Mamm's heart . . . Promise me you won't see him anymore."

Liesbet shrugged, the movement only a rustle in the dark. "Whatever you want." She turned and ran back toward the house, a shadow in the night.

Acknowledgments

It's always bittersweet to come to the end of a series of stories. With this book, we say goodbye to the Amish of Weaver's Creek, and their future lives are left to our imaginations. At the same time, the end of one story means I have the opportunity to invest my time in new projects!

I want to thank Vicki Crumpton, Barb Barnes, Michele Misiak, Karen Steele, and the other editors and staff at Revell and Baker Publishing Group for their tireless work to bring the best in Christian fiction to you, the readers.

I also thank you, my readers, for enjoying my stories and telling your friends about them. I love meeting you, and I hope we'll have the opportunity to meet in the future if we haven't already.

And as always, thank you to my dear husband who patiently listens to my story knots and often comes up with just the right way to untangle the thread at the right time.

Most of all, I thank my Lord and Savior, Jesus Christ, for his call on my life.

Jan Drexler brings a unique understanding of Amish traditions and beliefs to her writing. Her ancestors were among the first Amish, Mennonite, and Brethren immigrants to Pennsylvania in the 1700s, and their experiences are the inspiration for her stories. Jan lives in the Black Hills of South Dakota with her husband, where she enjoys hiking and spending time with her expanding family. She is the author of *The Sound of Distant Thunder*, *Hannah's Choice*, *Mattie's Pledge* (a 2017 Holt Medallion finalist), and *Naomi's Hope*, as well as several Love Inspired historical novels.

Don't miss out on the other books in
The Amish of Weaver's Creek series!

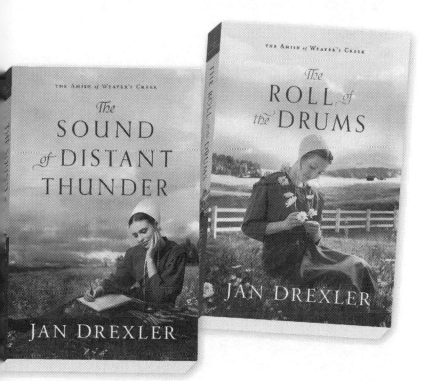

"The way Jan Drexler's Amish characters spring to life off the page will leave readers wanting to know more about the people in this Amish community. For sure and certain."

—**Ann H. Gabhart,** bestselling author of
These Healing Hills

Meet
Jan Drexler
www.jandrexler.com

Learn about the Amish—
find recipes, sewing patterns,
quilting patterns, and more!

Printed in the United States
By Bookmasters